Praise for CHRIS KRAUS

"The intelligence and honesty and total originality of Chris Kraus make her work not just great but indispensable. . . . I read everything Chris Kraus writes; she softens despair with her brightness, and with incredible humor, too."

—Rachel Kushner, author of *Creation Lake*

"I know there was a time before I read Chris Kraus . . . but it's hard to imagine."

—Sheila Heti, author of *Pure Colour*

"This woman is on to something most writers can't hope to get anywhere near. She is inimitable, sometimes infuriatingly distinct and perverse, magnificently obdurate in her singularity, smart as fuck, and usually brilliant, when she isn't just being smarter than most people."

—Gary Indiana, author of *Rent Boy* and *Vile Days*

"I could list dozens of reflexive, confessional, philosophical novels of the last decade that owe at least some of their existence to Kraus's work. . . . I admire Kraus's wit and rigor."

—Catherine Lacey, *Los Angeles Times*

"Reading *I Love Dick* made me laugh—cry—but most importantly it made me think about all the important issues of our time, DESIRE, AGING—Dick is a mere backdrop for this provocative meditation—it's edgy and deep."

—bell hooks, author of *All About Love*

"Chris Kraus . . . sets the bar."

—Maggie Nelson, author of *The Argonauts*

"Hardly anyone writes better or more insightfully than Chris Kraus about the lives of women and artists."

—Julie Phillips, author of *James Tiptree, Jr.: The Double Life of Alice B. Sheldon*

"Kraus's work is a bright map of presence. I'm grateful to her for deploying the materials of her life in rigorous and compelling ways; for holding vulnerability 'at some remove' in the face of those determined to read any act of self-disclosure as narcissistic or self-pitying."
—Leslie Jamison, *The New Yorker*

"[Kraus's] style is effortless, but deliberate, artful, colloquial, efficient—in other words, the antithesis of academic."
—Emily Gould, *The Guardian*

"Her work is strange and complete proof that intelligence can also be heartbreaking, moving."
—Javier Mattio, *La Voz del Interior de Córdoba*

"Her writing is not afraid to delve into the darkest areas of the human soul. In *Aliens & Anorexia*, Kraus fuses mysticism with politics, creating a narrative of pain and the search for transcendence."
—Juan Pablo Russo, *Escribiendo Cine*

"Chris Kraus [is] one of the most incisive voices in North American literature."
—Claudio Iglesias, Eterna Cadencia

"If America were to fling up a chain of roadside motels to be used as a needed neon refuge for girls too smart for their own good, the writings of Chris Kraus would be bitterly comforting Gideon Bibles tucked into the bedside."
—Michelle Tea, *San Francisco Bay Guardian*

"Chris Kraus is one of the most powerful independent voices in American criticism."
—Martí Manen, *La Vanguardia*

"Chris Kraus [is] one of our smartest and most original writers on contemporary art and culture."
—*The New York Times*

"Kraus has established herself as a cultural vanguard."

—*November Magazine*

"Kraus uses an interpretative lens to write through and around art, as if reimagining what art writing can be."

—*Los Angeles Review of Books*

"[Kraus's] writing is conversational yet critical, engaged yet incisive, with elements of chance, memory, and travel animating each entry."

—*The Brooklyn Rail*

"Kraus's text is not a collective call to arms, but an incitement to find art, to read in a heroic way, and to create a moment—as an individual or within a group—where one's relationship to the past is dictated only by the chance nature of what the present has thrown at you."

—*Glasgow Review of Books*

"Like all the great chroniclers of Los Angeles, Chris Kraus observes the city's emptiness, possibility and hallucination of meaning. But Kraus is Joan Didion cubed, writing herself into the narrative of the city."

—*Los Angeles Magazine*

"Writer and filmmaker Chris Kraus is searingly aware of the discourse in which she functions, and transforms it into something redolent of Simone Weil's poeticism and its daunting theoretical undercurrents."

—*Bookforum*

Also by CHRIS KRAUS

I Love Dick

Aliens & Anorexia

Video Green

Torpor

Where Art Belongs

Summer of Hate

After Kathy Acker

Social Practices

THE FOUR SPENT THE DAY TOGETHER

CHRIS KRAUS

SCRIBNER
New York   Amsterdam/Antwerp   London
Toronto   Sydney/Melbourne   New Delhi

Scribner
An Imprint of Simon & Schuster, LLC
1230 Avenue of the Americas
New York, NY 10020

For more than 100 years, Simon & Schuster has championed authors and the stories they create. By respecting the copyright of an author's intellectual property, you enable Simon & Schuster and the author to continue publishing exceptional books for years to come. We thank you for supporting the author's copyright by purchasing an authorized edition of this book.

No amount of this book may be reproduced or stored in any format, nor may it be uploaded to any website, database, language-learning model, or other repository, retrieval, or artificial intelligence system without express permission. All rights reserved. Inquiries may be directed to Simon & Schuster, 1230 Avenue of the Americas, New York, NY 10020 or permissions@simonandschuster.com.

As is true in many books of fiction, this book was inspired by events that appeared in the news. Nevertheless, the actions in the book, as well as the characters and dialogue, are products solely of the author's imagination. The names of some real people, companies and places appear, along with some real social media posts and messages, but they are applied to the events of this novel in an entirely fictitious manner.

Copyright © 2025 by Chris Kraus

All rights reserved, including the right to reproduce this book or portions thereof in any form whatsoever. For information, address Scribner Subsidiary Rights Department, 1230 Avenue of the Americas, New York, NY 10020.

First Scribner hardcover edition October 2025

SCRIBNER and design are trademarks of Simon & Schuster, LLC

Simon & Schuster strongly believes in freedom of expression and stands against censorship in all its forms. For more information, visit BooksBelong.com.

For information about special discounts for bulk purchases, please contact Simon & Schuster Special Sales at 1-866-506-1949 or business@simonandschuster.com.

The Simon & Schuster Speakers Bureau can bring authors to your live event. For more information or to book an event, contact the Simon & Schuster Speakers Bureau at 1-866-248-3049 or visit our website at www.simonspeakers.com.

Interior design by Kyle Kabel

Manufactured in the United States of America

1 3 5 7 9 10 8 6 4 2

Library of Congress Control Number: 2025937003

ISBN 978-1-6680-9868-4
ISBN 978-1-6680-9870-7 (ebook)

To B and A

Contents

Part 1—Milford
1

Part 2—Balsam
81

Part 3—Harding
"The Four Spent the Day Together"
185

Appendix
271

Acknowledgments
303

PART 1

MILFORD

1

. . . Just before she turned five, Catt's family moved from the East Bronx to Milford, Connecticut. It was winter, and she remembers exploring the yard while her parents cleaned out the house and unpacked their boxes. Carla, her little sister, age two, was probably stashed in a playpen. Winter-brown rosebushes clung to the garage wall and a big evergreen tree guarded the line between their house and the neighbor's driveway. The house beyond it was empty, boarded up for the winter. They wouldn't meet the Catalanos, their new neighbors, until they came up from New Jersey after Memorial Day for the summer. Catt picked up a bare frozen branch and dug holes in the snow. Under the evergreen tree, she found part of a small plastic sand pail. Buried inside translucent ice, it was frozen into the ground. She pushed and prodded.

Coming out to be sure Catt was still there, her father, Jasper, helped her dislodge it. *Look*, she said, *I found an ice toy! A nice toy*, her father replied. *An ice toy, a nice toy, an ice toy, a nice toy . . .* And she smiled, the elliptical meanings of words rolling around in their mouths like hard candy.

Their new house was on Wildemere Avenue, the last street to the south before the unguarded entrance to Laurel Beach, a private association. A long metal fence separated the residents of Wildemere Avenue from the more affluent Laurel Beach. *You Have Reached Laurel Beach—A Private Association for Members Only—Founded in 1903*, a big white wooden sign across the fence announced in cursive script. "A bunch of five-dollar millionaires," Sybille Brock liked to scoff. Sybille, as Catt's parents, Jasper and Emma, would soon learn, was the unofficial neighborhood historian. Unmarried in her early fifties, Sybille lived on Wildemere Avenue year-round in a tiny Cape Cod with her aged aunt. Nothing got by Sybille. She knew everyone in Milford at their worst.

Wildemere Avenue had once belonged to the now-defunct Wildemere Beach Association, a collection of beach shacks and bungalows built in the 1920s for prosperous, working-class Italian families whose kids and wives came up from Brooklyn or Hoboken for the summer. The elderly Catalanos were among the last of that seasonal tribe.

Over the years, storm windows and furnaces were installed in these old summer places and then they were sold to local, year-round families whose fathers worked in the trades or at the Sikorsky helicopter and Remington munitions factories in Bridgeport, less than ten miles away. These families were Catholic or else not religious. As US foreign policy flowed from the Korean War to the Cold War to the Vietnam conflict, these factories were flush with government contracts. With union pay and overtime, the assembly-line workers earned more than teachers and firemen.

THE FOUR SPENT THE DAY TOGETHER

At some point in a past no one but Sybille Brock recalled, Wildemere Beach had its own homeowner's association and a two-story clubhouse that hosted talent shows, card games, and bingo. As the old summer places were converted and sold to local families, the association disbanded and the clubhouse closed. Walnut Avenue, with its string of liquor stores, bars, and an amusement park that ran every summer, bordered the north side of Wildemere Beach. The hotels along Broadway had been turned into unlicensed care homes, bachelor apartments, and single-room occupancies. An Italian restaurant, Laruso's, reputedly run by the Mafia, opened their bar at noon every day to a handful of old-man boardinghouse customers.

To the south, the broad lawns of Laurel Beach were a parallel world. Inspired by the stately homes of Cape Cod or East Hampton, the Laurel Beach two- and three-story cottages all had ten or twelve rooms, skirted by gracefully curving Edwardian porches; dark cedar shingles, bay windows, and porticos. Each Laurel Beach avenue, numbered First through Eighth, bottomed out on Broadway with a gate leading to the private beach and boardwalk. On Fifth Avenue, at the heart of Laurel Beach, the association maintained a sprawling clubhouse known as the Casino. Flanked by tennis courts, the Casino was the place where they put on summer dances and hosted children's swim and tennis clubs. By the early 1960s, Laurel Beach seemed like a smart, contemporary choice for Milford's professional families. With the beach and the amenities, it was vastly preferable to the town's traditional center of wealth, a collection of drafty and stately colonial homes that lined the town green.

In the beginning, Catt's mother, Emma, wasn't aware of any of this. To her, Wildemere Avenue was an idyllic, quiet lane in the country. Looking out from her new front yard across the Laurel Beach fence, she could see a three-story house that to her seemed like a mansion, and a rambling white cottage covered in ivy where Dr. Malone, a retired GP, and his wife lived. Emma's house had a forsythia bush, a crab apple tree, and a magnolia. A row of sassafras trees lined the west side of the yard, separating them from their closest neighbors, the Pellicanos.

During their first week in Milford, while Emma was still settling into the house, Catt wandered into the Pellicanos' yard to explore. Bette Pellicano saw the lost child through her kitchen window—she had a son the same age—and asked Catt where she lived, but Catt didn't know. She just said, *We moved to the country*. Bette assumed she must belong to the new neighbors. Handing her back to Emma, Bette repeated Catt's answer. *Kids*, she laughed, *aren't they the limit?* and Emma blushed furiously. She'd hardly been out of the Bronx. She'd never considered the difference between country and town, but she knew right away that Milford was totally different from the Long Island suburbs of Massapequa and Levittown, where some of her old friends now lived. Milford had nothing to do with the city. It was strange and remote.

Jasper and Emma were among the last of their friends to leave the East Bronx. The neighborhoods they'd grown up in among Jews and Italians were now almost completely Puerto Rican. Of course Emma had nothing against them, they were just people, people like her and Jasper, but they kept to themselves and spoke only Spanish. Eight years into their marriage, until moving to Milford, she and Jasper still lived in the one-bedroom apartment on Tratman Avenue he'd shared with his late uncle George and late mother. Every night they pulled out the hide-a-bed couch while the girls slept in the bedroom that used to be hers and Jasper's.

She was thirty-three years old when they moved to Milford, with brown hair cut short in a bob that she maintained herself to save trips to the beauty parlor. By then she'd started to wonder if she'd ever have a real bed of her own to sleep in.

Growing up, she'd slept on the living room couch on Taylor Avenue, her mother asleep in the bedroom while her stepfather sat up talking back to the radio ten feet away from her, slurring his words, drinking and calling her to him. When she was small, Pat Kelley hadn't wanted her in the apartment. She'd been sent away for a whole year when she was four to live with her mother's childless widowed sister in New Jersey. Your mom and dad don't want you, her aunt Clara had explained then. But all that changed when she reached puberty.

Her friends knew something bad was going on at the apartment, but no one knew how long it had been going on, or the extent of it.

Pat Kelley—she could not call him Dad—couldn't hold any job for more than a month. The stench of his cigarillos filled the tiny apartment until her mom, who'd always had delicate health, couldn't stop wheezing. Her mother worked as a salesgirl at Macy's, selling shoes on commission. She'd held on to her job throughout the Depression, but as her asthma turned into emphysema she had to stop going to work. Emma was at the top of her class at James Monroe High School, treasurer of the Dramatic Society. Her best classes were English, Latin, and French, but she had to give up on her dream of going to college. She found a job as a statistical typist for the engineers building the new Bruckner Expressway. The engineers were mostly nice guys, very respectful, and her salary more than covered the rent.

Emma was twenty-five, a technical virgin, short, busty, and round like a ripe berry, with shiny brown hair that fell onto her shoulders, when Jasper dropped into the Episcopal Church of the Atonement one Sunday and heard her sing in the choir. The small white clapboard church with its black turret steeple was less than two blocks from Emma's apartment. Surrounded by well-tended bushes and trees, it was as if a wisp of some long-ago past had landed among the grimy brick tenement buildings on Taylor Avenue. All her life, for as long as she could remember, the church had been the only place where Emma felt completely clean. It was her refuge.

A year younger than her, Jasper did not even live in the neighborhood. He lived two stops away near Zerega Avenue and he went to St. Peter's, a much grander stone building, a cathedral almost, with its own chapel and cemetery. If Jasper hadn't decided to sample a different Episcopal church every Sunday that year they would never have met.

Jasper was tall, thin, and very distinguished, different from any man she'd ever gone out with. He wore a herringbone coat and took a monocle out of the inside pocket to look at the prayer book during the service. To Emma, this wasn't ridiculous. It was a gesture of infinite care. And Jasper knew how to ride horses! Not western but English. He volunteered most weekends with the New York City Mounted Police because that was the way to learn how to ride in Central Park for free. Although he lived in the Bronx, Jasper worked in Manhattan. He haunted the secondhand bookstores on lower Fourth Avenue between Cooper Union and Fourteenth Streets, in search of rare first editions and popular novels reviewed in the *Times* that week.

Exempted from military service to care for his mother during her long illness with Parkinson's, Jasper left school at fourteen and taught himself Latin while working full-time as a messenger boy in the jewelry district. In between errands, he discovered the Gotham Book Mart on West Forty-Seventh Street and even attended some meetings of the James Joyce Society. And to think: she'd almost married a butcher the year after high school! All her life, Emma had felt different from the people around her, and not just because of what had gone on all those years with Pat Kelley in practically full view of her mother. She wanted more than a late-model car and steak once a week. Jasper was the first man she'd gone out with who could talk about classical music and Shakespeare. Even his accent was different, as if he'd lived half his life in England or Europe.

Midway through their courtship, Jasper confided to Emma that the old man, Julius Greene, who had died when he was thirteen, wasn't really his father. Julius Greene (né Glaubner, from a Jewish industrial suburb of Prague) was a mason. Arriving alone in New York in his teens, he'd apprenticed himself in the trade and gone on to design ornate fountains and statues for city parks and Long Island millionaires. He'd waited to marry and he was fifty years old when Jasper was born. Jasper's fake father, Julius, had a workshop on Bailey Avenue, two workers, and a truck in Kingsbridge, a lower-middle-class section of the West Bronx. The workshop was just three blocks away from the new semidetached Heath Avenue duplex he'd bought for his family. Jasper; his big brother, Franklin; and their parents all lived downstairs. Their uncle George—a distant bachelor relation—rented the upstairs apartment.

But Julius's business never fully recovered from the Depression. People no longer wanted their lawns to be graced by funereal stone angels and fairies, odes to mortality that were popular during the *Great Gatsby* era. When he died at sixty-three the house was foreclosed.

Franklin had already fled the West Bronx to study at UC Davis and Jasper, his mother, and his uncle moved east to Westchester Square. For the rest of his life, Jasper would regret their exile from Kingsbridge (transformed by emotion in his stories and memory to the adjacent and vastly more affluent Riverdale) and the Heath Avenue town house (similarly transformed into a magnificent home set on rolling green lawns where deer grazed with bunnies) to the $24-a-month one-bedroom apartment on Tratman Avenue.

His mother's brothers, the four Hayman Boys, stockbrokers all, never offered to pay off the bank and stop the foreclosure. Maybe they'd had a rough time of it too, but they still had the Maiden Lane office. A year later, when his mother's Parkinson's became too advanced to ignore, all that they'd done was get him a messenger job in the Diamond District: to Jasper, it was a bewildering world where strange Jewish men in black suits yelled orders in Yiddish with breath that stank of pastrami.

But in the end, none of this mattered, he told Emma, because secretly he was a bastard—he liked the Shakespearean sound of that word: an illegitimate son of the British-born doctor Sir Edward St. John Jasper Lowsley. Jasper was certain his mother, Lillian, a vivacious and beautiful former journalist almost two decades her husband's junior, had had an affair with Dr. Lowsley, the Park Avenue proctologist his father consulted during the flush years before the stock market crash. Emma never questioned the likeliness of this story or the great doctor's complete absence from Jasper's life. Her father had abandoned her, too. Instead, she listened agape, as if this might explain Jasper's unusual accent, although if you actually thought about it (which she preferred not to do), it didn't.

When Jasper and Emma met, he'd already escaped the backroom squalor of West Forty-Seventh Street and moved down to Chelsea, where he assisted the manager of the Longines-Wittnauer warehouse. His job was inventory control, which meant keeping track of every Swiss timepiece that entered the warehouse and making sure no one was stealing. He was determined, he told her, to get out of the jewelry business and break into book publishing.

Eighteen months after the Sunday she'd written her phone number at the back of his prayer book, Emma and Jasper were married at St. Barnabas church. She thought about inviting her real father, the father who'd left when she was an infant, but he was somewhere out west and no one knew how to reach him. Still, she refused to let Pat Kelley give her away. She walked down the aisle with the head of the vestry. Her friends in the choir threw them a church hall reception. After the wedding, they caught the train at Penn Station to Niagara Falls and walked over the Peace Bridge. General Eisenhower had just beat Adlai Stevenson, the US had set off its first hydrogen bomb, and the Rosenbergs were in prison. It was the first week of November, cold, with thunderclouds overhead, and they saw a rainbow. Except for a few day trips up to Croton-on-Hudson with her girlfriend Marnie Beech, it was the first time Emma had ever been out of the city.

When they returned she moved into Jasper's apartment. Most of her old high school friends were leaving the city but at least she was finally free of Pat Kelley. Two stops or a long walk from the cramped tenement building that she'd grown up in, Jasper's one-bedroom apartment felt like a sanctuary. Trees lined the sidewalk and they had a view of the courtyard. She bought cookbooks and picked up groceries on her way home from work in the engineer's field office on the construction site that was to be the new Cross Bronx Expressway. After dinner they read, listened to records or radio dramas, played checkers and Scrabble. At twenty-seven and twenty-six years old, she and Jasper both felt like orphans. *Of course* they'd have children, but it wasn't time for that yet. Some Sundays they caught the train to St. Bartholomew's Church on Park Avenue to hear one of Bishop Sutton's excellent sermons. Jasper knew Bishop

THE FOUR SPENT THE DAY TOGETHER

Sutton because he'd loaned the diocese several rare prayer books from his collection for an exhibition. At the end of the service, as the congregation filed out and shook hands, he introduced her to the bishop. After that, they'd go for a walk in the park or take in a museum. She no longer sang in the Church of the Atonement choir. She and Jasper belonged to St. Peter's church now, and there was no room for her in St. Peter's semiprofessional choir. Over time, they saw her remaining old friends less and less. These friends were jokers and gossips with opinions all over the place. Their evenings together never quite clicked because Jasper didn't play cards and he didn't know how to talk to her friends. She could feel his discomfort. Perhaps he was shy, or just too far above them.

They'd been married a year when Pat Kelley dropped dead of a stroke and advanced liver failure. No one—not even Emma's mother—regretted his death. With Pat Kelley gone, her mother could live on her Social Security check. She wouldn't have to depend on her daughter's support, and Emma and Jasper could finally think about starting a family. Most of Emma's girlfriends already had toddlers. To be truthful, having a baby had never been one of her fantasies. As a girl, Emma daydreamed about travel. She read the *Arabian Nights* and imagined herself combing the markets of Mesopotamia, gathering shells on the beach in Gauguin's Tahiti, or sipping a café au lait at a railway café in Paris. She wondered if all those years with Pat Kelley had damaged her sex instinct, made her less of a woman. Didn't all women want babies? But, she knew, babies grew into children, and children were what made a family.

Jasper's dream of working in publishing was more realistic. Soon after Pat Kelley's death, he applied for a round of new jobs and moved to the warehouse at McGraw Hill Publishing Company as an assistant manager. An old friend from the Central Park Volunteer Mounted Police taught him to drive and they bought a used car. That summer, Jasper and Emma drove all the way up to Maine for vacation. They stayed in a housekeeping cabin surrounded by pines. By the time they got home, Emma knew she was pregnant.

Emma kept working long after she showed, almost until the end of her pregnancy. The baby, a girl they named Catherine, arrived within days of her due date. There were no complications.

Emma was thirty, about to turn thirty-one, by the time Catherine was born, but there was never a question in her or anyone's mind whether she'd have another. All her life growing up she'd longed for a sibling. Estranged from his brother or half brother, Franklin, Jasper and Emma were both only children. There were no nieces or nephews, uncles and aunts, grandparents or cousins. With no one to watch Catherine, there was no point going to work until the girl started school because most of her paycheck would just go to the babysitter.

She got pregnant again when Catherine was two and a half. This time it wasn't so easy, being pregnant while taking care of a toddler. The morning sickness was worse and she was

THE FOUR SPENT THE DAY TOGETHER

exhausted most of the time, hauling the stroller and groceries up three flights of stairs. During her second trimester she came down with mumps, which, Dr. Greenspan told her, was a stroke of good luck because if it had happened a few weeks before she could have miscarried. Still, she stayed in bed for nearly two weeks, too sick to watch Catherine, whom she reluctantly sent to her mom. Her mother still lived in the old apartment they'd shared with Pat Kelley on Taylor Avenue. Emma hated the thought that any part of her past could encroach on her new life or her children.

By the fifth month everything cleared. She felt stronger and better. At three, Catherine was already less trouble than she'd been before. Jasper was teaching Catherine to read and she spent most of her time in a living room corner drawing pictures and sounding out words from her storybooks. Emma already knew how to care for an infant. This time, she hoped for a boy, whom she'd name Kenneth.

That summer she gave birth to a girl. At the last minute the doctor insisted on a Cesarean birth but otherwise there were no complications. She thought about calling her Kendra but Jasper didn't care for that name, so they settled on Carla.

As soon as she went home and the anesthesia wore off Emma wondered if something was wrong. When she suckled her newborn she was clouded in bliss, just as she was with her first child. But the loop between her and the baby was never complete. When she held the child at her breast, Carla's small body remained tense ... the baby never melted onto her body the way the magazines said, the way it had been the first time with Catherine. And, even worse, Carla never looked into her eyes as she fed. The baby's wide eyes remained fixed and intent on the nipple as if Emma were just a milking machine, not the child's mother. Dr. Greenspan said there was nothing to worry about. She'd just given birth to a strong healthy girl; her weight was in the top quarter percentile.

But except in her sleep, the child never smiled. Carla cried all the time—not just when she was hungry or needed changing, but when she or Catherine made noise, or when Emma picked her up, took her out, tried to play with her, or even looked straight into her eyes. It was a loud, angry cry—as if Emma had done something wrong, something that hurt her. Jasper claimed to have no opinion. When Emma pressed the point harder, he said he'd tend to agree with Dr. Greenspan. After all, he was a pediatrician.

By now, Catherine was speaking in long compound sentences. Jasper bought her the Madeline books and together they memorized them. *In an old house in Paris that was covered with vines, lived twelve little girls in two straight lines, the smallest one was Madeline ...* She turned the text into a duet, assigning parts to him. After a long day at work, it was easier and more pleasant for him to converse with their older daughter and try to ignore Carla's screaming.

Jasper changed jobs when Carla was seven months old. At the new job with McGraw Hill, he assisted the office manager as well as the warehouse manager, making sure orders were filled and invoices were filed. No longer confined to the warehouse, he was learning more about publishing, talking to bookkeepers and secretaries as well as drivers and packers. When the weather was fine, he ate his packed lunch in the plaza at Rockefeller Center. Sometimes he skipped lunch altogether to look at rare books at the New York Public Library. At Scribner's on Fifth, he browsed the children's section for books to bring home for Catherine. Was *Monsieur Le Down*, the book about Gothic and Romanesque arches, too advanced for a four-year-old girl? He didn't think so.

In the Bronx, Carla wailed. She never seemed to sleep soundly for more than an hour. She cried in her crib and she cried when Emma held her. No matter what Emma did, it was wrong. She didn't crawl, she didn't say Mama or Papa, but she was growing, and fast. In fact, Carla's forehead seemed to grow bigger and much more pronounced than other parts of her body, which Emma hoped was a sign of intelligence. But when Carla started butting her head against the side of her playpen, Dr. Greenspan finally realized something was wrong. He referred them to a pediatric neurologist at Montefiore, who in turn sent them to Lenox Hill Hospital. And here began a long series of visits, tests, and procedures. Dr. Whitman, the specialist, warned them he'd need to monitor Carla's development before making any final assessments. But for how long, Emma wondered, riding the train with Carla finally asleep on her lap and Catherine in and out of her stroller.

When Jasper's boss at McGraw Hill was mysteriously fired, he was also let go by the new manager. Through no fault of his own, they lost their insurance. Until now, he'd distanced himself from Emma's simmering panic. But he had to get another job soon, if not immediately. The first thing he did was sell all his rare books to Ben Hackett, a kindly book dealer. Packing his entire collection into a suitcase, Emma's eyes misted up as she thought of the O. Henry story "The Gift of the Magi."

Unwrapping the books, Ben Hackett told Jasper he should talk to another collector he'd worked with, Giles Osborne, who was also the managing director of the American branch of Cambridge University Press. Jasper had already met Giles Osborne through Bishop Sutton. Osborne agreed to meet Jasper (Ben Hackett had called him) and two weeks later, Jasper began working at Cambridge. His job title, initially, was supervisor of manual inventory control. But even though the actual inventory sat in a shared warehouse space downtown near the Holland Tunnel, they offered Jasper the use of an extra desk in the East Fifty-Seventh Street office. Giles Osborne noticed Jasper's unusual passion for books. Clearly, the younger man idolized him and yet Jasper Glaubner, or Greene, unlike most of his kind, was reserved, never pushy. On a rare impulse, Osborne invited him to sit in on monthly editorial meetings. They served Riesling and told slightly off-color jokes. Jasper listened, enthralled.

Carla continued her tests. She was probed, scanned, measured, and sung to by student researchers. Finally, conclusions were drawn. Emma and Jasper were summoned to Dr. Whitman's office on the Upper East Side. *Your daughter*, he told them, *is severely retarded with an IQ of sixty-five. Do not expect much. Do*

THE FOUR SPENT THE DAY TOGETHER

not expect anything. With luck and good treatment, she might attain the mental age of seven by the time she reaches adulthood.

Jasper and Emma decided not to believe him.

Carla was two years old, barely a toddler, and things went on as before as if none of the testing had ever happened. Every morning, Emma unmade the sofa bed and reclaimed the living room. She dragged Carla's playpen out of the bedroom to keep an eye on her daughter while she worked in the bright yellow kitchen. Her best girlfriend Marnie and her engineer husband, Bob, had just bought a brand-new tract home in Massapequa Park on Long Island. The rest of the world had moved on, thinking big, making gelatin salads while she baked pound cake from scratch and invented new ways to get three meals out of a chicken. Most days she took the girls to the playground on Westchester Avenue where the nuns from St. Bridget's taught the kids free arts and crafts on the big picnic tables. There was no one to talk to. The other moms at the playground were young, Puerto Rican, even teenagers—girls with hoop earrings and glossy red lips talking and laughing in waves of fast Spanish. It occurred to Emma that the entire Bronx was an enormous dormitory for immigrant labor built in the late nineteenth century. Annexed to the wealth of the Gilded Age, each new wave of workers was a little more desperate. Her real father escaped with her mom to Salt Lake while she was an infant. He had big plans to move on to San Francisco but her mom was afraid of the unknown and she refused to join him.

Instead, she returned to the Bronx and married Pat Kelley. The Bronx would never change, and neither would she or her girls if they stayed there. The brightest boys in her class had been communists. Even her old friends from the choir were leaving for places like Garden City, Hempstead, and Hoboken.

While Catherine played on the swings and made pipe cleaner animals at the nuns' picnic tables, Emma rocked Carla's pram and wondered what had made her child different. Was it the mumps that she caught while she was pregnant, was it the Cesarean birth? She knew there was a full person, even an angel, locked behind Carla's scowling and squalling face. How could she help Carla's true spirit emerge? And why couldn't the doctors see it? Sometimes she thought all the way back to her daughter's conception: an October night, Indian summer, she and Jasper and Catherine had driven to Orchard Beach one last time before it closed down for the season. Was it something to do with her childhood, the way she held back, never giving herself over completely? But that couldn't be, it was not scientific. Every day she prayed that the doctors were wrong about Carla.

Carla's namesake, Carl Faiman, whom Jasper had known at the Longines-Wittnauer warehouse, retired the year that Carla turned two. Carl's two sons were grown and he and his wife, Erna, bought a big two-family house in Milford, Connecticut, one block from the beach. Carl, a Czech immigrant, was born in same Prague Jewish district as Jasper's late stonemason

THE FOUR SPENT THE DAY TOGETHER

father. The old man and the young man struck up a friendship. Perhaps they were even related, who knew?

Carl had considered his move out of the city for a long time. The old houses in Milford were cheap, a bargain compared to the suburban tract homes that all the young couples were buying. Carl could hardly believe his good luck once he and Erna moved into the house. He walked every day on the beach and with the rent coming in from downstairs they had more than enough to get by on. Still, he and Erna had long drifted apart and sometimes he wished for a friend. During these walks, an idea formed in his mind: he knew that Jasper was looking to get out of the Bronx—what if he and his family moved someplace close by? He could loan them the down payment. He invited them up for a weekend and proposed the idea.

As soon as they arrived at the small Milford station, Jasper knew that he wanted to live there. He forgot that their train had departed Grand Central a whole hour and forty-two minutes ago. The station was in the heart of downtown Milford, two streets away from the big town green. A stone tower guarded the Memorial Bridge, spanning a small branch of the Wepawaug River, with the names of the town's twenty-nine Puritan founders carved into big granite blocks: James Prime; Thomas Tapping; Frances Bolt; Ezeckial Fowler. It had been rebuilt and restored over the years, but the bridge dated all the way back to 1640, the year Milford was founded. The town green had a bandstand and a gazebo. A sprawling old two-story brick building housed the town library, across from a bank. Emma felt like she'd stepped into a dream—not hers, exactly.

Ducks nested and swam in the river that curled through the town. On the way up, more than an hour before, they'd passed Old Greenwich, where Jasper's boss, Mr. Osborne, had a house and some acres . . . and then Darien and Westport, where Chief Editor Bob Newbridge and Financial Controller Jack Sachmann had their homes.

Of course, things looked a lot different when they arrived at Carl's house at Naugatuck Beach. Big stolid houses built in the 1920s for summer residents who no longer arrived stood shoulder to shoulder, clad in aluminum siding. But there was the beach and the town green and the safe public schools and the library . . .

Three weeks later, Carl found the house at 49 Wildemere Avenue and put down a deposit before Jasper and Emma ever saw it. It was a twenty-five-minute walk south from his own house on Naugatuck Avenue—a charming one-and-a-half-story white bungalow with two small bedrooms and two dormers and an unheated sunporch. Emma bought her first double bed in nearby Bridgeport and they moved in a few days after Christmas.

As soon as they settled in she realized that she'd never been so isolated before, or so lonely.

2

Bette Pellicano invited Emma over for coffee to welcome her to the neighborhood: an event Emma dreaded, and with good cause. A tall brunette who wore stretch pants and harlequin sweaters, Bette was seven years younger than Emma. Her husband worked for Sikorsky Aircraft and she'd grown up in Milford so of course she already had plenty of friends. What would they talk about? Emma didn't like drinking coffee because it upset her stomach but she was afraid to ask Bette for tea.

Bette assumed Emma's husband had been transferred to Milford for work. Why else would they move here? She'd been to the city for shopping and shows but she had no idea what the Bronx was. Emma didn't begin to know how to describe it—she struggled to think what this pretty young woman would be interested in. The botanical gardens? The Bronx Zoo? They let the kids feed the seals for a nickel a fish if you got there at four. Catherine loved it.

Bette's son Kevin was the same age as Catherine and for a while, the two children played together, going into each other's rooms, climbing over the falling-down fence between their two yards. But when Emma discovered Kevin and Catherine playing Doctor and Patient underneath the forsythia bush, the two women decided it would be best if the children stopped seeing each other. They were both very careful not to express blame but after that there was no longer a reason to have coffee or chat.

Most mornings Emma drove Jasper to catch the six forty-five train to New York and picked him up twelve hours later. Ideally, these runs into town entailed dressing the girls and strapping Carla into her car seat while her little fists pounded the air. Sometimes, when they ran late she gave Catherine a book, put Carla into her playpen, and left them alone. How much could happen in less than an hour? It was better to risk it, because if she let Jasper drive himself to the station she'd be stranded on Wildemere Avenue all day with two kids.

The station was empty and dark when Jasper arrived in the morning. Four or five other men wearing topcoats haunted the New York–bound platform, flexing their fingers inside the black leather gloves their wives gave them for Christmas. The train wouldn't start filling up before they reached Fairfield and until Westport, the cars were half-empty. But after that, stopping at Darien, Old Greenwich, Cos Cob, the cars were all full of commuters who seemed to know each other by name, smoking and reading their papers. Jasper never saw Osborne or Sachmann or Newbridge getting onto the train. Did they drive into work? Perhaps they all caught the express out of Stamford.

THE FOUR SPENT THE DAY TOGETHER

When Emma got home she poured the girls' cereal, cleaned up the dishes, and made all the beds. From the hall window at the top of the stairs, she could see a slip of the Long Island Sound when the branches were bare. This was her house. *In Connecticut.* She bought an old Singer from the Goodwill and tried making curtains, an impossible project.

Carla was almost two and a half but she still wasn't speaking, not even a word. She wailed when Emma picked her up out of the playpen to change her. And so Emma sang, any song from her own childhood she could remember, "You Are My Sunshine," "Pack Up Your Troubles," "Row Row Row Your Boat," and often that calmed her. Once a week she did laundry on Naugatuck Avenue and shopped for groceries, combining her errands to save money on gas. In September Catherine would start kindergarten. Surely things would change then—she'd meet other mothers, go to PTA meetings. Sometimes on impulse she treated herself to a magazine at the IGA Foodliner checkout.

On the 5:15 New Haven–bound train from Grand Central, these same commuters—insurance salesmen, diplomats, advertising executives—bought drinks in the bar car and swung back the bench seats to play cards, four or six men facing each other. Sitting alone, Jasper looked out the window and leafed through a Cambridge University Press book he'd picked up at the warehouse . . . books about ancient history, molecular biology, quantum physics. At home, he ate dinner while Emma put Carla to bed. The house stank of small children. After that he read stories with Catherine, and then he and Emma talked for a while before going to bed. They would not buy a TV before Carl Faiman's loan was repaid.

Jasper and Emma knew the dangers of debt. They'd seen other people get into trouble, they weren't stupid. And besides, they had other pleasures. Filling the house with classical music all weekend on WQXR radio . . . playing their record of Carl Orff's *Carmina Burana* so loud the neighbors could hear it, the ribald songs of thirteenth-century clergy and nuns pouring out of the windows in Latin. Emma followed along with the English translation that came inside the sleeve and blushed when she heard it.

On Saturday mornings they went to the dump out beyond Naugatuck Avenue. There, flocks of white seagulls swooped over great mounds of garbage assembled by bulldozers. Householders tossed fresh bags of trash from their cars into the piles in a rushed orgy of freedom. After the dump, they'd sometimes go and have lunch with the Faimans. Erna, Carl's wife, served latkes and cabbage and barely spoke English. It was as if she'd never left Prague.

But the high point of each week for Emma and Jasper was the 10 a.m. Sunday service at St. Andrew's Episcopal Church. The priest, Father Luke, was no Bishop Sutton, but he was friendly and decent. His wife, Charlene, was the organist. She'd trained as a pianist and wore her long raven hair up in a loose wispy bun. Like her hair, Charlene gave the impression of someone forever just on the verge of becoming undone.

THE FOUR SPENT THE DAY TOGETHER

Distracted, forgetful, and breathless, she skipped from subject to subject as she made conversation with her husband's parishioners after the service over coffee or tea. Charlene's long oval face was forever marred by a harelip that everyone tried not to look at. Emma found Charlene very sympathetic and would have liked to be friends, although she realized this was impossible. The priest's wife couldn't be seen playing favorites among the congregation. Still, Emma sensed Charlene understood something about the worry she felt every day about Carla.

A few of their fellow St. Andrews parishioners lived in Laurel Beach. The Petersons, the Hoggs, the Conways were all virtual neighbors, with homes just a few streets away. In fact, Jasper realized after a few Sundays that Gregory Peterson was one of the men he saw every day on the New York–bound platform. Greg worked on Madison Avenue, a few blocks from the Cambridge office on Fifty-Seventh and Lex. After meeting in church the two men began nodding good morning. If the train came in late, they traded remarks about the weather or the New Haven Line schedule. But once they boarded the train, they were careful to claim seats at least a few rows away from each other. Neither one was inclined to make the first move or create a precedent they both might regret later.

That year, *Time* magazine published an interview with a famous psychiatrist, Leo Kanner, about Refrigerator Mothers and how they produced damaged children. Women who "just happen to defrost long enough to produce a child"; women whose maternal neglect lay at the heart of their children's mental illness. Could this be her? This new insight stunned her.

For a long time, everyone was talking about it; comedians cracked jokes about "re-FRIGID" women. But in the wake of this latest humiliation, Emma discovered a new seed of doubt or of hope: perhaps Carla was mentally ill, not retarded? Even though she didn't speak, didn't smile or react, she played with her Lego and magnetic blocks with fierce concentration, balancing them into intricate structures. Clearly the child had intelligence. Sometimes Carla reminded her of the structural engineers whose plans and blueprints she'd typed.

After reading the article, Emma scooped both girls up every day and brought them into the bedroom. *Do you want a little loving*, she'd ask, taking them in her arms, rolling around on the bed, and tickling Carla until they were all giggling and flustered. Still, Emma wondered if she'd somehow, unconsciously, passed the damage her stepfather did to her as a girl on to Carla. Pat Kelley used sex to hold her back, put her down, and humiliate her, and yet she had stayed. Her own mother was a weak, wounded woman, afraid of her own shadow. She didn't or couldn't help Emma, but if Emma had left, they both would have had no one. Everything in life that mattered, everyone said, could be traced back to the sexual instinct.

Emma became an avid Plaid Stamp collector. The IGA Foodliner gave out Plaid Stamps to shoppers for free. The stamps could be glued into books and then redeemed for free merchandise. Whenever she finished a book she put it into the

THE FOUR SPENT THE DAY TOGETHER

strongbox she kept in the closet, along with her ID and checkbooks. Emma hadn't held a job since her last pregnancy. She leafed through the catalog, looking at all the nice things she could earn with them.

On a rainy spring day when she was feeling even bluer than usual, she put the girls in the car and drove to the nearest redemption center. Looking out the window from the backseat, Catherine observed how abruptly the smug, sleepy houses and yards, the "colonial charm" of the town, disappeared after crossing the drawbridge in Devon. Car lots and commercial real estate signs with the words *Will Divide* loomed in the overgrown vacant lots of Connecticut Avenue. She wondered who Will Divide was. Passing the big Remington Arms factory and a tangle of train tracks, they stopped in a vast parking lot surrounding an old long, low warehouse: the Plaid Stamp redemption center. Inside, women with infants and strollers examined the merchandise in big open bins under fluorescent lights. Catherine knew then that this was a population she'd do anything not to belong to. She followed behind as Emma pushed Carla's stroller past TV stands and lamps, glassware and cocktail shakers.

Emma had eighteen books in her purse, just enough for a new Sunbeam toaster. The trip cheered her up. She was pleased with the toaster.

When summer came, the Catalanos arrived and parked their speedboat in the driveway next door. Emma took the kids to the beach when it wasn't raining. The gate to the Laurel Beach boardwalk was just a few yards away from the end of their street, across from Eighth Avenue. A narrow hedge-bordered path led from the gate to an open gazebo and a clean beach with white sand. A sign welded onto the gate said *Private Beach—Members Only*. The gate was always left open but still Emma walked over two blocks to the public, ungated beach on Ocean Avenue. Laurel Beach was a private beach. What if anyone asked where she lived and what she was doing there?

Wedged in between the cement retaining walls of two beachfront houses, the Ocean Avenue beach was frequented mostly by teenagers. Clusters of dry blackened seaweed divided a narrow strip of brown sand from the rocky shoreline. A few other women her age often arrived in the late afternoon. They spread out their blankets and beach chairs and sunbathed with aluminum foil wrapped over their noses. The women drank cocktails they brought with them in thermoses out of kids' plastic cups. As the sun softened around five, their laughter got louder and harsher.

Emma wanted to swim. As a girl, she'd learned how to swim in the Hudson River on her trips up to Croton . . . but she didn't trust Catherine enough to keep Carla safe while she went in the water so she just sat on the sand. On clear days you could see a strip of Long Island across the sound. Looking north, there was Charles Island—a magical place covered in forest that you could reach at low tide by walking half a mile out on a thin strip of sandbar.

THE FOUR SPENT THE DAY TOGETHER

In September school started and Emma's days became even more complicated. If they'd lived on Eighth Avenue Catherine could have taken the bus to Kay Avenue elementary school, but Wildemere Avenue was one block too close to qualify for free busing. At five, she was still too small to walk the half mile alone, which meant dropping her off at the kindergarten entrance just before nine and then picking her up when it finished at noon. Catherine was already reading and writing. Emma begged them to let her enter first grade, which went on until three. But that couldn't be done, the principal said, he wouldn't consider it. Didn't she understand that missing such a critical year would impede the girl's social development?

Catherine liked snack time and naptime. She learned to play Mother in the toy model kitchen and suffered through Story Circle, where Miss Morton dragged out the words from each infantile book as if she were sleepwalking. At home, she and her father were reading poems from *The Oxford Book of English Verse*. Sometimes he helped her to memorize them. When she learned to recite Blake's "The Tyger" by heart, Jasper brought her a beautiful illustrated children's edition of *Songs of Innocence and of Experience*. Jasper's own childhood had been cut so short by the Depression, he hadn't thought much about children until after Catherine began speaking. He was surprised by the porosity of a bright child's imagination and how easily he could shape it. When Catherine stumbled on words like "sinews" and "symmetry," he pronounced them for her out loud, his clipped faux-British accent truncating and yet somehow clarifying each syllable. Then, he took the *Shorter Oxford English Dictionary* down from the tallest living room bookcase and they looked the words up together. Marooned on Wildemere Avenue evenings and weekends, the girl was his project car, his familiar. Catherine knew what every word in the "Tyger" poem meant, but she did not always know what the words meant together.

When the congregation of St. Andrew's Episcopal Church decided to put on a variety show to raise funds for the vestry, Jasper saw this as a chance to showcase his work with Catherine. He signed her up for a Poetic Recitation and decided to teach her one of the limericks Giles Osborne shared during the Cambridge editorial meetings. This would be their secret, he told Catherine as they practiced together. It would be a nice surprise for her mother.

On the night of the show, Catherine stepped out onto the dark church hall stage wearing a starched little-girl dress and recited,

> *Weep not for Little Leonie*
> *Abducted by a French marquis*
> *Though loss of honor was a wrench*
> *Just think how it improved her French.*

Emma was mortified. The audience, already tipsy on spiked pre-show punch, roared with embarrassed laughter, the kind of deep, red-faced laughter that erupts when a banal interaction is suddenly sexualized. And then Father Luke and a few men from the vestry came out wearing wigs, makeup, and dresses

THE FOUR SPENT THE DAY TOGETHER

to perform Doris Day's "I Enjoy Being a Girl" and by the end of the night, all was forgotten.

In 1961, Cambridge University Press published *The New English Bible*, the first new translation of the sacred text undertaken since the St. James Bible of the seventeenth century. This event brought biblical concepts into the twentieth century and also changed Jasper and Emma's lives for the better. Orders poured into the office from all over America. The new Bible became Cambridge's bestselling title. Tens of thousands of copies were printed every few months and the shared warehouse space in Tribeca became too small to store them.

Osborne and Sachmann decided to give up the Fifty-Seventh Street office and move the whole operation to New Rochelle, a blue-collar town in Westchester County. Labor was cheap and it was only a half-hour drive from their homes in commuter Connecticut. They purchased a vacant industrial building with the idea that Jasper would set up a new warehouse and manage it.

Not only did Jasper receive a small raise, his commute was reduced from a four-and-a-half-hour to a two-and-a-half-hour round-trip every day. There were so many orders for *The New English Bible* that the office staff couldn't keep up with accounting and filing. Jack Sachmann let Jasper bring some of this work home for Emma. The kitchen table became her office, where she sorted the orders by region two or three hours a day for thirty cents over the minimum wage. They bought a second used car and a TV. Instead of taking the train, Jasper commuted to work on the thruway.

Without the twice-daily runs to the station, Emma's days became longer. Catherine was in the first grade, gone most of the day and big enough now to walk there alone or with other children. Alone all day with Carla, Emma now had the time that she'd craved . . . enough time to wonder how her life might be different if she'd gone to college, or if they'd moved to Long Island. Her friend Marnie had already gone back to work in Massapequa, teaching third grade.

The women she met at St. Andrew's church were friendly, but they lived too far away to become friends she could see on a casual basis. The other mothers in Catherine's class were younger than she and they'd grown up in or around Milford. Some of them worked full-time in restaurants and factories and they were so tough they frightened her . . . women with big broods of kids who worked opposite shifts to their husbands and drank on the weekends. Others, like Catt's friend's mom Mrs. Jackowski, were divorced or had never even been married. A cluster of stay-at-home moms in the new houses close to the school styled each other's hair and organized bake sales. These women dressed up their daughters like dolls. The Laurel Beach moms kept to themselves. Their lives were more interesting, Emma assumed.

By now, she'd met most of her year-round neighbors on Wildemere Avenue. Things with Bette were strained since the Doctor incident. There were the O'Briens, Joanne and Roger, older, retired devout Roman Catholics, and across from them there were the Shaminskis. The Shaminskis had five or six

THE FOUR SPENT THE DAY TOGETHER

children and a John Birch Society decal on their front door. Emma had never met Mrs. Shaminski, she'd only caught glimpses, but she'd seen Mr. Shaminski outside the house fixing his truck. The truck had a loaded gun rack and he'd looked at her with a Pat Kelley sneer. According to Catherine, who'd started running around with a group of the neighborhood kids, Jimmy Jr., who was her age, liked torturing squirrels and cats.

Emma didn't want to burden Jasper with these problems. But one night when the girls were in bed and he asked how her day had gone she started sobbing. *Why am I lonely, so bored and depressed?* Jasper looked at his wife, his long face detached and thoughtful, as she recounted how awful she'd felt when she dropped Catherine off at Holly Platt's birthday party. Mrs. Platt, Marybeth, offered to take Catherine's present as soon as they walked in the door, but Emma hadn't known until then that the kids were supposed to bring gifts. *My stomach hurts, each day is worse and what can I do?* And then a cluster of Marybeth's friends, some of the other moms, were sitting around in her kitchen talking and smoking and laughing. Marybeth hadn't even invited her in so she left all alone and returned two hours later to pick Catherine up.

Hmmm, Jasper said, clearing his throat. Why don't you call Lydia Bhattula?

She'd never thought about this. Jasper always knew what to do.

Long ago, before he met Emma, when he still worked in the jewelry district, Jasper took the train to West Fourth Street once a week to attend Introduction to Greek at NYU's Continuing Education Center. Lydia Bhattula, whose name then was Drakos, had been one of his classmates. A beautiful girl two years younger than him, Lydia had signed up to learn to speak with her Greek grandparents. To her, Greek was a living language. She wore her waist-length black hair in a stunning chignon and worked as a floor model and salesgirl at Bergdorf Goodman.

Jasper and Lydia were the only two students their age in the class. They began going out after class to have coffee, and eventually dinner and drinks. Lydia was an exuberant girl with a high trilling voice, vibrant but maybe a little naïve. She'd grown up in Bucks County and believed in world peace. She loved folklore, modern art, modern dance. They went out a few more times after the class ended. Things between them remained vague, and then Lydia met Gautam Bhattula at work. The eldest son of a wealthy Indian family, Gautam swooped in to win her and Jasper stepped back. Still, he and Lydia remained friends, sometimes meeting for lunch. After he and Emma had gotten engaged, he introduced them.

The two women became casual friends. Their first pregnancies overlapped by three months, but then Lydia and Gautam bought a house on a lake just south of Fairfield, Connecticut. After that they fell out of touch except for the phone calls that eventually dwindled to Christmas cards. Lydia's first child was a boy she'd named Michael. Her second, Danielle, was born around the same time as Carla.

Jasper was right. For almost three years while she'd struggled to make new friends in Milford, Lydia and her family were

THE FOUR SPENT THE DAY TOGETHER

just a half an hour away. Emma decided to call. It's been such a long time, Lydia trilled, and then invited the whole family next Sunday to lunch.

Danielle was a sweet little girl, but Emma saw right away there was something terribly wrong with six-year-old Michael. Tall and strong for his age, Michael's limbs flopped around him like jelly. Lydia had to settle him into his chair and then he wouldn't sit still. He couldn't speak words but he tried to communicate, emitting guttural cries, sometimes of contentment but more often rage. Michael's dark eyes seemed to smolder and his forehead was high and pronounced. Lydia had said nothing about her problems with Michael—but then again, Emma had never mentioned her worries about Carla in their few phone calls and notes.

Gautam took Jasper outside to show him the lake and their boat. While the little girls played in Danielle's room, Lydia and Emma caught up in the kitchen, with an eye on their two problem kids and the lunch.

Michael had been diagnosed with cerebral palsy soon after his birth, but Lydia wasn't sure she believed this. And even if the diagnosis was true, she refused to accept the doctor's prognosis: that her son would spend the rest of his life in a wheelchair, developmentally disabled, unable to work or make friends or have kids. Lydia wore a silk blouse, a long gathered skirt, and dozens of Indian bangles made out of amber and jade. She was still the same loopy idealist Jasper had known in New York but her passion for changing the world was now focused on one single goal, saving her son. Instead of being beaten down by Michael's special needs, Lydia seemed enhanced. When Emma brought up the Refrigerator Theory, she just laughed.

Didn't you know something was wrong that the doctors denied? Lydia asked. It's the same thing with us. When children are hurt, it's mothers who know.

When Michael was diagnosed with cerebral palsy, we were still living on the Upper West Side, Lydia explained. I knew I couldn't cope there. We decided to move here to the lake because it was more peaceful but I just kept him at home, there wasn't a plan or a doctor I liked.

When Danielle was born I tried putting Michael in daycare but he got too upset, it didn't work out. The director said I should try Fairfield Day Academy, a new school for special needs kids. None of the New York doctors had ever mentioned this place!

Gautam and I made an appointment to see Dr. Robert Gallo, the man in charge. They had all kinds of kids, age three to twelve, who'd been diagnosed with all kinds of terrible things—cerebral palsy, Down's syndrome, epilepsy, autism, retardation. Dr. Bob told us to forget about cerebral palsy. Whatever names the doctors attached to our kids didn't matter—they were all just hurt children, suffering from developmental delays, who needed our help.

He told us about a new treatment, the Doman-Delacato technique, designed to help kids with developmental delays. They had a center in Philadelphia, and Dr. Bob had trained

THE FOUR SPENT THE DAY TOGETHER

there. According to Doman-Delacato, children develop the same way that humans evolved from flowers and fishes millions of years ago! Each one of us recapitulates the entire history of man as we grow from infant to child, moving through stages that reprise our evolution—from a fish to an amphibian, to a reptile, a mammal, and finally a human. Dr. Bob said that Michael was stuck between fish and mammal but that didn't mean he'd have to stop there. They have a set of techniques that actually alter the brain through motor activity and move your child through the stages. Dr. Bob says every child has genius potential.

Emma didn't know what to think. She'd never heard of these theories. It was hard to consider Carla the same as a turtle or fish. But at the same time, no one had ever suggested a treatment for her. These men believed that instead of giving up on these kids or even locking them up in an institution, there were things you could do to help them catch up.

After the two families ate lunch, Emma followed Lydia downstairs to the den, which she'd transformed into a kind of occupational therapy room. She watched as Lydia laid Michael face down on a massage table. For the next thirty minutes, it looked as if he were swimming. She rotated his arms, moved his head. They did this twice every day. The technique was called "patterning," and it was true, Michael looked like a frog fighting his way out of the water and onto the mud. Patterning, Lydia explained, helped Michael with muscle control. The movements they made on the table were imprinting the pattern onto his nerves and his brain. After that, they'd move on to "crawling" and "creeping." When she was finished, Lydia sat Michael down on a beanbag and took out a bag of small objects. There were feathers and shells, rocks, sticks, plastic figures. Here, Lydia said, now choose one. Touch was the first sense, she explained. Touch, vision, and sound are the ways we perceive the world. By choosing and holding these things, Michael's brain would unclench and he'd be more receptive to the things he perceived every day, instead of shutting them out.

Watching Lydia work with Michael, Emma was completely transported from the minor humiliations of her life on Wildemere Avenue. Before they all left, Lydia offered to set up a meeting for Carla with Dr. Bob.

Jasper was irritable on the drive home. In his opinion, Lydia Bhattula had gone from flighty to batshit crazy. A human child wasn't a fish! And how could Emma compare Carla to Michael, who was so clearly retarded? To be perfectly honest, Michael probably belonged in an institution—did Emma really think this was helping him?

Yes, Emma said, I see what you mean.

She called Lydia the next day and a month later, Carla was enrolled at the Fairfield Day three days a week.

3

The Fairfield Day Academy campus was just a big, ranch-style house discreetly set in a quiet residential neighborhood. The treatment was new and Blue Cross didn't cover it. Except for the office secretary, Dr. Bob was the only full-time person on staff. Speech and physical therapists came in and out but most of the mothers volunteered one day a week. As Dr. Bob liked to say, they had less to unlearn than the professionals.

Emma met all kinds of moms at the academy—a Black woman and her son formerly diagnosed with Down's syndrome from inner-city Bridgeport; a white Smith College graduate from Westport and her daughter who'd been diagnosed mentally retarded. The only differences that mattered between them had to do with the kids and how they responded to therapy. The living room had been turned into an occupational therapy gym with monkey bars, weights, mats, balls, and patterning tables. Every morning a small team of moms helped the kids through a circuit that started with patterning therapy and ended up in the Listening Circle, where they listened to records of birdsong and thunder. As Dr. Bob said, by learning to hear and identify sounds, the kids were unlocking the part of the brain that controlled speech and language.

Emma knew right away that the treatment was good for Carla. Dr. Bob was the first medical authority to even believe there were things to be done that could help her. Just getting her there three days a week in a place with other children seemed to make a difference. Carla's mobility was already good—they just had to work on her verbal ability. Dr. Bob pushed her toward music and soon she was playing xylophone songs for the kids in the Listening Circle, and even composing them. At nearly four years old, Carla still refused to speak, but Emma was sure she was absorbing everything.

Emma's volunteer work gave them a partial tuition reduction. To cover the rest, she addressed envelopes, two cents apiece, on a big typewriter Jasper brought home from the office. But that still wasn't enough. They took out a second mortgage and borrowed again from the Faimans.

On Carla's Fairfield days, Catherine came home with a house key that she wore around her neck underneath her shirts and dresses. At eight years old, she was sensible and independent. She was careful not to lose the key, careful not to ever show it to the other kids or teachers. Emma worried sometimes that she was letting Catherine grow up wild, but what was the alternative? If the treatments failed, if Carla couldn't overcome her developmental delays, she'd ultimately become Catherine's responsibility.

Catherine couldn't stand to look at Carla. She didn't like to think about her sister much because when she did, she was overwhelmed with hatred. Her parents and the Fairfield people said over and over, There's nothing wrong with Carla, she's just different, but this was obviously untrue. You treat your sister like a vegetable, the visiting therapist chided her at Fairfield. She'd been trying, then, to hide the hate the way she hid the key. Because Carla was a little monster: squalling, screaming, and rocking; blowing air through her lips as if she were farting and then flicking her tongue with a small secret grin. Carla knew exactly how to annoy people. The cries and coos Lydia and all the other Fairfield mothers made around her little sister made Catherine sick. Carla's head seemed too big for her body, she had wide saucer eyes and thick bushy brows, and it looked like half her face was forehead.

She knew the other kids all knew that Carla was retarded. Her friend Margit told her this as if it was a secret, but it was a secret she already knew. Whenever Emma forced Catherine to take Carla with her to the beach and they passed by the Muller house, the Muller kids all shouted *Retard, retard!* But Carla did not, could not, react, and so they changed their taunts to *Catherine Greene, hey, Catherine Greenberg, your sister is a retard! What's for dinner at your house tonight, retard-burgers?* Catherine's face turned red. She didn't know what she thought about the Mullers, a big Catholic Laurel Beach family whose older daughters went to private school at Laurelton Hall, but suddenly the few dozen yards between Wildemere and Laurel Beach was turned into a stage and she was trapped within a spotlight. She wished she could be teleported out of Milford without any of her family.

Hoping to appease her older daughter's abandonment and rage, Emma let Catherine keep the stray black cat she found next door at the Catalanos'. Jasper hated cats, he disliked animals in general, but when Catherine tried to call her new pet Blackie he became interested enough to help her name it. Wasn't the name Blackie a little too pedestrian for this extraordinary feline? Not to mention racially insensitive? She should try the French, Noir, it was more elegant. Two days later, Jasper came up with an even better name: Trismegistus. Hermes Trismegistus was the god of the occult and magic, worshipped by the ancient Greeks in the Ptolemaic Kingdom. Jasper took out volume 2 of *The Cambridge Ancient History* and read out loud to Catherine about black magic and the emerald tablets. *What is below is like that which is above. And what is above is like that which is below*, she repeated. Were they casting spells? Her mother knew enough to leave the two of them alone when they were working. Sometimes Catherine felt her looking at them strangely. But then the young cat disappeared before anyone could learn his name and Catherine soon forgot about him.

Catherine knew her father was preparing her for a better life beyond Milford. He taught her how to swim in water far above her head and how to ride a bike by taking off the training wheels before she knew what he was doing. He told her stories about the *New York Times* arts columnist he'd briefly dated and

THE FOUR SPENT THE DAY TOGETHER

Catherine pictured the apartment that she'd have, two rooms in the East Seventies or Eighties, a big leafy tree outside the window. On weekends, when her friend Bonnie or Margit came over, Jasper led them in a game of Spelling Bee. Each girl moved up one step on the staircase for every word she spelled correctly. He made sure to give her friends the easy words. Catherine, spell "dissolution," he'd intone, and then his eyes met hers with just the slightest trace of a smile when he asked her girlfriends to spell "dog" and "ball" and "car." "Milford" was like a private joke between them.

When she was five years old, eighteen months after entering Fairfield Day Academy, Carla finally started speaking. Not baby talk: whole sentences. Emma was washing dishes, looking out the kitchen window at another bleak late-winter day, when Carla came up and tugged her dress and said, I'm tired of watching TV, can we go outside? Emma looked at her, then picked her up and spun around the kitchen. From that day on it was as if Carla had always had the gift of speech, just like any other child, but for reasons of her own, she'd decided to refrain from talking. At first she couldn't fully shape the words. Her speech erupted in a torrent of frustration, too powerful to be contained by the building blocks of language. She howled and gurgled. Jasper thought that she could overcome her speech impediment by putting pebbles in her mouth and speaking to the waves of the Long Island Sound, like the philosopher Demosthenes, but Dr. Bob referred them to a speech therapist in Bridgeport. If things went well, Carla could begin first grade next fall in Milford.

For Valentine's Day that year, Emma baked a heart-shaped yellow cake, frosted with an egg-white icing that she dyed pale pink and then decorated with a heart made out of Red Hot candies. Why was she still so depressed? She had every reason to be happy: a house, a loving husband, two normal, growing daughters. She missed the first years of her marriage in the Bronx, the way that Jasper sat beside her on the bed and read her stories when she was sick during her pregnancies. Except for church, there was hardly anything they did together. Jasper had so much responsibility at Cambridge, and he'd recently taken a Saturday job at a downtown jewelry store one town over to help pay back the Faimans. He refused to work at the new Milford mall where everybody went. What if someone from their church saw him?

The cake looked almost like the picture in the magazine and Emma was pleased with it. She'd put on so much weight the last few years. She had to learn to be more sociable and outgoing.

As a young adult Catherine struggled to remember anything about her Milford childhood. There were the Sunday drives, she guessed—her father at the wheel, her mother struggling to turn the aimless drive into an outing—and there were picnics, hikes, the mall. Dunkin' Donuts, Mister Softee, trips to Bridgeport with her sister and her mother, a shabby zoo or a museum. There were the games that everybody played one

THE FOUR SPENT THE DAY TOGETHER

spring, or maybe several springs, in the big dirt yard next to the Tiermans'. *It's getting late.* The games went on through dusk until everyone went home for dinner.

Catherine walked home alone from school beginning in first grade. She liked cutting through the marshy woods that started near the school and circled all the way to Milford Point, behind the houses. A cutoff from the main path took her almost home, to a vacant lot near the Shaminski's. Walking home one winter day in second grade, she saw a gang of boys ahead, running through the woods with sticks and branches. She felt a jolt of panic. As she approached they formed a human chain and blocked the path. Jimmy Shaminski looked at her and laughed. Now you've got to pay a toll, he said. They linked their arms and wouldn't let her pass. A toll? She was confused, she couldn't figure what they wanted. Jimmy was the leader but what scared her most was seeing all the other boys, boys she thought she knew, transformed into bullies, delirious with power.

Until now Catherine had stayed underneath the radar at Kay Avenue School. She wasn't popular like Pam Miller or Janice Romano, but neither was she ostracized like Deirdre "Grimy" Grimes or Fatty Patty. Catherine thought: if she ran back to school they'd chase her, but if she paid they'd make her pay the toll forever. But it was impossible to pay because she'd spent her money in the cafeteria.

Finally she offered them her mittens. They were nothing special, navy blue from the Goodwill or Kresge's. Jimmy held them up close to her face and spat into them. Then he tossed them down the line of boys to Wesley Hall, who threw them in between the cattails in the swamp. And then they ran away and she could not stop weeping. She stopped walking through the woods after that, told no one.

Third grade was a reprieve, an oasis of happiness, due to the arrival of Susanne McCoy, the only child of a literature professor from Bloomington, Indiana. Dr. McCoy was on sabbatical, researching his next book at Yale, and they'd rented an old summer house next to the beach on Naugatuck Avenue. Finally Catherine had someone to talk to! Susanne looked sweet and compliant with her blond, almost waist-length hair, but really she was a tomboy fiend in search of new adventures. The two girls talked nonstop in each other's bedrooms, they wrote plays and acted out the parts together, they pretended to be Russian spies.

Boris! Susanne would say, holding out both of her arms, and Catherine would faint into her arms and sigh, *Natasha!* They made friends with a lone radio announcer at a station near the school who let them sit in on his broadcasts. He even let them act out one of their plays on his program.

In June the McCoys went back to Bloomington and Catherine spent the summer moping. Emma tried to cheer her up, enrolling her in a class called Stretch 'n Sew where girls learned to make dresses from synthetic fabrics, but she refused to go. She could not think of anything more tacky or ridiculous.

Entering fourth grade that September, Catherine was surprised by how many friendship alliances had formed and shifted.

THE FOUR SPENT THE DAY TOGETHER

Blinded by her romance with Susanne, she'd virtually ignored her friends Bonnie and Margit and now they'd been recruited into Pam Miller's friend group. Everybody knew that Pam hated Catherine. Meanwhile, the other Wildemere Beach girls—girls from big blue-collar families whose parents partied on the weekends—had formed a tighter clique that Catherine never would fit into. Once, Catherine passed a note to Bonnie asking, *Why does Pam hate me*. Instead of writing back, Bonnie gave it to Pam, who passed it on to everyone who mattered.

Pam's family lived in Laurel Beach. Her father was an architect. Poised and icy, she styled her blond hair into a bubble cut and she wore the most conservative designer outfits. Margit and Bonnie drifted further into Pam's orbit and decided not to speak to Catherine, which made the lunchroom newly problematic. Everybody knew: the Wildemere Beach kids were afraid of stirring Pam's wrath, and anyway they had nothing much to say to Catherine, so they shunned her too. Which left just the bad kids' table—people like Juanita and Debbie, Tiny and Dale, whose families were actually poor and often absent. These kids failed every subject. But Catherine was still getting A's and they were not her friends yet. There were still the Outcasts—Lee "Needlenose" Nadel, Grimy Grimes, and Fatty Patty—who sat together by default, but Catherine couldn't bring herself to join them.

Instead, she left. Every day at lunch she slipped out the kindergarten entrance and over to Bill's Diner, a quarter mile from school just past the Naugatuck Four Corners. Her lunch money paid for a hamburger and Coke and she sat at the counter, reading the morning paper alongside commercial travelers and truckers. No one there knew who she was. She liked to think that she could pass as an adult. At times like these she could relax, she was no longer lonely.

Carla was safely enrolled in normal first grade and Emma hoped she'd be able to handle it. She didn't say anything about Carla's past. She hated to lie but she knew they'd put her straight into Special Ed if she talked about Fairfield Day Academy or her first diagnosis. She'd learned just how prejudiced the whole medical establishment could be when it came to neurological difference. Carla's just a late bloomer, Emma said lightly.

And for a while, Carla complied with all Emma's wishes. She sat at the back of the class and kept quiet. She carefully followed along with what the other kids did, knowing she was being tested. She even made two or three friends. Carla contained all her frustration and rage while she was at school. But then it exploded elsewhere. In the market with Emma, she ran through the aisles throwing boxes and cans into the cart, pounding her fists into the shelves when Emma tried to put things back. At home, she ripped the heads off her dolls and rolled them on the ground as if they were balls. Your sister is playing her Jacobin game, Jasper told Catherine wryly. But what disturbed Emma most was the way Carla would listen to conversations among them or on TV and repeat certain phrases and words over and over as if she were drunk, chanting her way to the ecstatic state of a born-again Christian. Was it mental illness? Or was she just trying to mock them?

THE FOUR SPENT THE DAY TOGETHER

One night that spring, the family went out for dinner, a rare treat. It was a Saturday night and the back dining room at Pasquale's was busy. Emma let herself order a single old-fashioned, her favorite drink. The conversation turned to scary stories, and then Edgar Allan Poe. Jasper had recently brought home the volume of Edgar Poe's works with the Gustave Doré illustrations. Emma had read Poe at school and he'd impressed her. She remembered "The Tell-Tale Heart" as one of the scariest things she'd ever read. The thump of the murdered man's heart beneath the floorboards—Poe was conveying a message, *our actions stay with us and guilt is eternal.* A story isn't a message, Catherine thought to herself, squinting hard and pursing her lips, it's an escape to a parallel universe. She hated the way her mother repeated popular phrases from Father Luke's sermons, TV, and *Newsweek*. It was so middlebrow. You have the potential, her father had said once, to be an original thinker. She treasured the thought. What about "The Masque of the Red Death"? Jasper asked, changing the subject. Catherine had recently read it. *Red Death, Reddeath*, Carla repeated, excited. Jasper, why don't you tell Carla the story? Emma asked, forcing a smile.

Oblivious, Jasper launched into the tale of the prince who'd gathered one thousand friends in his sumptuous castle to avoid the plague. What's the plague? Carla asked. "The Red Death" was Poe's name for the bubonic plague, which spread to England from France during the late Middle Ages, Jasper explained, looking at Catherine. The plague was a terrible, deadly disease, Emma elaborated. *Disease boy!* Carla laughed, looking at Jasper. But just when they all thought they were safe, Jasper continued, the prince threw a masked ball and at midnight, the red plague itself, which was disguised as a mysterious guest, was unmasked and contagion and death swept through the castle.

Would you say Poe was writing a parable or an allegory, Jasper asked in his most professorial voice. *Disease boy*, Carla taunted. Just as Catherine was preparing to argue for allegory, Carla pounded her fists on the table and began a new chant, *Daddy is a disease boy!* Shhhh, Emma said, but when Carla saw her family's shocked faces, she laughed. *Daddy is a disease boy, Daddy is a disease boy*, she chanted over and over until she was howling. By now everyone in the restaurant was staring. Emma took Carla out to the car while Jasper and Catherine finished their pasta.

One of the few scenes Catherine would remember from her Milford childhood was the Afternoon of the Coat. She must have been ten or eleven. Her mother left her to watch Carla while she went to the mall. Emma needed a new winter coat and it was the end of the season, the best time to shop for a bargain. She returned around dusk with a big plastic bag: I found myself a new coat, shall I model it? Catherine and Carla sat on the living room floor and Emma took the coat out of the bag: a knee-length winter garment in mustard-beige ribbed polyester with a Peter Pan collar, marked down several times, the kind of coat that looks old while it's still on the hanger.

THE FOUR SPENT THE DAY TOGETHER

Emma put the coat on, twirled around. Catherine and Carla looked at each other and shook their heads. For the first time they understood each other perfectly.

Around that time, Emma found a job selling *World Book Encyclopedia*s. She'd seen an ad in the *Milford Post*: *Calling All Housewives—Make Extra Money While Advancing American Education!* She went to the open-call meeting in Bridgeport and signed up for an interview. All of *World Book*'s twenty volumes were designed to meet the learning needs of students from first grade through high school. Acquiring a set was the most important investment a parent could make in their child's education. Adding *World Book* to your home was like owning a personal library, but better still—because each entry was geared to the official curriculum! It was the first step toward college. *World Book*ers scored 20 percent higher on college entrance exams than less privileged kids and they became learners for life.

World Book was something Emma thought she could believe in. And like the people at Fairfield Academy, they respected the moms. Who was more qualified to serve as an educational ambassador? You could sell the encyclopedias to your neighbors and friends.

Ever since Cambridge had opened the New Rochelle warehouse, Jasper's salary remained frozen. The girls fought all the time and he was afraid to ask for a raise. The house was so small. Maybe if Catherine had her own room she'd be less resentful? One of their fellow parishioners from St. Andrew's church showed them how they could build a new room on top of the sunporch. A full *World Book* set sold for $350 and the commission was 40 percent. Even if buyers chose to make payments, the ambassador-moms would get their full commission up front as soon as the contracts were signed.

World Book gave Emma a full set in advance of her first sale. No one in the family ever read it. Following the manager's instructions, she cold-called everyone on the Kay Avenue PTA list. Most late afternoons before dinner, Emma took up her station in the back of the kitchen on a stool next to the phone. Twisting the long beige cord around her wrists, pacing the linoleum floor, she used her best church-lady voice, cheerful and bright. *Hello, Mrs. Miller? It's Emma Greene, Catherine's mom. How are you? Yes, she's in the same grade as your daughter Pam. Um, I don't want to take up too much of your time—*

Catherine died. Her mom sounded just like Amanda trying to charm Laura's gentleman caller in *The Glass Menagerie*, a play they were reading at school. When the phone calls failed to yield meetings, Emma began wheeling her sample set through the Laurel Beach streets in an old shopping cart she'd kept from the Bronx—which was faster, she thought, than unloading all twenty books from the car. She called on Dr. and Mrs. Malone, strangers whose lovely home across the fence she'd admired since the first day they'd arrived. She called on the Mullers, the Pattersons, the Booths. When none of these tactics worked she reached out to people from church and sold a few sets but after that there was no one to call. Jasper suggested she put her *World Book* career to rest. Except for the day Carla said her first words, Emma had never been more relieved.

THE FOUR SPENT THE DAY TOGETHER

Except they'd already signed a contract to build the addition that spring! It would be wiser, Emma thought, to find a real job with real pay. She'd never waitressed before, but the Savarin restaurant at the West Haven truck stop gave her four shifts a week with no questions asked. She just had to buy her own uniform: a white apron, a pink belted dress, a pair of white waitress shoes.

When Catherine was ten, the conflict with Pam Miller escalated to a state of pure war. Was Pam slumming? Pam, Margit, and Bonnie joined up with Melissa and Brandy and the other Wildemere Beach girls and formed an alliance with Jimmy Shaminski and his gang. All of them met up at Ocean Avenue beach after school, even when it was cold. They saw themselves as a new family of orphans and spent hours drawing kinship diagrams in the sand. Family, like all children's games, was a way of manifesting irreconcilable conflicts and fears in the hope they might resolve. Pam was always the mom but the other roles changed day to day, from sister or uncle to second cousin, depending on where someone stood in the group.

Margit and Bonnie were no longer speaking to Catherine. The Greenes had recently gotten a dog, a black spaniel mutt they called Sundae. Whenever Catherine walked Sundae down to the beach the Pam clan closed tighter. Should she just walk past the group? Stop, say hello? Sometimes Jimmy or one of his gang would shout *Here comes ugly Catherine* and they all roared.

As weeks went by, Pam began drifting away from the Orphan Family, playing tennis and shopping with a few girls from Laurelton Hall. She even talked about transferring. Margit and Bonnie saw themselves stuck with the Wildemere kids and thought about ways to engage Pam. It was the mid-1960s. Demonstrations against busing, racial discrimination, and the Vietnamese conflict appeared on the TV news every night. What if they organized a big protest against Catherine Greene? Pam still hated her, that might pull her back in.

The whole gang got busy making placards and signs—*Catherine Greene Sucks*; *Catherine Greene Has Cooties and Lice*; *Burn Baby Burn*; *Greene Get Out Now!*—and then one afternoon they converged outside her house, chanting and waving their signs.

Catherine watched the whole demonstration through the kitchen window, standing behind Emma and trying hard not to be seen. Just ignore them, Emma said, and they'll go away. Go up to your room and turn on the radio loud.

Emma watched through the window a while longer. This was like nothing she'd ever seen growing up in the Bronx. Not all of the kids in her school liked each other, but they were civil. She couldn't believe the Milford kids could be this depraved.

Alone in her room, Catherine discovered she could get high by inhaling the office supplies her father brought home from Cambridge—bottles of Liquid Paper, tubes of rubber cement. No one knew she did this.

THE FOUR SPENT THE DAY TOGETHER

She began talking about suicide in a general way. How far would you need to swim out in the sound in order to drown? Would you die if you jumped off the roof? Alarmed, Emma contacted a child psychologist with an office near Yale. On Tuesdays after school Emma drove Catherine to see Dr. Caroline Sterne. Catherine loved the drive to New Haven, she loved walking around Yale to the psychologist's office. Catherine loved Dr. Sterne's haircut and plexiglass jewelry. She wasn't sure how she felt about the doctor herself. Dr. Sterne asked all kinds of questions about the Greene family and took constant notes.

Darling Natasha, Catherine wrote Susanne. They were still corresponding between Milford and Bloomington, even after two years. *I'm crazy—at least my mom thinks I am, hahaha!—I'm seeing a shrink. My stupid mother made me go because I told her I wanted to jump off the balcony to my death. You know how* literally minded *she is. Of course I would never do that.*

The letter was stamped and ready to post when Emma found it on Catherine's desk. She didn't think twice about opening it. She hardly knew Catherine anymore, she'd become so sarcastic and aloof and withdrawn. Blue Cross did not cover therapy. Every appointment cost more than Emma could make in a Savarin shift and all this time Catherine was just playing with them, which was what she should have suspected all along.

After that the trips to New Haven stopped.

In sixth grade Pam transferred to Laurelton and the Orphan Family fell apart. After years of being picked last for every team, Catherine discovered soccer and became good at sports. She still wasn't speaking to Margit and Bonnie. She began spending time with the "bad kids"—Juanita and Debbie, Tiny and Dale—whose parents were never around. She hung out in their empty houses. No one did homework. Often, they drank. Sometimes, they walked down to the cheap one-room apartments at Walnut Beach to see someone's big sister who'd just had a baby and dropped out of school. Everyone smoked. Catherine chose Parliament, the Intelligent Woman's Cigarette according to the ads. She liked the blue and white box. Briefly, she became Dale Caruso's girlfriend. Emma left her alone. And then Bonnie broke up with Margit and she and Catherine became best friends again.

Jasper brought home copies of *The Village Voice*, *Ramparts*, and *The New York Review of Books* for Catherine to read. They discussed Lenny Bruce and Norman Mailer, Susan Sontag, Malcolm X, Cesar Chavez and the braceros. The apartments at Walnut Beach stank of dirty diapers and trash. Catherine knew she didn't want to end up there. This is what happens, Emma warned, if you let a boy take advantage of you: you'll end up pregnant, then where will you be? You'd be a fool to believe it can't happen to you.

In seventh grade their class was split up into two different streams for the first time. Except for Bonnie, all of Catherine's new friends were in 7-B. 7-A read Shakespeare and held practice debates while 7-B learned how to plan balanced meals and fill out a check. Everyone knew the lives of the 7-B kids had been written off but no one discussed it. Catherine felt this

THE FOUR SPENT THE DAY TOGETHER

was wrong and unjust. On some nights when the weather was good she could tune in to the Manhattan underground station WBAI. Angling her pink bedside radio beneath the covers to pick up the waves, she listened to Bob Fass and Alison Steele as if they were speaking to her. She absorbed every word. She knew she had to get out of Milford but she didn't know how.

For Catherine's thirteenth birthday, Emma made baked chicken and a nice homemade cake with chocolate frosting. After dinner, they sang "Happy Birthday." After she'd blown out the candles, Emma gave Catherine a gift certificate to Floyd's Record Store and Jasper took two wrapped gifts out of his briefcase. The first, smaller gift was an orange and brown mosaic tile ashtray. She now had permission to smoke in her room. She wouldn't have to sneak out in the cold to sit on the Catalanos' front wall anymore. The second gift was a beautiful flat white lingerie box from Bergdorf Goodman tied with a purple ribbon. Catherine loved the box: it was an artifact of New York, a key to a glamorous Manhattan world where she wouldn't be jeered at, where she wouldn't feel like a freak. It was exactly this world her father had promised her secretly through all of their readings since she was three. She eagerly opened it. But when she saw the mauve lacy slip with its ruched, darted bust she was confused and embarrassed. Was this for her? She'd had her first period a few months before but she had no breasts to speak of and even if she did, she would never wear this. She saw her mother's jaw clench. She did not hold it up, but just folded it back into the box and hid it away in a drawer.

A few weeks later, aimlessly riding her bike before dinner, she found herself outside the seventh-and-eighth-grade wing of Kay Avenue School. There was no one around. The teachers and staff had all left for the day and the night janitor hadn't arrived. She put her bike down on the pavement. The doors to the junior high wing were unlocked and she just walked inside. Prowling around Mr. Sobanik's big desk in her homeroom, she saw the neat cardboard seating charts for her grade. There was one for each class—7-A, 7-B—with each person's name on a piece of white cardstock, tucked into a slot. She picked up the charts and shook them until all of the names were mixed up on the floor. Then she ripped up the posters about the Constitution and Our Nation's Flag. Outside, the grounds were still empty and her bike was still there. Without really thinking, she walked to the fields where she'd always been picked last for the games and started gathering rocks. Standing outside her homeroom windows, she hurled rocks at the row of new windows until they were shattered and cracked.

The principal called a special assembly the next day to discuss this heinous act of criminal vandalism. Police had already been called. Make no mistake—whoever dared to do this would be caught and dealt with severely. Days passed and nothing else happened. But then again Catherine no longer knew much about what went on at school. Except for going to homeroom at eight to say "present" when her name was called she stopped attending.

4

She didn't like being called Catherine so she changed her name to Catt. Girls in Milford changed their names and signatures from week to week, but Catherine's new name stuck because she was insistent.

During the first weeks of her truancy, Catt hung around a clearing in the woods she used to cut through on her way to Bill's that had become a gathering place for people in the grade above her cutting classes. Mostly they were boys. *Here comes tom tit*, they greeted her. *Look, it's Ugly Catherine.* Furiously embarrassed, she stood her ground and fumbled in her pockets for a Parliament and then, struggling to find her voice, asked if anybody had a match. *Yeah, my ass your face*, quipped her old neighbor Jimmy Shaminski. These were the same boys who'd thrown rocks at the magnificent Sam Sherman when she walked on the beach in a homemade caftan that was just a belted sheet. Sam wore a Campbell's soup can around her neck and Catt was probably the only kid at school who knew it was a nod to Andy Warhol. Sam (who'd changed her name from Candy) was someone Catt wished she could be friends with, but Sam was in the grade above, aloof and isolate, and so it never happened.

Reading *The Tibetan Book of the Dead* in the incomprehensible translation all the Yale hippies carried around in New Haven, she realized she was living, now, in Bardo: her real life would not begin until she was old enough to leave her parents' home and Milford.

And so she settled in to wait. She took down the stupid Beatles shrine she'd made above her desk with Christmas lights and Mylar and replaced it with a Chinese landscape poster she'd bought at the Yale Co-op. If her family lived in Darien or Old Greenwich like the Newbridges or Osbornes, things would have been different. She would have gone to a real school where there were other people like her.

There was nothing she could do about the cheap and girly dresser that her parents bought when she moved into the new bedroom. Shunning the ceramic ashtray she'd been given for her birthday, she let her cigarettes burn down until the white fake French Provincial top was scarred with yellow burn marks. She knew her mother hated her. The room became her prison. Emma didn't even bother yelling at her oldest daughter anymore. She didn't recognize this alien creature who flirted openly with her husband. Catherine had nothing but contempt for everyone and everything that Emma cared for. In fact, Emma was afraid of her. Her daughter was a powerful, corrupting influence and she was even more afraid for Jasper.

Following the instructions in a magazine, Catt made a mini-loom out of a pencil and began weaving a belt in an elaborate

THE FOUR SPENT THE DAY TOGETHER

chevron pattern. Looking out the window at the seasonal view of the Long Island Sound, she imagined she was Penelope, but instead of waiting for Odysseus she was waiting for the future.

By now she had outgrown the high she got from glue and typewriter correction fluid. What was the point? One quick huff, and two minutes later it was over. She knew that there were better drugs, and she knew that she could find them. Drugs were not the point, exactly. She didn't even crave the buzz, she liked it better being clear. Drugs were an experiment in altered states of consciousness, they were something people did to make sitting doing nothing in a room seem exciting. Still, she imagined shooting heroin and living underneath a tree near Harvard in Cambridge Common. She forgot that she was terrified of needles.

At thirteen, she was still too young to leave, but not too young to start preparing. She'd need to find some friends outside of Milford, she'd need to know much more about living in the world. And of course she needed money.

Catt filled out forms with her new name and applied for a Social Security card. As soon as she received it, she lied about her age and got a waitress job at a Friendly's ice cream parlor. Her father was surprisingly supportive of this enterprise. Realizing that a part-time job would remove her safely from the house and minimize the bitter conflict that he'd unwittingly unleashed between Catherine and her mother, Jasper drove her to the interview and even coached her. *Be sure and tell the manager that you're experienced.* The Jimi Hendrix LP of that name, *Are You Experienced*, had just come out that spring and it was playing everywhere. When Catherine introduced herself—*Hi, my name is Catt, I'm sixteen and I'm experienced*—the manager roared and repeated what she'd said for everyone to hear but then he hired her anyway. For several afternoons she was a Friendly's girl but when she dropped her tray too many times by walking out the in door to the kitchen, she was fired.

Work, she understood, was freedom and there would be other jobs. Arby's, KFC. She sang the Brecht-Weill song "Pirate Jenny" in her head while she was scooping fries and cleaning counters—

> *You gentlemen can watch while I'm scrubbing the floors*
> *And I'm scrubbing the floors while you're gawking*
> *And maybe once you tipped me*
> *And it made you feel swell*
> *In this ratty waterfront in this ratty old hotel*
> *But you'll never know to who you were talking*

—and combed the newspaper classifieds for better opportunities.

Catt used her Friendly's money to buy a batik shoulder bag from the head shop that had just opened near the high school. Big enough to hold her books and all the flyers she picked up, the bag was the first symbol of her independence. But her thumb, she realized, was the vehicle. There was another game occurring in the larger world. She longed to enter it, and at the highest level, and there was nothing stopping her from doing that right now. For the time being, hitchhiking helped her to forget about the future.

At first she started thumbing rides to save on bus fare to her jobs. But then she realized that her thumb could take her

THE FOUR SPENT THE DAY TOGETHER

anywhere, and so her range expanded to Cutler's Record Store and the Yale Co-op in New Haven, concerts and demonstrations on the New Haven Green, the Jewish deli, and the pawnshops in downtown Bridgeport along State Street.

Hitchhiking was fun and interesting and easy, and it was how she learned to talk to people. She didn't even really need a destination. Sometimes her rides were going other places, so she'd go there, too, and the new place would turn out even better than the destination that she'd planned. She fell in love with chance. Although that wasn't always true. Some of her rides brought her to a precipice of danger, although never more than she could handle.

As she was hitchhiking to a Black Panther rally in New Haven, a late-model Chrysler picked her up at Walnut Beach. The driver was a trim and muscular white man in his early forties with gray eyes and a taut unwrinkled face. She knew something about this ride was off even before he turned into the deserted state beach parking lot. For a moment they sat looking at the waves. Open the glove box, he told her.

The car was running still, in neutral. Catt's body froze as she tried to think ahead. Do it now, he said, smiling. I have something I want to show you. His voice was soft but firm, repressed but still insinuating. Until now she'd been chattering about the police murder of Black Panther Bobby Hutton but now she had the sense to stop. The air between them had turned heavy.

You need to do exactly what I say.

She reached and pushed the button and the door dropped open. The gun was in an open box.

Okay. Now. Do you want to touch it?

Reaching for the gun, Catt's arm was flooded with electric shocks but she sensed if she stayed calm and let him guide her with his voice he wouldn't kill her.

Running her fingers from the handgun's silver tip down to the handle, Catt found a voice she'd never known. I've never seen a gun before. She stroked it softly. It's so big and smooth and shiny. She let her mouth drop open wider. And it feels really, I don't know, powerful? The driver smiled and grunted softly. Catt looked at him with a shy smile. Would it be okay for me to put it back now?

Go on, he said. Get out. The car took off.

Shaken, shaking, she walked onto the beach and counted to a hundred. She looked. The car was gone. The next ride was a straight shot to the rally.

A week or two later, one of Catt's rides to Bridgeport let her off outside the Bard Diner near the Stratford thruway ramp. The Bard was a 24/7 place, a converted trailer with big booths and chrome and a thicket of Harleys parked outside. She decided to stop for coffee. The Bard was bigger and busier than Bill's Diner. No one there would ask her if she shouldn't be at school. She immediately felt safe here. Also—checking out the clientele—she felt a charge of possibility.

The Bard served as a satellite clubhouse for the Bridgeport Huns, a bunch of grown-up men who wore coonskin caps over their long, greasy hair and cut-off denim jackets with their colors. Tied to various criminal organizations, they were the victims and perpetrators of numerous fatal shootings, but to Catt, the

THE FOUR SPENT THE DAY TOGETHER

Huns seemed cool. She'd had no idea that there was anything like this so close to Milford. The Bard became a destination. She started hitching there, and if she couldn't catch a ride, she walked.

The Hunter S. Thompson Hells Angels book reported how they speed-faded jeans by pissing on them and then burying them for two weeks. She wondered if the Huns did this too. It hadn't worked for her but then she hadn't really given it a chance. *What the* hell *are you doing?* her father asked when he saw her digging a shallow grave underneath the sassafras trees for her new Wranglers. Just sitting in the Bard was interesting. Catt watched how the men moved back and forth between the booths they commandeered, transacting business. Eventually they noticed her. Sometimes, a couple of them would walk across the restaurant to the window booth she occupied alone and ask, *Hey, little girl, whatcha doing? Taking notes? Or are you waiting for someone? Somethiiiiing?*

On an April day that stank of summer one of the Huns asked if she'd like to go out for a ride, which may have been a joke but Catt jumped on it so fast he couldn't take it back, especially with all the others watching. Catt followed the man, who said his name was Randy, to the parking lot and he showed her how to get onto the back of his 1200 cc Harley. As soon as he started up the bike she was ecstatic: the open air, the speed, the power of the throttle. The tail of Randy's raccoon cap pushed up against her face as they drove around the roundabout and underneath the thruway toward the marshes.

Sun beat down on the small warehouses and factories as she hung on, drinking in the smell of fuel and pollen. This must be freedom. At that moment everything about her shitty life was vindicated. But the fact that Catt was underage was a lot more consequential to the Huns than to the manager at Friendly's. Much too soon, Randy circled back into the parking lot. *Now go on home, little girl, and do your homework.*

After that, Catt stopped going to the Bard so often. The magic ride was something that could only happen once. She didn't want Randy and the other Huns to laugh at her or call her greedy. Still, a seed was planted.

A few weeks later when she and Bonnie were in Bonnie's room playing the new Mothers of Invention, Catt talked about her Bard adventures. Bonnie was still more or less attending school. She'd never even hitched a ride before but she said she wanted to try it. Catt considered all the options. New Haven was too far and Bonnie had no interest in Yale but they could definitely try the Bard Diner . . .

It didn't take them long to catch a ride across the Devon bridge to Stratford. Walking in, Catt saw that Randy wasn't there. The other Huns pretended not to recognize her. But just being at the Bard seemed like enough for Bonnie. Her mom worked nights and she liked hanging out at home. She wasn't used to going to these kinds of grown-up places. The two girls settled into Catt's old window booth—two heavily made-up thirteen-year-old girls in short-short skirts and sandals, talking, laughing about what people from Kay Avenue would think if they could see them there. Smoking cigarettes and smashing the burnt meringue topping of a lemon pie with their two spoons, they were omnipotent. They felt like anything could happen.

THE FOUR SPENT THE DAY TOGETHER

Around five the diner started filling up. A couple of guys whom Catt had never seen before came over to the booth and asked if they could join them. They didn't look like college students and they definitely weren't hippies, just regular-looking guys in their early twenties—maybe they went to the community college? The two girls kneed each other underneath the table, laughed. *Okaay.* Before approaching Catt and Bonnie they'd been across the restaurant talking to the Huns, so maybe they were buying drugs or selling them?

Before catching their first ride, the two girls had decided that if anybody asked they'd use fake names and say they were in high school. The guys, Jason and Ritchie, slid into the booth and introduced themselves. Bonnie said, My name is Rose. And this is my friend Wanda. Which cracked the two girls up and left the guys confused. So, Ritchie asked, you live around here? You go to school? Uh-huh, Catt said, but only two more weeks. We're seniors. Yeah, we go to Milford High, Bonnie added, and we're about to graduate. Catt worried they might know some Milford families and start asking if they knew X or Y. Well yeah, Jason said. Then we should celebrate. Do either of you ladies feel like getting high? Bonnie looked at Catt, both of them feeling the excitement rise. Except for glue they were absolute drug virgins.

Sure, why not, Catt answered flatly. Okay then, "Wanda," Jason said, smirking. When's the last time you got high? I'm guessing never. You know you're right, Bonnie blurted. But we've been wanting to. Across the diner, several of the Huns were watching. Well then, Rose, let's do it up—there was this special gleam men got when they were encouraging a girl to do something that she'd never done before—it will be an honor. We could smoke out in the car, Ritchie said. But we've got some better shit back at the apartment so why don't we head back there since it's your first time? Everything was escalating fast into a whole new situation but neither of the girls could think of a way out of it. Jason said it wasn't far and afterward they'd drive them back here to the diner.

The apartment was on the top floor of a triple-decker house in a shabby neighborhood somewhere on the edge of run-down Bridgeport. The sun was setting when they got out of the car. They walked all the way upstairs and into a small combination living room and kitchen. Catt sat at one end of a Goodwill couch, Ritchie sat down on the other. An open archway led to a single bedroom. There were no posters on the wall, no stereo, no records—just an AM/FM radio on the counter.

Jason turned on the lamp with the red bulb and rolled a super-joint—weed laced with PCP and hash. He took a hit and passed it down to Bonnie, who was sitting on a cushion. She choked and everybody laughed. This is some righteous shit, he said. They passed it around the room and back to Bonnie. C'mon, Rose, you've got to hold it in. I can't!

No one was judging anyone and everybody laughed. But now the room was spinning, tingling. I've never felt like this before, said Bonnie. Catt's head felt so heavy that she couldn't hold it up and so she let it drop on Ritchie's shoulder. Bonnie was still sitting on the floor and somewhere Catt could hear her laughing. Ritchie put his arm around her shoulders and they were close, then closer. The radio was on, some talking. Everything felt very far away except for Ritchie's body and she could feel them drifting.

THE FOUR SPENT THE DAY TOGETHER

On the floor beside them, something else was happening. Bonnie on her cushion, laughing, and then Jason taking her by the hand, pulling her to her knees, then feet, to lead her to the bedroom. No—get off—I can't— Bonnie shook her head and stamped her feet, which was too weird for Jason, he abruptly snapped on the ceiling light. Ritchie, hey—they're jailbait, man. Don't be stupid. Time to get up now, little girl. This establishment is closing.

Catt and Bonnie sat together in the backseat of the car, legs touching. "A Whiter Shade of Pale" was double-playing on the radio and they thought the song was written just for them. Lights from other cars were flashing in their faces. They kept looking at each other, grinning. Had any of this really happened? Jason dropped them in the diner parking lot. Thanks, man, they called out after him.

Since it was late they took a taxi back to Bonnie's. Bonnie's mom was still at work, her parents were divorced, there were no issues. Catt had told her parents she'd be sleeping over that night at Bonnie's. By now, they'd given up on any attempt to influence or discipline her. Calling Catherine by her given name was their sole act of resistance.

The first job of a revolutionary is to not get caught, Catt thought when they were safely back at Bonnie's. In the end no one had missed them.

Catherine was a catalyst for Emma's rage but not the sole cause of it. Emma was forty-three years old. Where had her life gone?

Catherine's future had been one of their great hopes. When she was small Jasper imagined her attending Cambridge University. Now they'd consider themselves lucky if Catherine got an associate's degree at Housatonic Community College, or even finished high school.

Carla was still hanging on at Kay Avenue School, in the top quarter of her fourth-grade class, but at least once every month she came home with a teacher's note. Her behavior was erratic, disruptive, and frightening. Was there a history of developmental disability the school wasn't aware of? Jasper and Emma had chosen never to disclose this because she'd be consigned to Special Ed forever. There was nothing Emma could do but pray for Carla to eventually settle down, or at least get a teacher next year who'd be less aggressively inquisitive.

What Emma wanted most was to finally go to college and get her BA in literature but it was impossible to do this. Instead she took a part-time job at the Milford Public Library as a librarian's assistant, but since that only paid minimum wage she had to keep two shifts a week at the Savarin truck stop. She'd seen some of her coworkers climbing into the cabs of the trucks. She knew what went on but she turned a blind eye to it. Jasper hadn't had a raise in five years and now they were talking about bringing in an IT specialist to computerize his warehouse. And if they did that, where would he be? They wouldn't keep paying two managers.

When St. Andrew's Church co-sponsored an ecumenical teach-in event about racial equality and justice, Emma saw it as a chance to reconnect with her older daughter. Catherine,

THE FOUR SPENT THE DAY TOGETHER

she knew, cared deeply about politics. The main speaker would be Henry Harris Bowen, a brilliant young man from Harlem who'd just arrived to head up the Bridgeport Student Nonviolent Coordinating Committee. Pleased with herself, Emma bought two tickets and planned it as a mother-daughter outing. Finally, she was doing something Catherine would look up to.

The auditorium that night at Calf Pen Meadow Elementary School was almost two-thirds full—a larger audience than Emma was expecting, frankly, for a meeting of this kind in Milford. Father Luke introduced Rabbi Stein from Beth-Shalom, and Rabbi Stein introduced the speaker.

Without even thanking the rabbi, Henry Bowen surveyed the all-white audience of Episcopalians and Jews and proceeded to excoriate them. *It is a sign*, he said, *the Black Power movement has finally arrived when even the most privileged white communities are moved to educate themselves about the bloody racial history of this country and Amerika's systemic, absolute oppression of Black and brown people.*

Bowen went on to present a formidable and heart-wrenching list of facts about Black life in Bridgeport: the child poverty and illiteracy, the racist NIMBY opposition to school busing, the shocking overcrowding of families in substandard housing, and the historical exclusion of Black workers by the Irish-led trade unions.

A stunned hush descended on the room when he finished speaking. Finally, Rabbi Stein asked if there were any questions.

To her own surprise, Emma stood up. *What you describe*, she said—*well, it's just terrible. I sympathize with your plight, and I'm ashamed of Bridgeport, but, well—is there anything we here in Milford can do to help? What are your suggestions?*

Lady, he said, *we're not looking for your sympathy and we don't need your help. That's the whole problem with white liberals. They are so full of sympathy. We're talking about Black power and autonomy. We're talking about some deep systemic change here*—

Even Catt was shocked. Sitting down, blushing furiously, Emma wondered if Pat Kelley had been right when he ridiculed her for collecting money for war orphans and the children of the striking coal miners. *What are you*, he'd scoffed, *the Lady Bountiful? These people don't give two shits about you. Everyone looks out for themselves and maybe their families, and anyone who pretends otherwise is gaming you. If you were as smart as you think you are you'd hold on to your money.* What had happened to America? Nothing new. But to Emma, it had become almost unbearable.

That summer, Catt found a job harvesting tobacco on one of the small farms out by Wheelers Farm Road. The only American worker onsite, Catt took her place in the fields among a group of men who'd been brought up from the Dominican Republic. The men taught her how to chop and top the tall tobacco plants. By the third or fourth day, she was picking fast enough to not get fired. After work, they gathered in the bunkhouse to drink wine, play guitars, even sing. This seemed like an excellent opportunity to learn Spanish. Maybe she could move to Mexico or Cuba?

Friends from church spotted Catherine after work with her thumb out on the roadside. Instead of confronting Catherine again, Emma decided to pick her up after work. When she arrived at the farm, a foreman led her to the bunkhouse, where she saw her barely-teenage daughter sitting cross-legged on the

THE FOUR SPENT THE DAY TOGETHER

floor with a roomful of single men drinking cheap red wine out of jelly glasses. This was too much! Was Catherine *trying* to get raped? For the first time since she could not remember when, Emma dared to be parental. Catherine, get your pay. You're coming home with me. Right now.

. . . And then there was the blurry trip to Massachusetts, some college town where she and Julie Hudson ended up in bed with two guys in a dorm when they'd been trying to get to Julie's dad in Springfield.

Strong hash, and weather—snow and slush—the tiny backseat of a Volkswagen—a long walk through a quad, and then waking up or coming down alarmed that she had no idea where she was, as if she and Julie had been teleported to some generic TV campus. And then somehow getting back to Milford. She knew they didn't fuck. This is all that Catt remembered. If the capital of her female adolescent body was the animating force behind all of these adventures, Catt was not aware of it. Or maybe only dimly. She wanted to escape, she wanted to try all the drugs, she wanted to know everything. Losing her virginity was on her list of aspirations but in a lower place than learning to read French and tripping. If there had been women offering those things, she would have gone with them.

When her parents found the drugs, they decided that Episcopal church camp was probably the best thing for her. Camp

Jefferson: on the shores of Bantam Lake outside Litchfield, Connecticut—a sacred festive place where God's love for the world, made known to us in Jesus Christ, is shared through the ministry of hospitality. Everyone was white except for one Black girl named Tanaquil from Bridgeport attending on a Bishop's Scholarship. Tanaquil was expected to be friends with everyone and Catt felt sorry for her.

Swimming, sailing, chapel fellowship, and campfires . . . thirty of them sleeping in a loft in the log cabin dorm. Catt settled in for two weeks of this punishment. There were others who saw Camp Jefferson this way, and naturally they found each other.

Heather Kimmelson was sent to camp when her mother read her diary. Her father worked for an insurance company and they lived somewhere in the suburbs outside Hartford. Heather was even skinnier than Catt. She had masses of brown frizzy hair, naturally sun-bleached, and she wore perfectly torn and faded jeans. After bonding around their hatred of Camp Jefferson, they both signed up for crafts to get out of swimming. In the dark and relatively empty craft room, Catt and Heather told each other everything. Even though they lived almost a two-hour drive apart, they decided to be friends forever.

Emma and Jasper were relieved that Catt had finally found a normal, wholesome friend from an Episcopalian family. When the Kimmelsons invited Catt to spend a week in August with their daughter, they were relieved and then impressed by the Kimmelsons' big Colonial-style house in an upscale subdivision. Catt's heart sank when she saw the house. She knew

THE FOUR SPENT THE DAY TOGETHER

there would be pressure to do things the Kimmelson way, and anyway, what was there to do here?

On the first Saturday of their visit, Heather told her mother they were going to the mall and they hitchhiked down to Bushnell Park after she dropped them. Late afternoon, the park was full of people—families, couples, pretzel hawkers, hippies with guitars on blankets, newspaper sellers. There were ads for bands and posters for an upcoming demonstration, End the War. Obviously the hippie blankets were the place where the most interesting things were happening. The two girls gravitated to the edges of them, but the hippies were immersed in their own world and no one wanted to talk to them.

Finally they met two guys with enormous backpacks walking down the path. Damien and Jonathan had just gotten off the train at Union Station. They started out just asking Heather for directions but then they got to talking. Damien and Jonathan didn't know anyone in Hartford. They didn't know where they'd sleep that night, worst case they'd sleep out in the park—was that allowed here? They'd just arrived from Providence. It was the first day of the big trip west to San Francisco or Seattle they'd worked all summer to save up for. They didn't want any trouble. They could not afford hotels but if the Hartford pigs were piggy they could probably just panhandle for a while and sleep with the Salvation Army drunks in a flophouse.

Heather reached into her bag and gave Jonathan the ten dollars that her mom had given her and Catt for shopping. The guys were touched. They had a little weed... did the two girls feel like getting high with them?

Hanging out underneath some bushes, the four friends hatched a plan. Heather's neighbors the Johannsens were away on vacation. Heather was supposed to feed their cat. Her mother was holding on to the keys and she didn't want to ask for them, arouse suspicion, but she happened to know that the Johannsens kept one of their back windows unlocked in case anyone got locked out. They could all hitchhike back to Heather's street together, and then the guys could hide behind the Johannsen house while she and Catt went home for dinner. After that, she'd tell her parents they were walking over to a friend's to watch TV but instead, she'd stop and let them in. The guys could sleep in the Johannsen house, just make the beds before they left and nobody would ever know about it.

It was almost dark when Catt and Heather walked over to the Johannsens' after dinner. They were amazed to find the guys still there, waiting in the backyard with their packs just the way they'd planned it. Jonathan hoisted Heather onto his shoulders and the kitchen window opened, just as she'd expected. She slipped right in and unlocked the patio doors for them.

The Johannsen home was a wonderland of Danish modern furniture and expensive stereo equipment. They smoked some special hash the boys had been saving for the right occasion and went up to the bedrooms. Heather and Jonathan took the Johannsen parents' room with the big bed and Damien and Catt went into the daughter's. Catt turned the table radio on to WYBC and they got underneath the covers. A song was playing with the words, *I wanna ball you . . . I just wanna ball you.* Everything was swimming. Damien took off her shirt,

THE FOUR SPENT THE DAY TOGETHER

unzipped her jeans. Rolling, rolling. *Do you wanna ball now?* Catt didn't know the answer. She knew that Damien's body was bigger and more powerful than the college boys' she'd met with Julie. Nothing was ambivalent about it. She listened to the song and let Damien lead her hand to stroke his cock, ambivalently.

First the police turned on their flashing lights. They saw them through the window. They were still reaching for their clothes when the cops broke through the door and came upstairs. *Hartford Police! We need you to get up slowly with your hands up . . .* Heather and Jonathan came out of the Johannsen bedroom half-undressed. Embarrassed, Heather kept trying to explain things. *We are placing you under arrest.* And one cop said, *I think these girls are underage*, while the other called for backup. *Breaking and entering*, the first cop said. *Criminal trespassing, drug possession with intent to sell, contributing to the delinquency of a minor . . .*

The four of them were marched downstairs.

The last thing Catt and Heather saw was Jonathan and Damien handcuffed with their backpacks on the sidewalk. *We're so sorry*, Catt called out. *We'll try and get you out.* But Damien and Jonathan refused to look at them.

During the second week of school, Emma and Jasper were called into a meeting with Carla's new fifth-grade teacher, the visiting school psychologist, and the principal. The entire team agreed that Carla's needs could best be met by moving her to the Special Education module.

At Cambridge University Press, Giles Osborne and Jack Sachmann welcomed the arrival of Richard Donnegan, BS in computer science. Mr. Donnegan would lead them all in fully automating the warehouse. Jasper wasn't fired yet, but when they asked him to give Donnegan his office he saw the writing on the wall. At forty-two years old, with no degrees, he was practically unemployable.

Grounded and forbidden to ever speak to Heather Kimmelson again, Catt considered suicide as penance for what they'd done to Jonathan and Damien.

After dinner, on an October night before Halloween, Jasper and Emma told the girls they had big news. Their applications for assisted passage to New Zealand had been approved. Catt and Carla didn't know anything about these applications, or about New Zealand. Jasper would be working as the office manager for New Zealand's premier publisher, A. H. & A. W. Reed. Emma showed the girls a photo book produced by Reed about this marvelous tiny country. Two Pacific islands ten thousand miles away—a country with six million sheep and half as many people.

They'd sell the house and cars and get the girls their passports. As soon as that was done, they'd leave for Wellington.

PART 2

BALSAM

1

The first time Catt saw the gray house in Balsam, she was sick with desire. It was an old-fashioned cottage, one and a half stories tall, perfectly located. Set halfway up the hill of a big rolling meadow, it sat a few hundred yards back from a small oval lake. Whoever built the house here had obviously thought about it. The dirt driveway stopped at a two-car garage. Through the woods to the left, there was an unfinished guest cabin, hauled on a trailer from a girls' summer camp by a son of the original homesteaders. The son—by then an old man—had worked as the maintenance man before the camp went out of business. There was an outhouse behind the garage, and a few hundred feet north, up next to the lake, the original one-room log cabin the first homesteader had built with a chisel and axe when he'd arrived there from Finland.

A long cement walkway joined the garage to the cottage, where a doorway off the front deck led to a sunroom. The afternoon sun filtered through pine trees, and Catt thought she heard a faraway cackling loon. She'd decided to take the afternoon off from writing a museum catalog essay to go swimming at Scenic State Park up in Bigfork. After stopping for lunch at the diner at Balsam Four Corners, she'd seen the For Sale sign across from the Bible Church, alongside Route 7. Getting out of her old Ford Ranger truck, Catt's first thought was: We could never afford this. But that didn't stop her from walking up to the house to look through the windows.

It was a Wednesday in late June 2012. A few days before, white Shasta daisies had bloomed overnight, everywhere—in the small yards of the Iron Range mining towns, along the bike trail and roadsides, and outside the rough summer cabin overlooking Twin Lake, where Catt was staying.

Late June was also the tail end of turtle season in northern Minnesota. Emerging from a long hibernation, wood turtles and snappers foraged in tall, uncut grass along roadsides before building their nests. Unaware of the dangers of traffic, they liked to bask in the sun on the freshly tarred two-lane highways. For two or three weeks, at least twice a day, Catt pulled her truck onto the shoulder and got out to rescue them.

This was Catt's fourth Twin Lake summer. She'd found the cabin on Craigslist in 2008, the year she'd followed her partner Paul Garcia to Center City, Minnesota. Paul was about to start a one-year graduate degree in addiction studies at the Hazelden Betty Ford treatment center. Catt and Paul met in 2005 and maintained a long-distance relationship between LA and Albuquerque, where Paul was finishing his BA in psychology. The Hazelden year would be their first chance to actually live together. Catt quit her visiting job in the UC San Diego writing program to work on an unfinished novel. They sublet her house in LA and rented an empty three-bedroom house, month-to-month, in the small town of Lindstrom, ten miles from the campus.

The split-level ranch house was set on a lake, and Catt imagined them hosting fondue evenings for Paul's colleagues in front of the fireplace. But after unloading the truckload of furniture she'd packed from her house in the sub-zero darkness, Paul went into a mysterious fugue state. For the rest of the night and half the next day he withdrew, refusing to speak to her no matter how much she pleaded. Finally, his dark, sullen mood erupted in rage: *Don't you see? I've made a mistake! I love you but I'm not in love with you. I don't want to live with you.* Catt did not understand. Was there a difference between loving and being in love? She'd just quit her job, paid the tuition for Paul's first semester, driven two thousand miles, and sublet her house until next January. Frightened of drowning in his unstoppable anger, she considered all her options. He could withdraw from the school and move back to Albuquerque. Or, he could stay and she'd go back to LA, or maybe even Mexico City and sublet an apartment? When he got his first job he could start repaying the tuition.

The cloud passed. Paul changed his mind and apologized. None of these solutions were necessary.

They never spoke of that first night again. Through the long winter, Catt worked on her book every day while Paul went to classes. At night, they made meat loaf and northern bean casseroles. Catt never met anyone from Paul's cohort. *It's not like art school*, he told her. Most of his classmates were local and kept to themselves. During the weekends, they took to exploring the strangeness of Minnesota. Staying at roadside motels, playing cards late at night, they invented a game: which of the places they passed through would win the Saddest Town contest? By midafternoon, night fell over hundreds of acres of corn husks. Thick-coated horses foraged stalks in the soy fields. The old IGAs and appliance repair stores on Main Street had either closed or been turned into food pantries and thrift stores. Bars remained open.

When the management company unexpectedly told them they'd have to leave their house in June, Paul moved in with a classmate to finish his internship and thesis. Eager to finish her book and explore the Northwoods near the Canadian border, Catt scoured Craigslist until she found Cheryl Thorsen's Twin Lakes cabin.

No shower, no internet—Cheryl and her husband had come up from the Cities and built the place themselves back in the sixties. Now that her husband was dead and she lived a two-day drive away in South Dakota, Cheryl no longer used it. A retired schoolteacher, she lived alone and worked part-time at a Walmart. Crammed with knickknacks and family memorabilia, the cabin was all that remained of happier times and she was reluctant to sell it.

That summer, Catt walked and wrote every day, rode her bike through the woods on the paved eighty-mile trail, and read on the screen porch every night until ten watching the long, blood-orange sunset. The sky and the trees and the bottomless

THE FOUR SPENT THE DAY TOGETHER

lakes were the same impossibly deep blues and greens Catt recalled from growing up in New Zealand. The next summer, and the ones after that, she saw no reason not to go back again. She woke up most mornings just after dawn and walked with her dog up the quarter-mile driveway through deep woods, sipping a hot mug of coffee. From there, she walked down to the dock of the cabin next door that was forever for sale, the only spot at Twin Lakes that had cell service. Watching the morning fog lift from the lake, she called Paul to give him a wildlife and weather report while he was driving to work. Paul was leading five groups a day on the locked ward of a psychiatric hospital, getting the supervised hours he needed to take the exam for his therapy license. He envied Catt's freedom, although since he'd always worked regular jobs, if push came to shove he would probably not know what to do with it. Gray herons nested high in the trees. Catt watched the loons skim the lake as the sun rose and her coffee grew colder.

Twenty eleven, 2012, 2013 were the years in LA when it seemed like everything escalated. Was it because everyone was online all the time? UberX, promoted by the Obama administration, was launched, driving medallioned taxi drivers out of business, into debt and suicide. Uber, in turn, lobbied for Obamacare. No one talked about how the invisible mesh of surveillance and data control that surrounded the world was tightening. Time sped up, a continual stream of cascading events that meant less and moved faster.

At home in LA Catt felt most alive in front of the screen, seething with rage at her quote-unquote friends' Facebook humblebrags. It was completely addictive, everyone checking their privilege while flaunting it. It made no difference how transparently self-serving these posts were. People who'd once prided themselves on their distrust of authority dove like lemmings into social media, hungry for approval from their new online communities. Inflamed by her feed, Catt reluctantly logged out to read *The New York Times*. From there, she checked email and wrote numb automatic replies until finally, completely drained, she logged back on to social media. Reading used to be her great escape, and books her solace. Now she had to force herself to leave the screen and even open one.

And then there was the long string of untimely deaths among people she'd grown up with. One friend fell to his death while hiking in the Cascade Range, another friend was bludgeoned to death by her epileptic son in their New York apartment. An old friend from New Zealand died of a heart attack while on tour in Amsterdam. A new friend in LA died of mad cow disease. Her old acting teacher died in New York after a short battle with cancer; another friend died of a rare blood disease. Most troubling of all, her old best friend Leslie died in New York, Catt guessed of an overdose, but there was no way of knowing for sure because there was no trace online of her death, much less her life. Leslie had married a famous director and given up acting and by the time Catt sought out their last mutual friend, he'd died of cancer. Many of these deaths were publicly mourned over Facebook.

Catt found it strange to see outpourings of grief rewarded by the app's trademark gold star: a yellow thumbs-up emoji.

THE FOUR SPENT THE DAY TOGETHER

Didn't past generations handle this better? she wrote in her notebook. *Avoid, a-void. The people we knew are disappeared into oblivion.* But by the time the crying-face emoji was introduced in 2016 she'd gotten used to it. The echo chamber was sealed, there was no longer any way out of it.

Automation, the mathematician Norbert Wiener warned an oblivious world in 1950, will end the economic and political basis for a stable social democracy based on human values other than buying and selling. Still, at the same time, the migration of all things online gave a big boost to Catt's career as a writer. Things that she'd written more than a decade before were being discovered, posted and tweeted by a new generation of younger women. *You're getting to be a famous writer,* her friend Bettina remarked when a TV star posted one of her books on her Instagram. Catt and her friends were doing more work for more people, so busy they barely had time to mourn their missing contemporaries. But what would that even mean? Sometimes they talked about this escalation, but the only conclusion they reached was to keep going.

The dive bars and hole-in-the-wall galleries where they used to present work to a handful of friends were being replaced by sumptuous, quietly capitalized spaces. There were conferences, seminars, launches, and openings, all of them well received and then quickly forgotten by larger, more affluent audiences.

The summers Catt spent at Twin Lake were the only part of the year when she felt herself swimming in time, instead of drowning in it. Walking down to the lake in the late afternoon with her kayak, she read, wrote, and drove into town once a day to check email. By the end of last August, she'd started to wonder if it wouldn't be better to find her own North Country cabin . . . a place she could leave all her books and skip the half-hour drive to the Greatwoods Y to take showers.

In less than three days she'd be leaving the cabin to teach in the Swiss Alps for a week with her soon-to-be-ex-husband Mikal, a critic and philosophy professor. She and Mikal had done this trip every summer for the last several years. Now in his midseventies, Mikal seemed to Catt like the Last Humanist, an avatar of the European twentieth century. He'd read Bakhtin with Lucien Goldmann, studied literature with Roland Barthes, and protested the French war in Algeria. In New York, he'd studied and taught post-political politics. Catt could tell Mikal resented her recent cultural currency, though she could not understand why. He of all people must have known that internet fame meant next to nothing. Once, they'd imagined being buried alongside each other under a tree like Virginia and Leonard Woolf's ashes. Now the shared teaching gig was pretty much all that remained of their deep alliance.

On Saturday morning, Catt would leave Cheryl's cabin and drive four hours south to Minneapolis to catch the overnight Amsterdam nonstop. At Schiphol, she'd connect to a midmorning regional flight to Zurich. Arriving at noon, she'd catch a taxi to the Kloten commuter rail station, get off at Zurich Central, and catch a train to Lausanne, stopping at Brig. Two and a half hours later, she'd get off at Brig, exit the station, and wait for the bus that went all the way to Saas-Fee, where the school was. Throughout the long trip, she'd watch the landscape become progressively more alpine and beautiful. When the bus reached Saas-Fee a man from the hotel would be waiting with a luggage cart. She'd unzip her bag before handing it over and put on a light winter jacket.

Four days later, she'd retrace these steps back to the cabin with an envelope bulging with cash buried deep in her backpack.

The East German philosopher who directed the school had established the custom of summoning faculty members to his hotel room one at a time late at night after their last day of teaching. After reviewing their seminars he'd open the safe and pay them in crisp, fresh large bills, as if they'd just finished a topless bar shift or a burglary. Catt and Mikal liked this arrangement. They loved the students the school attracted, who were almost autistically bright and came from all over the world. In Saas-Fee, they felt like they'd found their people.

Now that their divorce was practically final, it seemed more important than ever for Catt to find a house she and Paul could purchase together. Paul was ten years younger than Catt and everything in their lives predated their couplehood. He'd been sober two years when they met. Before that, his life was a mash-up of alcoholic catastrophes.

But by 2012 finding another place in LA was out of the question. Prices had gone up—people were arriving in droves, priced out of New York and San Francisco. Catt had bought her sprawling old house in Westlake near MacArthur Park more than a decade earlier. Developed in the 1920s, Westlake evoked the Bronx of Catt's early childhood with its tall brick apartment buildings and once-stately hotels with long yellow canopies. The neighborhood was originally mostly Jewish but during the great exodus to LA from Guatemala and El Salvador during the dirty wars of the eighties, it became home to the largest Central American community outside of Central America. Storefront parcel delivery services lined the streets, with photographs of TVs and stoves delivered by burro to remote villages in the Guatemalan highlands. Walking around MacArthur Park, Catt could almost pretend she was back in the Bronx or in Central America. It was like time travel. Hidden behind a wrought-iron gate at the end of a cul-de-sac, her house was one of the jewels of the ungentrified, crime-and-gang-ridden neighborhood that Catt loved and Paul hated. But now that LA had become so expensive, the move to a more middle-class part of LA would mean trading her lovely art deco house for a condo. And so they stayed.

Recently it had occurred to them both that buying a house two thousand miles from LA in the Northwoods might be the answer. Except for Catt's parents, who now lived in Palm Springs, they had no family ties to LA or really anywhere. Paul had worked at his hospital job long enough to apply for a mortgage. Even if he could only come out every summer for two or three weeks, they both loved the deep blues and greens of the flat northern prairie, the forests, the clouds and the weather.

The Minnesota North Country was how Paul imagined the landscape in Oregon where he was born, before his family slunk back to Albuquerque. Paul was the youngest of six in a large Mexican-Lebanese Catholic family and according to family legend his birth was the cause of their descent into real poverty. While his mother was pregnant with Paul, his father was hired as the director of Spanish language studies at a small Jesuit college in Silverton, Oregon. They'd been there less than a year when his mom, who had acute schizophrenia, attacked one of the nuns in a postpartum rage: *You filthy whore, you've been sleeping with my husband.* The next year his job was eliminated and for the rest of his life, his dad supported them all teaching high school in Albuquerque.

Catt loved northern Minnesota because it reminded her of Thurman, the southern Adirondack town where she and Mikal had spent the most isolated, intimate years of their lives together. They'd moved to Thurman in the late 1980s before cell phones, internet, and cable television, when old-timers lived according to a rural calendar marked by signs and each month was defined by agriculture, trapping, hunting, animal migrations. In northern Minnesota, Catt discovered, wildlife was even more intact and plentiful. Hundreds of miles of forest and lakes spanned the north-central portion of the state far beyond the Canadian border. Eagles and cranes, hawks, egrets, and white pelicans circled Twin Lakes every summer. Once, she'd seen a timber wolf along the bike trail. In northern Minnesota Catt could almost forget the ecological apocalypse. When she attempted a small joke about global warming one summer after a full week of rain, the woman who punched cards at the town dump erupted into a dance of climate denial.

That's all wrong! Changes in weather are cyclical, our minister said so. If you think the globe's warming, try spending a winter up here! It's been like that for thousands of years, just read the Bible.

By the time she found the gray house, Catt had almost abandoned her on-again off-again search for a Northwoods cabin. The lakefronts were studded with enormous glass and cedar lodges, used as vacation retreats for big Minneapolis families. Along Highway 169 between Greatwoods and Harding, there was a string of little towns with shambling wood-frame houses built by the mines in the 1920s and leased to their immigrant workers. When the ore was extracted the companies left and the houses were sold to local families. Over the decades, as the region declined, these former mining locations became the last source of cheap housing for the disabled and semi-employed. Those with good jobs or good pensions moved into new double-wide trailers or manufactured homes further out in the country. Unlike the stately retreats that lined the big lakes, these places were set within feet of the road, making it easier to plow your way out during the six months of winter.

In Thurman, Catt remembered, she and Mikal had immersed themselves in a parallel world of Adirondack bands, amateur historians, singer-songwriters, and storytellers, but here it seemed there was no regional culture beyond mining. The Iron Range had four museums devoted to mining, even though the old mines were closed and the new ones were completely automated. Whatever other histories may have occurred were hidden deep under the surface.

THE FOUR SPENT THE DAY TOGETHER

Until now she'd never seen anything on the Range remotely like the gray house—a small compound with three outbuildings and a dock, but modest, discreet, flanked by towering pines and meadows—like something you'd see in the Berkshires. It was the kind of place she'd dreamed of when she was broke and living in New York during her twenties.

Catt parked and walked up the long path to the house. She found the front door locked so she circled the house, checking for unlocked windows. There was an old back door behind a lilac bush, swollen shut. Catt pushed it open and entered. There were maple plank floors in the living room and kitchen, louvered windows facing toward the lake, an old wood-paneled door that led to a small bedroom. The kitchen had been modestly updated: the appliances were old but money had been spent on a deep farmhouse sink and glass-fronted wood cabinets painted burgundy. A half-story staircase led to a big boat-like loft room. Catt felt a sense of return that was also the beginning of something. She wondered who the former occupants were and where they came from. Anyone local would have spent on a stainless steel fridge and a dishwasher.

Standing in the downstairs bedroom with its two narrow windows, Catt pictured herself writing a book here, maybe several. The big boat-shaped loft room upstairs was sweet and enveloping, with low plaster walls and a pitched ceiling. A small room at the north end of the loft looked over the lake—Paul could use this as his home office! Her heart raced as she reached for her phone—it was two thirty in Minnesota, which made it 12:30 in LA, he'd be on his lunch break—but there was no cell service beyond Balsam Four Corners.

Closing the door tightly behind her, Catt walked down the hill to a lopsided wooden pier at the foot of South Jonas Lake. Lily pads, wild irises. She counted a few other piers but the houses were hidden behind the thick June foliage. There was no one around. Catt took off her shoes and put her feet into the water. Two loons ducked up and down between the small choppy waves. She couldn't imagine this incredible place costing less than $350,000. There was no point even thinking about it; it was impossible.

Still, as soon as she drove back in range she called the number she'd seen on the sign and the broker answered immediately. South Jonas Lake? It had been on the market for over a year but last month the seller finally accepted an offer. When Catt asked the price, the number was less than half what she'd imagined. She kicked herself and made him promise, please, to call if anything changed or fell through.

Paul and Catt met in Albuquerque in April 2005. He was staying in a new Northwest subdivision with his sister Pam and Daniel, her ten-year-old son. One month before that, he'd been released from Los Lunas state prison for charging $953 on his former employer's fuel credit card. He'd been working for Halliburton, driving a big gas field truck up in Farmington, New Mexico. Donnie, his AA sponsor, had hooked him up with the job but then he relapsed. Paul stopped going to work

THE FOUR SPENT THE DAY TOGETHER

but it took his bosses three weeks to shut down the card. Until then, he'd been hanging around Circle K pumping gas at half price for anyone who didn't tell him to fuck off. Initially he spent the money on Jack Daniel's and Marlboro Lights but eventually he moved on to crack; it was more cost-effective. He totaled his car, the whole thing was a shitshow. When he was finally arrested no one would loan him money for bail or a lawyer. The public defender promised he'd get off with probation if he pled guilty to Felony Class 3 but the judge sentenced him to thirty-two months, the maximum penalty. Halliburton controlled everything in that town. Except for a few DUIs Paul had no prior charges.

He got sober on his first night in jail and earned early release by going to AA, the sweat lodge, Bible class, and chapel. After working his way from Level 3 medium security in Santa Fe all the way up to Level 1, the Los Lunas farm, he initially moved back to Farmington. But when he saw how old friends there were going to pull him back into trouble, he decided to move back to Albuquerque, where his sister Pam let him stay with her. The most functional of his five siblings, Pam was a staff physician at a big hospital. She was also very critical of Paul, who'd always been smart and should have been more successful. Pam and Daniel lived together alone in an enormous McMansion but she did not help Paul out with a lawyer. When he was completely dying in Level 3 medium, trying to stay clear of the gangsters, she took Daniel to visit thinking the sight of his uncle behind bars in an orange jumpsuit would "scare him straight." Daniel still had the photo.

Albuquerque had changed a lot in the ten years since Paul fled to Farmington to escape a few problems caused by his drinking, as well as his family. It used to be, he could walk off the street and talk his way into almost any job or apartment. But now it was all online applications, credit and background checks. No matter how well an interview went, everything changed when he answered the felony question. Thanks, they all said, we'll get back to you. He was beginning to wonder if he'd ever find a real job, let alone an apartment. And then he saw Catt's newspaper ad for a resident manager of some apartments. The ad offered good part-time pay and a rent-free apartment in a ten-unit complex.

Albuquerque, as everyone knew, was split sharply between Good and Bad. As a child, he'd gravitated toward Good Albuquerque, making friends with the upper-middle-class kids, learning about boating and tennis, but drinking had mixed him up with the Bad. Catt's apartments were set in the heart of Bad Albuquerque, just three miles from downtown and the university but riddled with crack dens and gangsters. Paul knew: he'd often bought drugs there.

Paul couldn't match his impression of Catt with the apartments she'd just acquired. With her nice boots and haircut, she clearly belonged in Good Albuquerque—and yet she seemed different from most of Good Albuquerque, freer and lighter, maybe more like someone from Taos?

Before even meeting, the first time they talked on the phone, something clicked and they connected. When they finally met, she offered him the job immediately. Like him, she'd never had

THE FOUR SPENT THE DAY TOGETHER

kids, which was almost unheard of for someone their age. She lived in LA, wrote, and taught part-time at a college. He had no idea what she was doing with all these apartments in such a dangerous neighborhood.

She'd arrived from LA with a crew led by her friend Vernon, a carpenter-handyman in his late 40s, to fix up the apartments. Paul began helping out. Almost immediately, they began flirting, but before their first date, Catt told him that she was married. She and Mikal, she explained, no longer had sex or even lived together but they were still each other's best friends and they still shared their money.

Paul had a hard time understanding this. Once he broke up with a woman, it was as if she had never existed. He and Catt had been "together" for a few weeks when Mikal came to visit and see the apartments. He was French, old, European, and he seemed like a really nice guy. He invited them both to a cloth-napkin restaurant for Paul's fortieth birthday. Paul had never seen anything like that. Mikal seemed completely content to see them together, as if he were Catt's dad or big brother.

Catt had acquired thirty-six run-down apartments in some of Albuquerque's worst neighborhoods that spring in a spirit of misguided optimism. She'd been dabbling in small real estate ventures ever since she and Mikal—priced out of New York—moved to Thurman. Mikal's mother had given them two gifts of money and since it wasn't enough to buy a New York apartment, they chose instead to invest it.

The money had come from Mikal's older sister Jacqueline. In the postwar building boom around Paris, Jacqueline had saved her immigrant parents from an impoverished old age by purchasing condos with no money down and building a modest real estate empire. Jacqueline, a secretarial school graduate, was stylish, ambitious, and smart—a Maria Braun figure, relentlessly charming, who even looked a little bit like Hanna Schygulla. Mikal and Catt loved and admired her. Under her influence, they'd bought and fixed up a small rental house and eventually acquired a one-bedroom East Village apartment.

By the time Catt moved to LA in the mid-1990s, she already knew quite a lot about plumbing and sanding and painting. So instead of renting a house she bought a falling-down cabin at the foot of Mount Washington. It was the first thing she'd ever owned in her name and her adjunct teaching job more than covered the mortgage. Since she couldn't afford to hire a general contractor, Catt decided to remove the old asbestos shingles herself and re-side the whole cabin. Vernon, the counterman at the lumberyard, offered to come over one weekend to teach her how to install the new cedar shake shingles. He kept coming back and they finished the cabin together.

Vern and his wife, Felicia, became Catt's new Los Angeles friends. They were all around the same age, and the two of them lived in a mobile home park east of LA in Upland. Catt was already wildly conflicted about her life in the Los Angeles art world and her visits to Vern and Felicia became her new secret escape. Vern was a kind of savant—a high school dropout who had perfect taste and could fix or restore almost anything.

THE FOUR SPENT THE DAY TOGETHER

When Catt and Vern both lost their jobs around the same time, they decided to keep working together. After the riots and earthquake, there were so many old houses for sale that no one else wanted. They found and fixed a trashed chalet in the San Bernardino Mountains sixty miles east of LA, and then a duplex in Atwater Village. Credit was cheap and it was easy to pay herself and Vern and make a small profit without raising rents or displacing people. She bought, and they fixed, her house near MacArthur Park and a big empty duplex around the corner that was caught up in a lawsuit. She'd been so poor in New York, working the most menial jobs, before she and Mikal got together. Her teeth had been crooked, she had to cover them up with her lips when she smiled because until she was forty years old, she couldn't afford to fix them. *The universe*, Catt thought, *is telling me now to make money*.

But eventually LA woke up from its slumber. The warm buzz of capital pulsed through the streets like caffeine, all the old diners were closing and being replaced with high-concept cafés. Artists she knew snapped up shabby ranch homes and doubled their money, turning them into midcentury masterpieces. The rents on these places could not stay the same. A new demographic swept in and took over. Catt craved stability—she'd loved these old shabby neighborhoods for what they had been and the people who lived in them, and hated the idea of becoming a part of this tsunami of gentrification.

Around the same time, she'd begun dating a maverick real estate lawyer she'd met on a plane. Hank Forster was from Appalachia and hadn't been able to get his teeth fixed until after law school. He was a Robin Hood figure, representing the city and county in deals with foreign developers. Hank was charmed by her little empire and encouraged her to professionalize it. So she sold the Atwater duplex and bought a twelve-unit building near the Mojave Desert two hours northeast of LA. There, things were more stable. She could fix up the apartments without totally gentrifying them and rent them to working-class people. Vern and Felicia moved up and became the resident managers.

Two years later the Los Angeles boom spread to the desert. When a professional developer offered her three times what she'd paid for the complex she knew she'd be a fool not to take it. But she couldn't just take the money and exit. She'd bought the twelve-plex with tax-deferred funds from the duplex. To maintain the deferral she had to buy other rental apartments of equal or greater value. The brokers advised her to go to Las Vegas or Phoenix but she hated those places.

When she saw the old Route 66–style stucco buildings in Albuquerque, she fell in love. The thick casement windows, the sunlight and dust . . . trace elements of a lost Americana. The apartments had been listed for months, with very few paying tenants, which she naïvely saw as a plus: she could fix them all up and start fresh without raising rents and displacing anyone. With thirty-six tenants she could afford to use ceramic tiles in the kitchens and baths, pave the parking lots, and paint accent walls in Southwestern colors. Unlike the professional management companies in town, she would rent the apartments to homeless agency clients and people with felony backgrounds.

THE FOUR SPENT THE DAY TOGETHER

She imagined people restarting their lives in the sanctuary of these graceful old buildings.

After helping her rehab the buildings in Albuquerque, Vern and Felicia would move back to the desert. Catt loaned them money to buy an old Craftsman home of their own and three rental units. It would be better, she thought, to separate the toilets-and-leaking-hot-water-heaters part of her life from her life in LA as a writer.

When Mikal came to see Catt and the new apartments that May, they talked for a long time about Paul and about everything. They'd just sold their old house in Thurman. Soon, Mikal would retire from his tenured job in New York. This was the first summer in twenty years they wouldn't be spending together. Mikal would visit his family in France and then travel on to an Italian residency.

Catt had vague plans to travel but after she met Paul, she started rethinking them. She'd just closed the door on the sexual part of her friendship with Hank, who was almost the same age as Mikal. Mikal wondered how serious Catt's involvement with Paul could actually be but he didn't directly question it. Instead, they talked about politics.

It was late spring 2005: since the Iraq invasion two years before, they'd watched in horror as George Bush and Dick Cheney imposed a permanent state of exception. New anti-terrorist laws encouraged the prosecution of acts of good conscience and civil disobedience. The government targeted powerless people, people the media didn't care about—cabdrivers and drywallers, ecological activists in the Pacific Northwest who attended state colleges. There were the roundups and preemptive arrests of Muslim immigrants and the harsh federal sentences imposed upon kids who'd destroyed a few gas-guzzling SUVs at a Ford dealership. One out of every hundred people in the US was incarcerated. There was scant recognition of these events, much less resistance. *The poor must exit*, Catt remembered Jean Baudrillard said of the Reagan years in his book *America*. Eleven years before the election of Donald Trump, six years before Occupy and the Arab Spring, activism hadn't acquired much cultural currency. Mikal and Catt thought about these things every day but like everyone else they felt isolated, estranged, and powerless in their frustrated rage.

Because look at what happened to Paul! Catt said to Mikal. *He spent sixteen months in prison for stealing $953 from Halliburton, Dick Cheney's business that supplied the Iraq War and probably embezzled billions.*

Mikal nodded intently. Despite his sophistication as a critical theorist, he was deeply moved by accounts of injustice. *And Paul doesn't even see his own case as political!* Catt continued. *He's embarrassed, ashamed. He takes everything personally. But any middle-class person with their own lawyer would never have taken a felony plea! They'd have been arraigned and sent home within hours.*

Catt believed in Paul passionately. She wanted to help Mikal understand her excitement about meeting him, and better still, share it. As a hidden Jewish child during the French occupation, Mikal's default impulse was to act always on principle.

THE FOUR SPENT THE DAY TOGETHER

Hadn't his parents' friend Esther, a single woman in the French Resistance, thrown herself out a fourth-story window when the Gestapo knocked on her door in order not to betray her comrades? The war was Mikal's past and he immersed himself in it. Hidden safely in the countryside while his father was arrested, Mikal grew up so traumatized that he never knew how he felt about anything while it was happening, or if he felt at all. His life was more easily arranged around ethical imperatives. *It's not enough,* he liked to say, *to be merely intelligent.* More than anything else, Catt still craved their deep understanding.

Paul's dream was to go back to school and get his BA in psychology. He'd written that down as an affirmation in his prison diaries. Catt was touched by this and stunned by how many obstacles stopped him from doing it. There were so many things he had to pay for: drug testing fees and fees for probation; an expensive Breathalyzer device and another $120 per month for it to be monitored. He couldn't receive cheaper in-state tuition until he paid off a three-thousand-dollar loan he'd taken out for community college, many years earlier, which had since metastasized to a debt of eighteen thousand dollars. *The poor must exit.* And weren't these charges and fees a soft form of incarceration?

Before Mikal left Albuquerque, he agreed, passively, when Catt suggested they pay off Paul's bills and give him a credit card. It would be a fresh start, a political action. She'd managed to escape her own past, why shouldn't everyone? Mikal and Catt both had computers they'd found on Craigslist, but they took Paul to the Apple Store in the uptown mall and bought him a brand-new MacBook. *Welcome to the professional class,* Mikal said wryly.

Seven years later, Paul had completed his BA and the Hazelden master's degree and was working full-time at a psychiatric hospital. Their bet on him had paid off, it seemed—but at the cost of their own estrangement.

In Saas-Fee, Catt settled into the comfortable hotel room the school provided. Mikal would arrive early the next day just before classes started. As usual, they'd been given adjacent rooms, but that summer they hadn't seen much of each other. In fact, since signing their separation agreement on a napkin at a Jewish delicatessen two months before, they'd hardly spoken. He and his new partner Claire were always traveling or busy.

We'll have time in Saas-Fee, Mikal assured her. *Just wait. Things will go back to normal.* And yet, they didn't. They never talked on the phone anymore over coffee. Their emails about business, Catt felt, had gotten terse and colder.

Mikal was exhausted after traveling all night when he arrived on Monday morning. He didn't have time to have coffee with Catt because he had to prepare his first lecture. And so it went throughout their stay. Mikal's job was to lecture on poststructuralist philosophy for six hours each day.

His teaching style was improvisational. He could never prepare enough. He had to immerse himself in the texts so he could extemporaneously synthesize them. Since Catt just

THE FOUR SPENT THE DAY TOGETHER

taught writing, she didn't have much work outside the classroom. *My whole life,* she liked to think, *is the preparation.* She just had to show up on time, hand out some readings, invent a writing prompt or game, and then listen while everyone read what they'd written. According to Saas-Fee custom, the faculty ate lunch with the students. But even at dinner, Mikal avoided Catt, sitting down at the faculty table.

On their last night in Saas-Fee, they were going to have dinner at a fondue restaurant a few blocks away from the school and safe from interrupting students. As soon as they'd sat down at the bar to order drinks while waiting for a table, Volker, another faculty member, walked in and sat between them. A renowned filmmaker of the New German Cinema, Volker had been born the same year as Mikal. A German and a Jew: he and Mikal were both children of the Second World War, although from opposite sides. The two men had much to talk about.

Mikal asked Volker if he'd like to join them for dinner. As the two men talked, Catt watched the chance of ever reconnecting with Mikal ebbing. She left before they ordered coffee. The next day she caught the bus alone to Brig and then traveled on to Zurich.

Catt refused to buy the special SIM card for her phone to work in Europe so it wasn't until she arrived back in Minneapolis that she saw the missed call from a northern Minnesota number. The Jonas Lake broker had left a voicemail: the buyers had backed out, the house was hers and Paul's, if they still wanted it.

Paul had already used his two weeks' annual leave from the psychiatric hospital, so he could not come out to see it. Trusting Catt's intuition and enthusiasm, he signed the contract and the mortgage.

At Christmas they drove two thousand miles from Los Angeles to Balsam, with all the things that they'd collected for the house packed in a U-Haul trailer.

2

They drove through Nevada and Utah, Idaho, Wyoming, Montana, and North Dakota with their little dog Blaze dressed in a red hand-dyed sweater. Catt had bought it for him from an expensive new ethical shop on the Lower East Side the last time she'd read in New York. How much, she'd asked herself then, can one spend on a scented candle? The answer was $73. The sweater was lovely, but still she imagined the bewildered contempt of the Bolivian woman who'd knitted it.

They stopped around one on Christmas Eve night in an empty motel near the oil fields outside of Bismarck. A strand of old-fashioned lights with thick colored bulbs hung from the eaves. The lights were the kind both Paul and Catt had grown up with, their parents too cheap to invest in the new twinkling kind. Small blobs of color shone through the dark prairie night and the air was so cold it was painful to walk through the parking lot.

Paul was angry that night and Catt didn't know why. Was it the spat that they'd had at the China Buffet seven hours ago? Catt swore by the China Buffet as the only real chance to eat fast, healthy food on long road trips. As always she half-filled her plate with white rice and vegetables. Paul clocked her despair as he loaded his plate up with pork, fried rice, and egg rolls. She wanted to talk, then—about anything. *Paul*, she'd whispered as he shoveled the poison into his mouth, *can you slow down, please?* He'd glared and grinned at her tightly and then returned to the buffet for seconds. Since then he'd been wrapped in a silence that could explode anytime into rage. She'd tried cracking a joke and then playing a car game they both remembered from childhood. In Montana, she found an NPR station playing Bach's Christmas Cantatas. Paul loved baroque music—as a young woman his mother had trained as a pianist—but he switched it off angrily. When these black moods descended there was no way of coaxing him out, although she stupidly tried to.

There was a road trip they'd taken together—was it before this, or after?—when Catt sat on the floor and tried to make herself disappear into the corner of a motel room in Nebraska or Kansas. He'd yelled at her till she wept and then got into bed and slept like a dead man. Catt was afraid of his anger but she still hadn't learned how to prevent it. She'd already learned not to bring it up later, because if the subject was broached he'd snarl, *Why are you always so negative?* and the rage would start up all over. Eventually, a day or week later he'd find his way back and make a veiled, joking reference to his "bad mood," which was his way of apologizing. Googling *Is my partner abusive* into the night, sometimes Catt felt Paul's revolving moods diminished her agency. But, then again, wasn't agency overrated? She had so many other things going on—writing and teaching, her writing career, the apartments in Albuquerque—so long as the moods weren't too frequent it was easier just to ignore them.

Paul stayed in the truck while Catt went to the office and traded some cash for a room key. They unloaded their overnight bags and carried the dog upstairs underneath a blanket. This ghostly sixties motel Catt found so interesting was just like the places Paul used to smoke crack in. He cranked up the heat and without saying a word disappeared into one of the two double beds.

When they woke up it was Christmas. Paul put on his parka and boots and went out to the truck for the coffeemaker. He brewed up a pot and gave Catt a big mug of black coffee with two spoons of raw sugar, just how she liked it. *Merry Christmas, kitten duck!* He scooped up the dog in his arms. The black mood was over.

The sky was as gray as the house on South Jonas Lake Lane when they pulled into the driveway. Thick heaps of snow sat on the tall Balsam pines. It was the first Minnesota winter they'd seen in the five years since Paul finished his Hazelden master's degree. Even though he'd gone on to get his PsyD in LA, Paul never fully bought into the concept of school or even psychology. Sometimes he made extra money writing service-dog letters under his MFT therapy license—*To Whom It*

May Concern, Patient X consulted my office presenting with symptoms consistent with moderate depression and I prescribed a therapy animal. It was ridiculous. Still, it was better to attend school and have a profession than not, if he wanted to function in life and live comfortably. And it had paid off! The gray house was a dream. Who would've thought he'd have his own lake house when he got out of Los Lunas state prison less than ten years ago? The grant deed was in their names jointly. Catt was a freelancer—she could never have gotten the mortgage without his pay stubs and high credit score.

The broker had had the house cleaned and put the heat on for them. Unloading the U-Haul and carrying the furniture they'd been collecting for months into the house, they couldn't believe how good it all looked. Catt warmed up some hot apple cider and they walked down to the lake with their mugs through a few inches of snow. *It's so quiet*, Paul said, taking it in, *so clean here*. The lake was a perfect white egg ringed by white birch and pine trees. It was like being reborn. Catt couldn't wait for him to come back and see the place in the summer.

Still—in the back of his mind, Paul was already dreading the end of the break, when he'd have to go back to his job on Skid Row with a new mobile mental health team. Skid Row, Death Row, Skideath Row . . . it wasn't even a district, per se—the borders kept shifting around downtown LA. When he accepted the job, he'd thought that driving around in a shiny white van every day would be a reprieve from the locked ward of the hospital. But there was just so much suffering, wherever

THE FOUR SPENT THE DAY TOGETHER

he went in the field of psychology. The energy flying around in his therapy groups had been desperate and crazy, and he felt it, but at least after group he could go back to his office. As soon as he stepped out of the van on Skid Row, he knew he couldn't escape. The air on the streets locked him in. He kept his mouth closed; he did not want to taste it but still the smell stuck to his skin. Everything dirty and wrong. Wherever he looked hundreds of people were pushing carts full of possessions that were really garbage. Their hair was matted, their skin was so dirty it looked like a whole other color. Torn rotting clothing covered in stains from old food and shit, the smell of piss in the alleys, everything stank. All day long, it felt like something bad stuck to his skin and it itched. He didn't tell Catt this.

She and her friends thought this was an important, even glamorous job. Of course: they did not have to do it. The new mobile mental health team was charged with triaging those who were closest to death and bringing them into a new clustered care program, where medical doctors, prescribing psychiatrists, therapists, and housing specialists worked together to ensure their survival. Once accepted into the program, new clients were whisked off the streets and given free medical treatment, psychiatric supervision, food stamps, and brandnew apartments. During the two months he'd been on the job, they'd saved eight or ten people. But there were so many more. The pain that he witnessed was infinite.

The gray house stood on the snowy white hill like a dream. *This* was what he had worked for. If he could just find a way to actually live here! He held Catt's mittened hand tight in one of his new leather gloves, the gloves that her parents had bought him for Christmas.

They dropped off the U-Haul the next morning at Nuttal's Garage in Greatwoods. Greatwoods was smaller and nicer than Harding, the next major Iron Range town, about thirty miles down the highway. There was a still-working paper mill, an arts center, a Y, and a vegetarian café. Of course the town had a big Walmart, but there was also a yoga and dance studio next to the jail and the courthouse. You could tell there were people in town who'd lived other places. The broker had told them Greatwoods was twenty-five minutes from Balsam, but driving the trailer on ice took them almost an hour. The guy at the U-Haul seemed surprised they'd come out to the Range from California. Most people moved in the other direction.

From there, they went to the hippie café and had Thai curry soup and cranberry muffins. Catt was determined to cross-country ski at least several times on this winter vacation. She'd researched the trails and packed all the gear they'd bought five years before during the Hazelden winter. Driving north on Route 38 out of Greatwoods, they followed a map onto snowy back roads and eventually pulled into a small parking area. There were just a few other cars. But behind a big metal gate they found a nicely groomed wilderness trail that ran for six miles through a handful of lakes and the woods to an

THE FOUR SPENT THE DAY TOGETHER

abandoned estate. They put on their skis and took off over a series of up-and-down hills that passed by two lakes. It was around 1 p.m., the heat of the day, about 10 degrees Fahrenheit. Ice-coated branches of larch, maple, and oak laced high overhead, and through them, the sky. Catt zoomed down the hills, ecstatic. When she and Mikal moved to Thurman she'd set out to learn all the middle-class skills she'd missed in her childhood. She learned how to ski, ride a horse, and roast a French chicken, and took ballet lessons. *You have to glide, Paul, glide!* she called out to him from the tops of the hills. Trudging up every hill on the edges of his skis, Paul was a good sport. He could see how much she loved this.

In the basement that night, Paul found an old wood-burning furnace. He loaded it up and they both fell asleep with the dog at their feet, warmed by wood heat. Late that night, Paul heard several loud bangs on the chimney, as if someone were striking it with a big metal pole, but Catt couldn't hear well and she didn't hear it.

The vacation was almost over but they still hadn't had sex in the new house. Catt was concerned but did not want to push it. The question, or matter, of sex had become so fraught and sensitive. Paul was tired most nights from work or depressed on the weekends. Once, in a black mood he'd snarled, *If we were the same age and I was attracted to you, our relationship would be perfect.* But then he apologized and explained he was just looking for something ugly and hurtful to say. He was so sorry she almost felt sorry for him. *Oh, kitten,* he said, holding her close under the covers, *you are my favorite person.* There were patterns of frost on the window beside them and beyond that nothing but snowfall.

In the morning they woke up to a note on the door—

Welcome to Balsam!—Come up and say hello anytime—we're the white house at the end of the road.
Walter & Heather Lapke

The Lapkes were their closest, in fact their only, year-round neighbors at South Jonas Lake. Walter and Heather were home when Paul and Catt walked up the dirt road and knocked on their door, along with four of their five homeschooled children.

The Lapkes were missionaries. Before the birth of their first they'd served in Namibia and Central America. Now Walter edited a Christian blog and Heather served as the Balsam town treasurer. They also sold goat milk.

Paul and Catt took off their boots and followed Walter into the living room. In his late forties, he wore a fleece vest over his plaid shirt, dad jeans, and a cheap pair of bifocals. Heather, about seven years younger with curly brown hair, came out from the kitchen wearing an apron. Pink-faced, robust, and stolid, they looked like middle-class people of the last century who'd taken up hobby farming. A bright, cheerful living room: a dining table next to the windows with pale yellow curtains; a TV and bookcase; a long couch and two recliners all facing the woodstove. The sun shone but outside it was 3 degrees

THE FOUR SPENT THE DAY TOGETHER

Fahrenheit. Walter asked how they were settling in and enjoying the weather after California. The broker had told them the new owners would be driving out from Los Angeles.

For no reason—no one had asked—Paul and Catt struggled to explain their presence in Balsam. Catt was a teacher and writer—she'd be up here summers—they'd discovered the North Country while Paul was in grad school at Hazelden.

We were starting to think, Heather said, as she brought out some hot mugs of tea and home-baked Christmas cookies, that the Ellison house would never be sold.

Before you came along, it had been on the market almost two years, Walter added.

All this used to belong to the Ellisons, Heather said. A hundred and twenty-five acres, it was the old Maki homestead.

As soon as I saw the gray house last June, Catt confessed, I pictured us there. It was *exactly* the place that I'd dreamed, I was almost sick with desire.

It was the same way for us! Heather said, smiling. We'd just gotten back from Zaire when Walt Jr. was born. We were renting in St. Paul and looking all over Minnesota for a house with a barn on a lake that we could afford then. We bought our place from Theresa Ellison just after she'd gotten divorced.

Was she from the Cities?

No, she came from somewhere in England! She had big plans for turning the whole Maki place into a horse farm. They cut trails back by the creek that they used for cross-country skiing. Of course they're long since grown over. But when she and her husband divorced they split the place up into parcels.

A fellow from Harding bought the back forty-five acres that he uses for bear hunting.

Bear hunting? Paul asked.

Yeah, that's right, Walter said proudly. You'd better be careful back there.

Where are the Ellisons now?

Well, Heather said, I think he moved down to the Cities. I don't know where Theresa is now but for a while we were neighbors. After Walter and I bought this place Theresa moved over to your house and we got to know her a little. Her daughter Mariah was living with friends in Greatwoods, she'd partly grown up here. And then Theresa had to go back to England to take care of some family things, so she put your house on the market. It was originally going to be your house plus the metal horse barn and sixty-five acres. She let Mariah and her boyfriend move into your cabin rent free—that old summer camp cabin that one of the old Maki sons hauled here. The idea was, they were going to fix the place up and then Theresa would cut a half acre out, sell it, and give them half the money. But then it didn't work out that way.

Apparently things got a bit out of hand, Walter said, over the winter. Of course they didn't bother us much—

But when Theresa got back and saw the state of the place, she was just done with it, Heather added. She changed things around, put the cabin together back with the house and the barn and the acres for five hundred thousand but nobody bit so she split it again, the barn and the acres, the house and the cabin, and then you came along—

THE FOUR SPENT THE DAY TOGETHER

Speaking of bit, Walter said, turning to Paul, do you fish? Because, wow. The lake is eighty feet deep in the middle, which given its size you'd never expect. This summer you're in for some great bass and walleye.

Can't wait, Paul said, forcing a smile. In fact he'd only fished once as a child. He'd thrown his first, his only, fish back in the water, and they'd called him a pussy but he couldn't stand watching it suffer. He didn't say this to Walter.

The temperature reached the high teens that afternoon—it was going to snow again. Walking home, Paul and Catt stopped to look at the cabin. Snow had piled up by the front door. Paul pushed it open and they walked into a small room with electric and plumbing supplies: a toilet, a sink, a hot water heater, a microwave. Someone had started to rough in a kitchen and bathroom. Through a door, in the main room, sheets of plywood panel had been haphazardly screwed to the studs, but whoever had started siding this room had left it unfinished. A pile of dead leaves had blown through a torn screen door into one of the corners. There were a few cans of spray paint and a thin mattress jammed into an unfinished closet. Paul had a powerful feeling that something bad, even evil, had gone on in this place, but Catt didn't see that. It was a whole bonus cabin—six hundred square feet with electricity, plumbing, and water! They could fix the place up, invite friends to stay over the summer.

That night Paul dreamed he was in a big empty park: *It was a very nice park, very green, I felt surprised and even lucky to find it.*

I saw a big centipede-looking thing crawl through the grass past two newborn puppies. A big human hand reached out of the bushes, trying to push the centipede back toward the puppies, but it crawled safely past them. Walking on, I turned to look back and there was the centipede, eating the puppies. They screamed in its mouth while being devoured.

Waking up, he still heard the sound. But it was only a screech owl outside the window.

Paul quit his job on Skid Row after a long string of hot days that descended in May. It was not even summer but already the heat and the stench, the noise and the chaos, of the unhoused mentally ill were making him panicked and desperate. Every day that he spent on those streets pitched him back to his childhood. It was like seeing his raving-mad mother throwing a brick on his six-year-old foot, multiplied thousands of times in different races and genders. Now that he had his degrees and his therapy license he could get a job anytime, and hopefully one he liked better. He dreamed about taking off the whole month of July to hang out with Catt at their lake house in Balsam. To his surprise, she was on board with that. They could camp and go kayaking, build a bonfire, maybe fix up the cabin.

Paul left in late June for Balsam and drove for two days without stopping. The summer of 2013 . . . Catt was still in LA, planning to join him a week or so later.

She and Mikal signed their divorce at a café in Eagle Rock the day after Paul left for Balsam. She'd thought the divorce would drag on another few months with the lawyers, but Mikal and his partner Claire abruptly decided to file it themselves. He sat on a couch reading a book while Claire walked Catt through forty pages of documents. When her hand shook and strayed from the signature line by a couple of millimeters, Claire, who'd grown up in Austria, worried the papers would be rejected and sent back by the authorities. *Are you trying to sabotage this?* she asked Catt. *Oh, Claire, she's not*, Mikal said, looking up, defending her for the last time. After signing the rest of the papers Catt left with her copies in a bulging pink folder. The next day, Mikal sent an angry reply to her request for some airline miles that he'd borrowed. *I canceled my debt out to you by procuring you a free trip to Baltimore*, he wrote—he meant a museum speaking engagement that he'd recommended her for after declining it—*a good dinner, hotel, a $1,000 fee, and extra adulation. I think it is a fair trade.*

They talked many times after that, but not really.

In Balsam that summer Paul and Catt fell in love with the north: the constantly changing patterns of clouds in the sky, the wild orchids and dragonfly wings, the modest and homely lavender cornflowers.

When they stepped outside on their first night in the house together, the sky was lit up with fireflies. Thousands of pinpricks of light flashed in the darkness. They thought about catching some in a jar but that seemed too cruel and they decided against it. Instead, they named the house Firefly Pond. They talked about posting a hand-painted sign at the foot of the driveway.

Catt found some old lace crocheted curtains at the Harding Goodwill. They set up two deck chairs facing the lake and watched the mist rise while reading the *Harding Tribune* and the *Greatwoods Herald*. Their little dog, Blaze, rolled around on the hill in the thick bright-green grass. Paul bought some tools and a lawn tractor and set up the garage while Catt read Paul Bowles and began to think about writing.

Her last book had come out the summer before. She'd written about meeting Paul and the apartments in Albuquerque, criminal justice and American poverty. It was her first book set outside the art world and the reception was tepid but she believed in it totally. Since then, she'd written nothing but art essays: commissioned and turned out every two or three weeks.

Catt's life as a critic had begun when she moved to LA to teach at an art school. She'd gotten the job through a series of favors. People assumed she knew something about art, which she did not, given the prestige of the program. Catt did not even like art, especially. Given a free day in a strange city, she'd always choose the botanical gardens over museums or galleries.

At first she'd considered her work as an art critic a kind of glorified scam. Writing a column for an art magazine, she challenged herself to see how few words she could devote to the art itself while describing the city, her moods, and her newly adventurous sex life. But as time went by, she came to respect the art and the artists she wrote about. All artistic work was made with intent. She learned to look more closely. To her surprise, she began receiving awards and commissions

THE FOUR SPENT THE DAY TOGETHER

to write about serious artists for major museums. Given this small power, she wanted to use it to support underrecognized artists and work she believed in.

Consequently, since finishing her last novel two years ago she'd written only about visual art, and for hire. All of her fiction so far had come from her life—the people and things she'd observed—but her position right now felt uncertain. Had she used up her life? She started to think she should write about somebody else's.

Almost two decades before, she'd started to work on a biography of the American writer Kathy Acker. Acker died at age fifty, around the same time that Catt's first book came out. They'd only met once or twice and had not even liked each other, but she came to believe their fates were connected. Like everyone else in the East Village, Catt read Acker's self-published books in the late 1970s and her writings shot straight into her heart. When she read Acker, she felt like a better, more intelligent self was speaking for her. Catt had just arrived in New York from Wellington and she didn't know anyone. Forcing herself to go to readings and screenings and concerts alone, she often saw Acker—perfectly dressed and flanked by an entourage—but she was too shy to approach her. And anyway what would she say? She just watched in awe as Acker sucked every room's anxious energy into her personal orbit. Later on, Catt discovered that Acker had been Mikal's most important and serious girlfriend before she left New York for Seattle and London in the wake of a misunderstanding between them. In eighties London, Acker became very famous. All of the years she spent with Mikal, Catt felt the shadow Acker had cast over his life and respected it.

In LA, two decades later, when Catt heard that Acker had collapsed in a San Francisco motel alone with metastasized cancer, she was devastated and empathized her way into a hospital too with a Crohn's disease flare-up. Acker was moved to an alternative clinic in Tijuana and Catt prevailed on Mikal to fly out to visit. She drove him across the border and waited outside while he paid his last visit. All of her adult life Catt had admired, observed, and envied Kathy Acker. And yet the arc of her life seemed to carry a message, and it wasn't a good one. In the months after her death Catt interviewed some of Acker's close friends, thinking she'd write about her.

The transcripts had been sitting in a box for sixteen years. Now, as she kayaked and took bike rides with Paul, she started to think about how she might use them.

The weather that summer was perfect: long rains overnight, breezes that smelled of fresh grass during the day. Catt and Paul bought an atlas at the Balsam Four Corners Store and set out to kayak some of the one thousand lakes in Itasca County.

Kayaking one evening on their own lake, they met Bob and Dolores, the old couple who spent every summer in their ranch house on the highway side of the lake. Bob waved and invited them in and Dolores served iced tea and cookies. Their house, Paul and Catt learned, used to be the old general store that later moved down to Balsam Four Corners. Bob walked

THE FOUR SPENT THE DAY TOGETHER

them around and showed them where walls had been added and counters removed. The old owners, he said, sold up and moved out of state right after the tragedy. Bob was surprised that no one had told Paul and Catt about the missing boy when they asked him about it.

It was in the late eighties, Bob said. July, summer. The store had been here forever. A couple on vacation from the Cities stopped in to buy bait and I guess they got distracted. They had a six-year-old son, he walked down to the lake to catch turtles or something, they weren't watching him. And the boy just disappeared—his body was never recovered. Did you know our lake is eighty feet deep in the middle? Everyone knew the only way he could have disappeared was by drowning. The sheriff closed the case early.

Hiking deep in the woods at Scenic State Park, they saw their first showy lady slippers, the Minnesota state flower, a magnificent low-growing orchid with white angel wings and bulbous pink bells. Kayaking at Two Rivers, they passed through a grove of nesting gray herons. A young deer stepped out of the woods and stood perfectly still. During these outings, Catt felt she was storing up pieces of happiness, cocooning herself for the time Paul would leave and she'd stay alone for the rest of the summer to write.

But what would he do when he returned to LA? They talked about this a lot. There was no question he had to find work. It's what he'd gone back to school for, and they needed the money. Things were not going well with the apartments in Albuquerque. After being gouged by a couple of management companies, they'd hired a couple, Sammy and Patrizia Chee, to work for them directly. Patrizia was really Patricia, a white working-class wannabe chola, and Sammy, part of a large Gallup Navajo family, had spent numerous years in prison for petty drug-and-alcohol-related offenses before getting clean. In a sense, they were Paul and Catt's lower-class doppelgängers and for this reason, Catt felt compelled to help them: loaning them money, paying for work on Sammy's old Chevy Blazer, buying them plane tickets so they could connect with long-lost relations. Although it was really Patrizia in charge, because Sammy worked full-time in inventory control at a Best Buy. When Paul managed the apartments, he'd leased them to all kinds of people and things had run smoothly. Either Patrizia was completely inept or she was stealing. Because now, people—most of them Patrizia's friends and family members—moved in, stopped paying rent, and destroyed the plumbing and floors, windows and walls, before leaving. And then a new round of repairs by Chee family members would begin. Whenever Catt questioned Patrizia she threatened to quit on the spot, which, since she had all the leases, receipts, bills, and checks, would have been a disaster. In order to clean up the mess, Catt would have had to abandon her other commitments and move to Albuquerque.

 Paul had always assumed he'd have his own private practice. During the blissful long days of the summer of 2013, they decided that this was their chance. Instead of finding another full-time job that he hated, Paul could rent a small office and set up a practice, make his own hours, and even travel

THE FOUR SPENT THE DAY TOGETHER

to Albuquerque once every month to keep an eye on things. Catt would not have to worry. She could stop accepting all these commissions and start writing a book again.

At the end of July they camped on the shore of a wilderness lake. Watching the sun through the trees in the aqua-gold late afternoon, Catt felt like a lid had been removed from the box of the world. As soon as Paul left for Albuquerque, she began making notes from the interview transcripts.

But in the end Paul's practice didn't work out. They hired a practice consultant who promised to fill up his calendar and within three months, she did—with in-network insurance patients. After paying for billing and charting and taxes and rent, Paul made just a little bit more than the minimum wage. The only way a private practice could work was to see private patients, but he had no clue how to recruit them. Likewise, his trips back to Albuquerque were pointless. There was money flying all over the place between five subaccounts and a half dozen Chee family members. It would take a forensic accountant to figure it out. The shitty Bronze Plans he and Catt bought cost more than their mortgage. At least the Skid Row job had provided insurance.

At the end of 2014, Paul accepted a full-time job as clinical director of Sunrise Recovery, a new treatment center out in the Valley. A great title, full benefits, an almost-six-figure salary.

But the treatment center wasn't really a center at all . . . it was a suburban house with twelve patients bunked in four bedrooms.

The big-screen TV in the living room played all day except for the hour when Paul or one of the unlicensed counselors roused them all for "group therapy." Once a week, the patients rode in the van over to Chatsworth, where they received "equine therapy" at a friend of the owner's mini-ranch. Everyone looked forward to this afternoon of brushing the horses and feeding them carrots. The rest of the time, the patients sat in the yard or hung out in the living room watching TV. Upstairs in a room that none of the clinical staff were permitted to enter, the Armenian owner and two of his nephews conducted the center's real business, whatever it was—and given their large personal fleet of luxury vehicles, Paul guessed it was shady.

Since all of the rooms were needed for patients, Paul did not have an office. An essential part of his job was providing one private therapy session a week to each patient—all the insurance carriers required this—but there was nowhere to do this. Wherever he looked in the house, there was a cluster of patients hanging out. The only way to see someone alone was to give them a ride to the vape shop, so he used the van as his office. A few of the patients he saw actually wanted recovery. The rest were there under court orders, or to placate their families, counting down the twenty-eight days until they could leave and get high again. The owners insisted he be there from eight until five, Monday through Friday, so each discouraging day at the center was bracketed by a hellish one-hour drive through rush-hour traffic. Sometimes he brought their little dog, Blaze, to work with him. Blaze provided "pet-assisted therapy," which lightened things up but never enough. Everyone petted him.

THE FOUR SPENT THE DAY TOGETHER

He was beginning to wonder if he'd chosen the wrong profession. None of the jobs he'd had since getting his license were what he'd imagined. Treatment had nothing to do with care or sobriety. It was all about money. Anyone who really wanted to get sober could just go to AA. That was what he'd done . . . although he'd stopped going to meetings. Did everything always have to be about drinking and drugs? He was sick of the rhetoric; after a full day or week at work he preferred to stay home than go back out into traffic.

Consequently, he hadn't made any friends in the five years since he'd moved to LA. Catt was his lifeline, but she was almost always away. If she wasn't on tour, she was writing in Balsam or teaching in Europe. As another lonely summer approached he tacked a flyer from Blaze's veterinarian onto his corkboard, hoping she'd get the message: *Canine Abandonment Disorder (CAD): Know the Symptoms.*

Soon it would be stinking hot in LA and he'd be alone again. His mood darkened. When he wasn't at work he sat in his living room rocking chair, watching TV and vacantly rocking. *Why can't you leave me alone?* he'd explode if she tried coaxing him out for a walk or a drive to the market. It was even worse when she tried to strike up a "real" conversation: *Why are you so unhappy?* she'd timidly ask. *What would you rather be doing?* As if every problem must have a solution. *I think I'd enjoy being an actor*, he said, scowling. *Or maybe a long-distance trucker.*

One Saturday morning when he couldn't stand hearing her fake-cheerful voice, he grabbed the end table next to his rocker and threw it. Not *at* her exactly, but toward her. This was a first. She fled the house, weeping. She was frightened to stay and frightened to leave him alone. *You're right*, he said, when she returned hours later. *I'm know I'm depressed. I need to do something about it.*

That afternoon they went to an urgent care where a physician's assistant gave him prescriptions for Prozac and Xanax. The Xanax, she said, would help him get through till the Prozac kicked in, and it did.

And then Catt left for the summer, somewhat relieved but uneasy. Maybe things would get better?

Paul liked the calm, steady feeling he got after taking one or three Xanax. No one was there to judge or observe him, so instead of watching TV he could let himself fall into a dark easy sleep after eating his takeout. Since he was no longer abstinent—the old AA mandate—he saw no reason not to start smoking weed, a drug he'd always enjoyed that gave him no problems. Staying more or less high every day helped Paul to tolerate life at the rehab.

By the time Catt got back from Balsam he'd managed to find just the right balance between Xanax and weed and things were more peaceful. Besides, new things were starting to happen. TV rights for Catt's first book, *I Love Dick*, the one with the cover everyone posed with and tweeted, had been optioned. A month later a pilot was funded and on the basis of that, the book was being commercially published in the UK and a dozen other countries.

Paul was truly happy for Catt. He was proud of her success and, even more, of her writing. If only he could enjoy it . . .

THE FOUR SPENT THE DAY TOGETHER

the prospect of attending more dinners, art openings, and book events made him glacial with terror. Everyone at these events drank and nobody talked to him. He was acutely aware of being there as Catt's partner: a social appendage people only acknowledged as an extra dose of politeness if they wanted something from her. And it would only get worse.

What if I drank? Paul asked her one Sunday evening while they were driving home from Palm Springs after seeing her parents. He pitched it just right: his voice was so easy, mature, charming, and casual. *You know how socially phobic I am*, he said with a laugh. And she did, and felt nothing but pity. *Just on special occasions—I'll have one or two drinks so I can feel more like the others.*

Catt had no idea what to say. She had endless compassion for Paul's outsider status because, she felt, it mirrored her past. *Of course I won't, if you think I shouldn't.* Still, she knew enough about twelve-step programs to know that the choice between drinking and not was a private decision. Perhaps Paul was right? His life in LA was so different from his old life in Farmington. Before he'd had nothing to lose. Now he had his degrees and his license, his work and their life together. *Well, um, I guess.*

She felt estranged from the people she knew in the art world as well, people who'd always been rich or felt underprivileged if their parents were merely professors or lawyers. *You have to do whatever you think is best.* Paul shone his most radiant smile. *Why don't we go out for dinner tonight? I'll take you out for sushi.*

Paul ordered a single large flask of hot sake. They solemnly toasted each other's success. The warm glow of the sake felt like a balm even before the alcohol hit. Paul knew he'd come home again. He would not drink beyond this tonight, he told himself. There would be other nights, many.

You know, Catt, he said, *we're lucky people. We have a good life. And I'm promising you now: if it ever gets out of hand, I'll stop whenever you say so.*

3

A few days later, Paul had a troubling dream.

I was alone in a room and there was a large, flesh-colored spider on a table in front of me. Suddenly it jumped up in the air. I swatted it down to the floor, but then it was watching me. Still, I thought I was safe but then it jumped onto my fist. I tried to remove it but it was like we were locked in a standoff. The spider was big, and it held on really tightly.

Then a Chinese man came into the room, for whatever reason. I asked him for help, and he grabbed on to the thing and tore it off from the middle. But the legs were still sunk in my hand, the head was still there, trying to bite me. I watched while he tore the whole thing apart and it died on the floor, with liquid dripping out of its mouth. And its legs just fell out of my hand, kind of limply.

Was the spider his drinking? He didn't want to be bitten but he did not want it dead.

He managed to keep it together for Christmas with Catt's parents out in Palm Springs, but only barely. Sitting through the forced conversation, the presents, the niceness, the overcooked dinner, the unwanted dessert, with only one glass of white wine? He could not wait to leave.

Catt's parents had moved back from New Zealand on the cusp of the twenty-first century, thirty years after emigrating. They were seventy-one and seventy-two years old and they felt like someone had switched on a light and woken them up from a decades-long slumber. Even in Palm Springs, where they moved to be close to Jasper's niece, Elena, they were frightened and shocked by the compression of time. Arriving in Wellington had been like falling back into the world of their childhoods. Now they were thrown into a digital future where robots answered the phone, SUVs prowled the wide empty streets, and no one knew how to give directions.

New Zealand had been the right thing for their daughters, but their own lives as middle-aged immigrants hadn't exactly worked out. It was a small, closed society, and no matter how hard she tried, Emma couldn't master the accent. Within months of arriving, Jasper was fired from A. H. & A. W. Reed for taking a principled stand over author royalty payments. After that, there'd been a short downward cascade of warehouse management jobs that ended in unemployment. Emma supported them both by working full-time as a typist while Jasper struggled to start his own business. When an old colleague from Reed offered to cut Jasper in on a new publishing venture, they sold their house, gave him the equity, and moved up to Auckland with just enough left for a down payment on a small tract house a half hour north of the city in a suburb called Sunnynook. Jasper's old colleague disappeared soon after their

THE FOUR SPENT THE DAY TOGETHER

move and stopped returning his calls. For years, Emma worked full-time in the city and Jasper received an unemployment allowance until they were finally able to get superannuation at sixty.

Living on their modest pensions, Jasper and Emma shared a constantly breaking used car and published a yearly poetry journal. Catt helped when she could. Her sister, Carla, was living in a Hindu religious community in the Pacific Northwest and working part-time after giving up on the idea of becoming a classical cellist. Catt understood that part of her fate might be to eventually support the whole family.

But just before she turned seventy, Emma received an unexpected inheritance. Her birth father, Warren, had died in Northern California one year before. All her life, he'd been a mystery, but with the help of the internet she'd finally located him. A few months before Warren died she and Jasper flew out to meet him. Warren had left Salt Lake for San Francisco after Emma's mom returned to the Bronx. He'd made, lost, and remade several fortunes. With Catt's help Emma traveled to California again for his funeral. As his only living blood relative, she signed the death certificate. Emma didn't dare to have expectations but, still, she was devastated when she learned he'd amended his will after their meeting to specifically disinherit her. The lives of their suburban neighbors were filled with big extended families. They were the only people their age who didn't have grandchildren, and their two daughters lived half a world away in California. Even though Catt and Mikal were no longer exactly together they were thinking about buying her parents a house in Crestline or somewhere affordable not too far from LA.

When Interpol knocked on Jasper and Emma's Sunnynook door and asked her about Violet Taylor, she didn't know who they were talking about. But Violet Taylor—Emma's aunt, Warren's unmarried sister—had died alone in a Banning, California, trailer park with nothing of value except for a folder of shares her brother had bought her. The shares were worth 1.5 million dollars, and since Emma was the sole family survivor she would receive them.

Jasper and Emma moved to Palm Springs on his niece Elena's advice and bought a house near an Episcopal church in the old Movie Colony. After succeeding in various enterprises, Elena and her husband, Mack, retired to Palm Springs and Cancún in their early forties. They believed Palm Springs would be perfect for Jasper and Emma and they were right. Emma made all kinds of new friends at the church and Jasper rose to their reversal of fortune immediately. His Oxbridge accent became more pronounced and he called their new Palm Springs home the "American offices" of their New Zealand poetry journal.

Emma was nice, but Paul never felt fully accepted by Catt's parents. There was this way Jasper had of looking at him, as if he knew exactly who Paul was and what he was up to. He'd been with Catt for more than a decade, but the only framed photos her parents kept were of her and Mikal together. When he and Catt married in 2014, they chose not to attend their small backyard wedding. Sometimes he wondered if they even liked Catt all that much. They'd sent her a letter asking her to remove the down pillow she kept in their guest-bedroom closet—*We do not want your things in this house . . . we find you far too abrupt and controlling*—written, no doubt, by Jasper, but cosigned by Emma. Jasper was an odd duck and Emma was sweet and compliant.

As usual, Christmas in Palm Springs meant a big lunch at Catt's parents' house with Elena and Mack. All afternoon, Paul had deprived himself of a real drink. Mack was on his third bourbon by the time Elena served the dessert. Clearly as eager to leave there as Paul was, Mack started ranting about how great Donald Trump was . . . which was so passive-aggressive, given Mack knew Catt's parents were liberals. Mack had watched the debate and he thought Trump was right: Americans had to unite and ban Muslims now that ISIS had taken over the internet. Given that Mack had a master's degree from UCLA he probably didn't really believe this—he was just looking for something offensive to say. As an alcoholic, Paul understood this, but still, being half Lebanese, he was offended. Everyone knew Trump was a clown and a liar.

Driving back from Palm Springs at ninety-two miles per hour Paul couldn't wait to get home, have some drinks, and relax. But then he lost all the time that they'd saved when a cop pulled him over for speeding. The early days of Paul's drinking were like dating a popular girl back in high school—you had to be careful not to show how much you liked her, because then you'd lose everything.

He'd set up some home drinking stations . . . a fifth of Jack Daniel's behind the barbecue grill under the ivy, a bottle of vodka behind the clothes dryer. That way, he could enjoy a nice glass of wine during dinner with Catt and then "do some laundry" to actually relax. Always, he was careful to avoid drinking himself to the point that he actually craved, which was total oblivion.

For New Year's they drove down to Baja, arriving New Year's Day at a lagoon where the migrating whales had just given birth to their babies. And it was bliss, a new morning—everything limpid and fresh, the whales and their calves swimming up to the boat so close you could actually touch them. But as soon as they reached the hotel Paul felt an unstoppable urge to go home again. It was too hard to drink on the sly while he was with Catt on a road trip.

In another five days he'd be starting a new nonprofit job in South Central. The job at the treatment center hadn't worked out. He'd had one too many fights with the owners and they let him go just two days before his first paid vacation. After that, he'd called his old boss from the mobile mental health team. The agency had since expanded and right on the spot she'd asked him to be the deputy director of an outpatient clinic for the formerly homeless.

The clinic was located in the heart of South Central, ten blocks south of MLK Boulevard. MLK was the border between the USC campus, with its cafés, Trader Joe's, and student housing, and the South Central ghetto. South Cen—as they called it—was a whole other world from Skid Row and completely

THE FOUR SPENT THE DAY TOGETHER

different from Albuquerque. Everything took place out in the street. At first, it looked like absolute chaos, but after a while he saw it was all highly organized. Clusters of boys and young men hung out on the sidewalk selling drugs, taking bets, talking and laughing. Women in hoodies and braids acted as messengers, carrying children and babies. Walking around the wide, four-lane street you could feel traces of other centuries . . . a boarded-up news and cigar stand; an old hotel called the Broadway, no longer open, with an ornate terrazzo entrance.

Every day Paul could feel the neighborhood changing. He began taking photos to document it. Two blocks from the clinic, they'd just finished building the station for a new Metro line that would connect downtown LA with Santa Monica. A new Target sprung up beside it. Up and down Vermont Avenue, vacant lots were reclaimed to build new apartments—the same stucco boxes with balconies that had already sprouted all over Echo Park and Koreatown.

Like everyone else, Paul knew this change would not be for the better—at least not for the people who already lived there. Every day, crazy violence erupted from nowhere: a gunshot, a stabbing, a scuffle. He called the police when a knife-wielding meth-head threatened one of his case managers. Still, an old man who sat every day on the stoop two doors from the clinic let Paul know he'd be safe. *We know you're doing good work in there.* He could park his new Subaru out on the street and no one would fuck with it.

Some of the clients were people he'd helped off the street in Skid Row. Two years later they were alive, stable, and set up in apartments. There was Barbara McBride, who'd tried jumping off the Mission Road bridge before a passing police car stopped and sent her to the hospital. And there was Paul's friend Mr. Featherstone, an elderly man with a white beard whom he called Feather. During their first session Feather told Paul that his new meds did not stop the voices, they just muffled them. Together, they considered how Feather could use his brain as a switchboard. When the voices gave good advice he might as well take it. But when they told him to hurt people, he could choose to ignore them.

Paul loved Mr. Featherstone. One of the best parts of the new job was spending time with him, taking him shopping at Target for monthly supplies. Although the last time Paul came, Feather didn't come to the door. He heard the old man's faint voice—*Dr. Paul? Help me, I fell over twice.* Paul ran downstairs for the master key. When he finally got inside tears came to his eyes to see his friend so helpless, lying there on the floor. For once, the paramedics came right away. But it was only a blip, nothing serious.

Promotion for the TV show pilot based on Catt's book began in the spring, and it was everywhere. Foreign editions of *I Love Dick* would be released around the same time the pilot dropped in August. People, mostly girls, tweeted photos of themselves holding the book in all kinds of public places. Crafters rendered 3-D versions of the cover art in Play-Doh, Rice Krispies, and makeup. One reader keyed the book title onto her ex-boyfriend's car and got thousands of likes from her followers.

THE FOUR SPENT THE DAY TOGETHER

There were translation questions, interview requests, and photo shoots. Mainstream media outlets invited her to weigh in on subjects like menopause, summer romance, and feminine aging . . . *Which part of your aging body do you like the least?* Catt emailed with European publishers throughout the spring about a monthlong summer tour. A writer she respected asked if she could profile her for *The New Yorker*. *My parents will die*, she emailed Paul at work. *I'm ambivalent*.

Because what she was finally surmising was that the interest in the book had hardly anything to do with the book she thought she'd written. Writing love letters to a man who didn't love her, she'd poured out her thoughts and feelings about rural poverty in the US, the Central American civil wars, the absence of working-class artists in American culture. She'd tried to memorialize the lives of some artists she'd loved who'd been so marginalized they became completely crazy. By doing this, Catt had written her way out of her own invisibility. But two decades later, it was the phenomenon of the book that interested people.

What is it like to have I Love Dick *achieve success after so many years?* people asked her over and over. Twenty sixteen was the moment of the aging, underrecognized white female artist, and journalists wrote coverage of the coverage. *How does it feel to be an icon?* Catt understood she was being called upon to become a motivational speaker and she found she could excel at this. Some nights she lit up and felt herself becoming a transmitter, drawing people's energy into her heart and bouncing it back to them. Other nights she felt fraudulent and cheesy. Lost and drained, like so many other people, she had finally achieved success—just not the kind she'd wished for.

In February 2016, Donald Trump, already the front-runner for the Republican nomination, told an Iowa crowd to knock the crap out of any protestors. I promise you, I will pay the legal fees. Three weeks later at a rally in Nevada, he pointed out a lone protestor and exclaimed, I'd like to punch him in the face. But like their friends, Paul and Catt weren't paying him much attention. Trump was a total clown. They were more interested in the race between Hillary and Bernie Sanders, the candidate they both supported. Targeting their Latino neighborhood near MacArthur Park, Hillary's tone-deaf marketers sent out flyers about how Hillary Clinton es como mi abuela!, which was absurd. The hashtag #Notmyabuela bloomed overnight. Meanwhile Bernie kept banging on about her speaking fees and her emails. Inevitably Hillary would become the Democratic nominee, but badly damaged, because once things are said, America was coming to understand, it no longer matters if they're true or even pertinent. *Stones may rot but words live forever* . . . Catt remembered the Samoan proverb she'd learned in New Zealand as a teenager.

Things in Albuquerque were spinning out of control. The neighborhood had become worse. Catt used some of the money from the TV show to repair the apartments but there was no time to address the real problems. The automatic security gate they'd had installed to protect residents was vandalized over and over again. The vacant lot alongside the sixteen-plex had turned into an open-air drug mart. Catt agreed to let one of Patrizia's

THE FOUR SPENT THE DAY TOGETHER

ex-husbands live there rent-free in exchange for providing "security" but still there were gunshots and overdoses. Apartments reported as vacant appeared to have multiple occupants.

Catt was afraid to question Patrizia too closely because whenever she did Patrizia got angry and threatened to quit. Instead, she sent her carefully worded, twice-proofread texts, to which Patrizia would reply something like—

week before last 10 had a hole in ceiling and dripped down to living room which went into chuys threw electrical out cpl days on that then painted 5 by self cleaned 12 at lomas so yes Sammy lots of hours Sammy needs pay now. 6 will pay Friday death in family had to pay for funeral 15 will pay Friday he had cut hours 3 says also pay they moved from las cruces—

Paul and Catt had a sick sense of impending doom, but they were eight hundred miles away and there wasn't much they could do because they were always too busy.

Sometimes Paul thought he should just quit his job at the clinic and go back to manage the properties. But doing that would be such a huge step backward—it took seven years to get his degrees and his licenses and besides, the whole mess in Albuquerque just made him sick.

One night that spring Catt's friend Eloise called, hysterical and panicked. Her boyfriend had just died of an overdose on her kitchen floor . . . she'd called 911 and watched the paramedics zip him up into the bag and wheel the gurney out to the street. Once a prodigious art-world phenomenon, Eloise was a great artist who'd pretty much lost her career to poverty, drugs, and mental illness. Since she and Catt had drifted apart Catt read her call as a crisis. Her first thought was to ask Paul to step in. She had no idea of the extent of Paul's drinking yet and he and Eloise had gotten along whenever they'd met. Catt was in awe of Paul's gift for connecting with people who suffered acute mental illness on their own terms, in a genuine way.

When Paul arrived he found Eloise huddled in back of the small storefront cave where she was living. The room was covered with artworks she'd recently made even though she no longer had a career. She was completely distraught but still, the idea of receiving a therapy house call struck her as funny. They sat in the kitchen together—the same spot where she'd tried to revive her dead boyfriend less than twenty-four hours before—smoking a joint and winding down to a point where she could even consider what happened. Her long hair was matted and her arms were scarred with infected bedbug bites. Paul wondered if Eloise expected him to make the first move, was that what was happening? Well okay, that's better, Eloise sighed. But also maybe a pill? Within two weeks she'd be dead of an intentional overdose. She giggled and opened the bottle. You want one? The pill, a thirty-milligram oxy, was fantastic. Why had he been so cautious? The pill brought him back into the zone that he'd craved since that first sip of sake.

In May Donald Trump was declared the presumptive nominee. Catt begged Paul to fly out to Albuquerque to meet with the

THE FOUR SPENT THE DAY TOGETHER

new management company she'd hired to replace Patrizia and Sammy. *You've been hearing me say it's a rigged system, but now I don't say it anymore because I won,* Trump joked on CNN. Paul resented this waste of his holiday weekend and at first, he resisted. But upon further reflection: the three days away would give him a chance to drink and get high and get a Golden Pride green chili burrito. *It's true,* Trump laughed. *Now I don't care.* Paul didn't show up for his meetings and didn't cancel them either. He stayed at the motel getting wasted and treated himself to an outcall massage when it all started to feel kind of lonely.

A week later the new manager emailed Catt, *Today I got into a confrontation with the tenant in #7 . . . I'm doing my best but with tenants like these that threaten you I'm taking it easy. I wasn't going to go too far and get myself stabbed, etc. They can't print enough money to deal with these people . . .* Catt wired more money to get the sagging balconies fixed, the same balconies that had supposedly been fixed six months before by one of Sammy's half brothers.

Back in LA Paul knew he had to get on top of his drinking, and fast. He had too much to lose. At work they were talking about promoting him to clinical director. Once Catt left on tour he filled the fridge up with beer, a much smarter choice than Jack Daniel's or vodka. He decided to let himself drink two beers a night, although most nights it was actually four. He forced himself to abstain on the nights when he'd had six the night before. Worn out by these calculations, on weekends he allowed himself to relax and get really fucked up.

At the same time, he launched a campaign to get Catt on board with his drinking. She was always nagging about how he should go out more, take up a hobby, make some new friends. He decided to take up astronomy and bought an expensive new telescope, although he couldn't be bothered to look through it much. Then he sent a series of sweet, supportive emails laced with upbeat reports of his new, alcohol-enhanced activities. *Robbie and I went to a local neighborhood bar and played a few games of pool*, he wrote her in London. *Hang in there, little kitten*, he emailed when she was in Stockholm. *Hank and I had a great time last night at the LA Philharmonic. We went for dim sum afterward and had a beer . . .* He wrote her in Amsterdam about his solo road trip—*Driving here I had such a deep sense of peace and belonging. I stopped at our favorite restaurant but it was too early to eat so I had a beer at the bar . . . By the way it seems like someone smoked all our pot. There's a little left, I'm going to smoke it right now, do you know who took it?*

How do you like talking about this book after so many years? people asked Catt over and over. It's better than waitressing, she wanted to say but did not. In Amsterdam she tripped on her shoe in the street when they let her out alone for a sandwich. Traveling most days and performing other people's expectations almost every night, Catt let herself be comforted by his emails.

I know how to meet a plane! Paul wrote back when Catt sent her flight details. The phrase had become like a mantra for

THE FOUR SPENT THE DAY TOGETHER

them—it was the first thing Paul said when she'd had to fly back to LA for a few days after they had gotten together in Albuquerque. And she'd been touched. She'd never known anyone who was so naïve and openly eager. Paul had considered greeting her with a bunch of red roses but finally decided that was too much, too gauche, for a seasoned traveler. Still, she never forgot the pure relief and joy of his embrace—*You came back!*—when she walked into Arrivals.

The first Friday night she was back, they drove up to Tujunga to visit their new friends Johannes and Astrid, an artist couple they'd met through Catt's friend Bettina. After that, they'd take a cool evening drive into the Angeles Crest Forest. It was a hot, dusty late June afternoon and Johannes had brought back a case of imported beer from the German market. He and Astrid were renovating the beautiful midcentury house they'd bought in the Descanso Tract at the foot of Mount Lukens. The two had a flair for all things midcentury. They were expert hosts, able to talk with anyone for hours about anything, and they were never afraid to have a few drinks.

Catt and Astrid caught up with news from Bettina—she'd just moved from K-Town to Oakland and Catt was flying up to see her the next day. Meanwhile, Paul seemed to be happily talking with Johannes. It wasn't until they'd moved on to Bettina's ambivalence about dating that Catt noticed Paul had already finished three beers. And then he drank another, and another—his conversation with Johannes about free will and determinism, one of his favorite subjects, getting louder and louder. In another half hour he was obviously drunk.

As darkness fell over Johannes and Astrid's suburban half acre, Paul remembered their plan to drive his new car into the mountains. He wanted their new friends to come with them! *This is the night that Jupiter will be rising in the western sky,* he insisted. *I've got my telescope—we can all take the Subaru!* Catt couldn't imagine anything worse than Paul driving drunk around steep hairpin turns on the small mountain highway. And yet Johannes and Astrid seemed almost willing . . . She looked at them pleadingly, hoping they'd intervene and spare her the anguish of incurring his rage, but they remained neutral. Veterans of many nights in the conversation pits of the Descanso Tract that had gone south after too many drinks, they knew it was best to step back. Finally Catt grabbed Paul's keys. *It's getting late. We need to go home now.*

Why don't we all take a rain check on that? Astrid smiled as she led them down to the carport.

They drove back to MacArthur Park in silence. Catt tried cracking a joke. I thought you wanted me to make friends, he sneered back. Once home, he slammed the door to their room and disappeared into bed.

Catt stood in the hallway: shaking and super-alert, her nerves jangling, as they did every time Paul released his rage and then escaped into sleep. She didn't know where to go, what to do next. She was catching the plane up to Oakland early the next morning. In eight more days she'd start the long drive up to Balsam, where, god willing, she'd finish the Acker biography by the first week of September. And she had to finish it then because once the pilot dropped in late August she'd be too busy

THE FOUR SPENT THE DAY TOGETHER

to work. In the six months since Paul asked her "permission" to drink she'd seen him drunk once or twice, but never *this* drunk and never in front of their friends. Still jet-lagged from Europe, she felt the walls closing in. She couldn't sit still long enough to watch TV, read a book, even look at the news on her laptop.

It occurred to Catt then that she might as well just take the drive that they'd planned. She could drive up to the Angeles Crest and chill out, listen to music, maybe look at the sky near the Mount Wilson Observatory? Lacking a better alternative, she drove her old Fiat Pop forty miles through the mountains to Red Box. It was pitch-dark and cool when she stopped in the parking lot—the sky full of glittering stars—and she was completely alone except for a couple. She thought about walking the trail but decided against it. Time and distance had helped her calm down. Maybe things would be all right; there was nothing to do now but go home.

Their front door was locked (they never locked it). Except for a light in Paul's office the house was dark. She banged hard on the door—but no answer. Catt crossed the patio to get the spare key from the lockbox. While she was punching the keypad a skinny white girl, wearing a halter and missing two of her teeth, darted out of the house through the gate and disappeared up the street. Paul stood in the doorway, wearing only his gym shorts. *Why, kitten duck, you're home! I was worried. I didn't know where you went.*

She stormed downstairs to his office and saw an uncapped bottle of lube on his desk. *I was just interviewing a prospective patient—it's not what you think!* he insisted.

During the trip up to Oakland, Catt would replay these events over and over, but they didn't make sense. Paul knew she was staying overnight at Bettina's. If he'd just waited a day she'd never have known, he would've gotten away with it. Clearly he was sending a message, he'd wanted her to walk in. The message, her friends all agreed, was to divorce him immediately. She thought back to the half-assed prenup they'd downloaded and signed before getting married with dread. Was it even valid? To divorce Paul she'd have to stay in LA and get a real lawyer, which would mean giving up her summer in Balsam, and then who knew if or when she'd ever finish the Acker biography? And she'd promised to write an *Artforum* Passages piece that was due in next week, her friend Eloise's obituary . . . Cass, Catt's closest friend, took a more nuanced view of the situation—*But, Catt, don't you see? It's a cry for help. I feel so sorry for him*. Hank, always her champion, said to protect herself and then wait and see.

Paul called Catt's number thirty-five times over the weekend. Leaving Bettina's on Sunday, she finally answered the phone. Deeply repentant, Paul seemed confused by his actions and swore if she gave him a chance he'd stop drinking and go back to AA. On Monday Hank drafted a legal-ish document reprising Paul's promises and the terms of their prenup, and then Catt left for Balsam as soon as they'd signed it.

Melania Trump's old porn photos were hitting the internet while Catt drove to Balsam. Trump/Pence 2016 signs lined the road of each little town she stopped in once she left California. Catt wrote the *Artforum* piece in a Kansas motel and copied two

THE FOUR SPENT THE DAY TOGETHER

lines from a Peter Handke book into her notebook: *She walked and walked until she was so tired she had to sit down again. But soon she had to stand up and go on.* And then she added: *Terrible loneliness. So long as I am working my mind's absorbed and I'm displaced from it. Don't stop. When stop, a sad chasm.*

In Balsam she cleaned and swept dead mice off the porch. She felt a lump in her throat, as if something was stuck. Pale amber light streamed through the trees outside her bedroom each morning, casting shadows of leaves onto the cream broad lace curtains. The curtains—found at the Harding Goodwill—were just like the ones she'd seen with Mikal the first time they traveled to Brittany. They'd gone to Quimper to visit the poet Max Jacob's archives, reciting his poems on the train ride—*L'enfant, l'enfant, l'elephant* . . . She wondered if the gray house in Balsam was just a monument to her former illusions.

Paul went to AA in LA twice a week and refrained from drinking. At the beginning of August he finally received his promotion and became the new South Central clinical director. He wanted to celebrate but he was alone so he let himself have a few drinks . . . although Catt wouldn't know that until later. On August 30 she finished her book right on schedule, two days before Paul arrived for their long-awaited September vacation.

September is the most golden month in northern Minnesota. The lakes are still warm from the August heat and white-and-yellow pearly everlasting stalks line the roadside. The temperature drops close to freezing at night but the afternoon sun is the color of honey. Leaves start to turn and flocks of wild ducks and geese circle loudly overhead before beginning their migration.

That September, a Trump rally in the little town of Wilmington, Ohio, drew a crowd of 5,500 people. The Minneapolis *StarTribune* began taking the Trump campaign seriously. In a guest editorial, a professor of public policy examined his promise to reverse the devastating effects of neoliberal globalization.

Catt picked Paul up in Harding from his late-night regional flight the Thursday before the long Labor Day weekend. All summer she'd been looking forward to the things she and Paul did the best—playing with their dog, hiking and kayaking, collecting autumn leaves, and spending long mornings talking in bed with hot mugs of coffee. Last summer they'd even written haikus to the birds. She had their vacation all planned: a trip to the bear preserve, the Friday Night Walleye Special at the Dam Restaurant in Orr, two or three nights in a rustic cabin at an old-fashioned lodge on Pelican Lake.

But that Friday night, driving the network of two-lane roads from Balsam to the Dam Restaurant, Paul's mood darkened. As usual, Catt tried to cheer him up, and as usual, he couldn't or wouldn't respond. In the restaurant he got up as soon as the server took their orders. Catt waited, and then waited some more. Finally, riding a deep wave of dread, she forced herself across the room and into the bar, where Paul was finishing a double vodka. She caught her breath. Panicked, she ran back for her bag and out of the restaurant to stand next to the car. A few minutes later, Paul joined her.

THE FOUR SPENT THE DAY TOGETHER

There was nothing to fight about anymore; their agreement was broken. Paul said, I'm an adult and I'll drink if I want to. Catt said that was true but that didn't mean she could live alongside his drinking. I guess that's an irreconcilable difference, she said, and they agreed that divorce was the best solution.

But what about the rest of the vacation? Catt's mind was racing. She had tickets for a short-leg Midwestern tour that began with a flight out of Harding coming up in two weeks, she couldn't just go home to LA. Paul felt like dog shit. That double had not been enough. He hated hurting Catt and he didn't want to leave the beautiful cool North Country weather to shuttle between his home ghetto and work ghetto at the sweltering start of September. *What if I just don't drink?* he said.

They both agreed that this would be the best solution.

In the morning Paul made coffee and swore to give up alcohol forever. In the afternoon he took advantage of a solo trip to the Harding Lowe's to grab a quart of vodka and a thirty-pack of beer.

That evening, Catt stumbled across his improvised drinking station when she went to clean out the shed.

The deal is off! she screamed.

It was still only Saturday, the start of the long three-day weekend. Delta's flights out of Harding were booked until Wednesday morning, which meant she was trapped. Finally, she came up with a plan. Since they were stuck here until Wednesday and Paul had to drink, he could move out to the cabin and drink freely there. She'd cancel their reservations at

Pelican Lake and get back to work on another catalog essay that was almost due.

Okay, Paul said, *I'll stop. Just—please.* In reality Paul hated himself drinking. He didn't want to cancel the vacation! The simple years of his sobriety felt so far away.

Solemnly they poured out the remaining beers and vodka. All these events left them both feeling drained and empty. It was already five o'clock—too soon to start dinner, too late to get back to work on the cabin. *I know,* Catt ventured. *Why don't we take a drive? We could go and see the trumpet swans at Scenic.*

Scenic State Park had two big wilderness lakes. The park was in Bigfork, about twenty miles north. By now, Paul was sober enough to drive. Relieved and exhausted, they drove in silence until a deer ran onto the road from the woods, clipping the driver's-side headlight. The airbags didn't go off but the deer was hurt badly. Limping and wounded, it disappeared back into the woods. Pulling onto the shoulder, they got out and saw the headlight smeared with its blood. *The deer—* Catt said. Both of them were close to weeping. *It was a sacrifice!* Paul swore on its blood that he'd stop drinking now, for good.

On Monday night Paul got up abruptly while they were watching a movie. He had to load up the kayaks. *But why?* It was raining and late. Heart pounding, Catt stood on the sun-porch and watched Paul back the truck out of the driveway. He could not back out fast enough. She considered following him in the car, but to where? There were bars in every little town. Still—even though she knew that Paul was drinking,

THE FOUR SPENT THE DAY TOGETHER

she couldn't know until she knew it for sure. *What to do?* she texted Hank. It was still eight o'clock in LA. *Advise!!*

Just go to sleep, he texted back. *Pretend it's not strange. Thank him in the morning for loading up the kayaks.*

Sitting on the screen porch of their little cabin at the Northwoods Lodge, Paul and Catt watched the long slow sunset over Pelican Lake, drinking mugs of strong black tea. Strands of pink and purple cloud were streaked across the orange sky.

Catt, Paul said, *I don't want to get divorced. All the worst things in my life go back to alcohol. Drinking has been terrible for me. I need to stop.* His eyes teared up. *I don't want to lose you, I can't just throw the life we've made away—*

The next morning they rented a big motorboat and went out on Pelican Lake. Cruising on the far side of the lake, they saw a flock of beautiful white pelicans rising from a thicket of wild rice. Their boat was bobbing on the choppy little waves.

You know, Paul said, *when we're seventy, we'll have a boat like this*. He'd just turned fifty earlier that summer.

Catt looked ahead to another twenty years of alcoholic breakdowns, repentances and promises, betrayals and interrogations. She knew that she'd betray herself if she agreed but questioning him might incite his rage.

Do you think? she asked him, smiling.

The next morning she found an empty quart of vodka underneath the mattress while she was packing.

4

Yes, he confessed, *I've been drinking. I drink. Don't you get it?* It was late Friday night. They were back home in Balsam and Paul would be catching the 6 a.m. flight from Harding back to LA and his job in South Central. *And I want to keep drinking!* Drunk and enraged and backed into a corner, he took off his gold wedding ring and threw it down on the table. *I don't want to be married to you. I only ever married you because of your money. You're old and you're ugly.*

The next day he called and profusely apologized.

Did I sleep that night? Catt wrote in her notebook much later. *I don't remember. The usual feeling of filth that surrounded these episodes.*

He was drunk and upset, he didn't mean any of it.

And soon I was weeping, confiding, lamenting, Catt wrote. *I'd wanted so badly for this to be over—I didn't realize then I was being led back into the cage. And I was leaving again in two days for Detroit, Chicago, New York, and Champaign-Urbana.*

Alcohol is an evil spirit, Paul would tell Catt on the brink of yet another relapse several years later. *Why kill the addict? It would be a waste of suffering.* It would be the last relapse she witnessed. *The evil spirit would rather use the alcohol to destroy everything and everyone around him.*

For the next few months Paul did his best to stay sober but something always prevented it. The world was like the North Country sky, forever changing. He tried holding himself in a calm and clear mental frame but then thunderhead clouds rolled in through the edges.

There was the time he'd been sober for ninety-five days (he was forever counting) but then he saw five cops beating a man outside the clinic. It was so fucked up, it could have been one of his patients, and there was nothing he could do about it. Paul watched the man's face go rubbery soft from the pain before they hog-tied him. And then his mind flashed on a plan to stop at the liquor store on his way home that afternoon and pick up some vodka. Every relapse began with a plan, and once the plan entered his mind he was helpless to shake it. No matter how much he tortured himself by questioning the plan, he knew eventually he would fulfill it.

I Love Dick season 1 began shooting that fall soon after they dropped the pilot. Catt read the scripts, visited the set, and abstained from forming any opinion. It was another world— one that had nothing to do with her, even though the main characters shared her and Mikal's names. The Acker biography would be published the following fall, 2017. In between traveling to events to support the TV show and the new foreign editions, she had to edit the new book and work on the index.

Paul sent Catt a steady stream of opaque and effusive emails that fall while she was touring. *Hi kitten haven't heard from u. Just checking in. Hope u r having a great morning!* She wondered if he was drinking. Every night she googled *How to leave your alcoholic spouse* and dreamed about getting lost in foreign cities. In Indiana her dad emailed about a strange and troubling phone call he'd had from Paul—he sounded drunk, was he drinking? Getting out of the taxi home the next night, Catt saw someone scavenging empty Bud Lights from their trash bins. She walked through the door determined to pry the truth out of Paul. *You're like a pit bull!* he screamed. *This is just too intense, you're fucking crazy.* According to the separation agreement Hank had prepared for them, Paul would move out if he started drinking. She was desperate for proof—

Heart pounding, Catt went back out and dove deep into one of their trash bins. And it was there she found one of their blue drawstring bags triple tied, full of old mail and three empty quart bottles of vodka.

But now that she had it, what use was the proof? She couldn't just throw Paul out of the house. Where would he go? Besides, they were legally married. Even though she'd kept the house in her name alone, they'd signed a new mortgage together. Eventually she would prevail but it would take effort and time and she wouldn't be able to do all of the things that were expected of her. The stress would push Paul to the edge:

he'd go on a binge, stop going to work, and be fired. Things would get worse before getting better. When Paul swore again that he'd stop drinking, it was easier to just believe him.

And so instead of filing for divorce, she grabbed her laptop and files, threw some clothes in a bag, and drove five hours south to Baja California. There was a beach camp south of Ensenada where she'd gone to write in the past. Settling in at the La Joya Trailer Park and Beach Camp for the rest of the fall, she did all the promotion online and finished the index.

On election night, November 8, Catt went to watch the results at Sharky's Bar in Punta Banda. The TV was tuned to CNN and by the look of the place you'd think it was any night. Most of the regulars—American retirees who'd moved south to drink and live on their Social Security checks—were playing pool for small bets, as usual.

Catt slipped onto a bar stool alongside a thin, thoughtful man who looked like an artist-turned-carpenter. They started talking. The man—a former surfer in his midforties—told her he'd been diagnosed with terminal leukemia. Instead of doing the chemo he'd decided to move down here and spend his last days where he used to surf in the nineties. *It's not looking good*, he said when Wolf Blitzer called Florida for Trump. Together, they watched Trump take North Carolina and then Utah. *I don't think I can watch this anymore*, Catt said, and went home when they called Pennsylvania.

The next morning Catt's Facebook feed exploded with posts from people seeking and offering solace. *We will protect each*

THE FOUR SPENT THE DAY TOGETHER

other . . . *We will take care of our community.* By midmorning the postmortem analysis kicked in. Arguments erupted among friends. Was Trump's shocking victory due to the misogynistic Bernie Bros and their enablers, or to the corrupt, out-of-touch Democratic leadership? *Whenever I hear the word community I think of Shirley Jackson and "The Lottery,"* a lone contrarian posted.

Two weeks before Trump's inauguration, Catt's mother, Emma, had a stroke and then a heart attack. She died peacefully at home and did not live to see it.

Friends traveled to DC for the Women's March the day after Trump's inauguration. Almost half a million people filled the Capitol, three times the number that attended the inauguration. *It was ecstatic!* Catt's friend Lucia texted. The vast sea of heads outside the White House was blanketed with pink knitted pussy hats, invented by activist Krista Suh, who'd shared the pattern online after Trump's victory. By late afternoon, social media users across every platform began to debate whether these hats were actually racist and transphobic. Since this controversy was vastly more entertaining than the actual march, it received most of the coverage. It occurred to Catt that nearly half of the stories in *The New York Times* comprised reports and analysis of remarks made on Twitter, as if reality itself had shifted onto social media.

As early Trump advisor Steve Bannon gloated later: *We got elected on Drain the Swamp, Lock Her Up, Build a Wall. This was pure anger. Anger and fear is what gets people to the polls. The Democrats don't matter. The real opposition is the media. And the way to deal with them is to flood the zone with shit.* Catt remembered the once-famous remark widely attributed to Karl Rove in 2002, a remark that Rove later disputed, before the US invaded Iraq: *We're an empire now, and when we act, we create our own reality. And while you're studying that reality—judiciously, as you will—we'll act again, creating other new realities.*

Paul hid his drinking from Catt until a few days before Christmas of 2016. They'd bought tickets to fly to Belize but as their departure approached he could no longer conceal it. Catt went alone and on New Year's Eve, Paul checked himself into a hospital detox. After detox he entered an outpatient treatment program and remained sober for a few months after that. And then he relapsed.

We're in the Subaru driving on a snowy road through some low mountains, Catt told Paul one Sunday morning while he was sober. Since her mother's death, she'd wanted nothing but sleep and remembered all of her dreams. *The car skids and rolls down the hillside several times. Eventually some people come and then we're taken to a hospital where they're triaging people according to degrees of trauma. We're separated then—I'm told I'm in the severe group but I can't understand the instructions fully. I can't understand why they don't understand that I can't understand them. My brain's working slowly and I'm upset that I'm not making connections easily. Finally I find the severe trauma group but I've already missed the meeting . . .*

Billboards for the TV show went up all over LA in May when the first season streamed. The actress playing Catt looked a little like her, only younger and prettier.

THE FOUR SPENT THE DAY TOGETHER

And then Catt left for the summer: first, to direct a summer art program in Winnipeg and from there on to Balsam. Between classes she rode around Winnipeg on an old borrowed bike and went to daily Al-Anon meetings. No one, they said, can tell the spouse of an addict whether to stay or to leave. Still, she was beginning to see that she would never really be happy while living alongside an addict.

Just before Catt's program ended, Paul lost his job for calling in sick once too often. She knew it was now or never. *We need to get divorced*, she said on the phone, summoning all of her courage.

Paul was only half drunk when the server came with the papers. There was no point to staying in LA if he and Catt weren't married. He didn't want to go back to Albuquerque and he had no idea where else he could be except for Balsam. He and Catt co-owned the house, she would not throw him out. With all his licenses and degrees, he'd have no problem finding work there. Since they'd bought the gray house in 2012, he'd longed to be up there all year and watch the changing of seasons. They had the kayaks and the lawn tractor, and if he were up there alone he would not have to hide his drinking. He could go to work sober, relax in the evenings, and get wasted on weekends.

Paul loaded his car and drove for two thousand miles. The world as he'd known it for years was falling apart but this was a new beginning. When he arrived Catt was already there. It was early July, North Country high summer, with loons on the lake and long sunny days, everything warm, gentle, and quiet.

Chasing their little dog, Blaze, around the meadow that circled the house, Paul realized he'd been completely sober throughout the long drive. Why not stay sober? Maybe then she'd change her mind and they'd stay married. They were pretty much a long-distance couple now, anyway.

He found an AA group in the next town, cleaned out the garage, and barbecued meat raised on a neighboring farm. Evan, his new sponsor, lived just two miles away. Together, they reworked the steps and he applied for new jobs every day.

Paul was still sober a month later when Catt left for Europe. He'd just been hired as a frontline counselor at Lake Resort, a residential rehab facility on a big beautiful lake just a few miles away. When Paul drove Catt to the Minneapolis airport he asked over dinner if she'd rethink the divorce. The summer so far had been blissful. She said, *Let's wait and see.*

Since the Acker biography was coming out, Catt arranged events throughout the late summer and fall. After two weeks in Europe she flew back to Balsam before leaving again for Canada and then Bard College in upstate New York. During the few days she stayed in Balsam, Paul was doing so well she agreed to withdraw the divorce. From Bard, she'd catch the train to New York for a discussion at CUNY and then on to London for a few more events. After that she'd go home to LA to do a conversation with her writer friend Bruce at an art-project space at 282 Boyd Street near downtown LA.

In London Catt got a troubling email from her Mexican friend Beto Pena. They'd met when he was living in Tijuana and running a cultural center there, but he'd since moved back

THE FOUR SPENT THE DAY TOGETHER

to LA. Beto and Catt hadn't stayed closely in touch, but she remembered how shocked he had been by how much rents had gone up in his old family neighborhood, Echo Park. Houses had changed hands several times since he'd left—ragged front yards strewn with kids' toys had been thoughtfully landscaped with native plants and enclosed behind new stained cedar barricades. Laundromats had been replaced by upscale cafés. The neighborhood was almost unrecognizable and he could no longer afford to live there. After a very long search, he found the last studio apartment under $1,000 in the rapidly gentrifying, Mexican working-class neighborhood of Boyle Heights.

Hey, Catt, Beto wrote. *You've probably heard about the boycott against all the galleries in Boyle Heights. The boycott was called because the presence of these galleries is complicit in hiking up real estate prices in a way that endangers the historically working-class Boyle Heights community. This is a time when artists and arts organizations need to show where they stand against gentrification, capitalism and neo-colonialism. I know you may have friends at 282 Boyd Street but I think working with us will prove an essential truth that culture belongs to the people . . .*

It was a friendly and courteous email, but still—it was an email, not a phone call. Catt was surprised, even shocked, to see that Beto had joined, or at least embraced, BHG, the Boyle Heights Guardians, an activist group comprised largely of CalArts students and recent grads. Not all of the members even lived in Boyle Heights, but they'd set their sights on a few select targets: a single proprietor of a new coffee shop; a Chicano legacy workshop called Self-Help Graphics & Art that was founded in Boyle Heights before the students were born; and the nonprofit art project space 282 Boyd Street. Members of BHG harassed and heckled all who dared enter these targeted places and waged viciously personal online campaigns against their directors. The purported crime Self-Help Graphics committed was that the nonprofit director's wife worked as a real estate agent. Blue-chip galleries like Hauser & Wirth had opened just a short way away, but they left those places alone. It was 2017, Trump's first year in office. ICE was sweeping through all LA's Latino neighborhoods, rounding up those without papers, and passions ran high.

Still, Catt found it hard to believe that Beto would actually think these measures addressed the very real problems of gentrification. They'd shared, she thought, an understanding about culture and politics, both of them relative outsiders, autodidacts who'd attended state schools. So long as there was a profit to be made in Boyle Heights, it would be made. Elderly people who'd lived there for decades were selling their modest homes for more than they'd ever expected, and who was to blame them?

BHG's bullying tactics rubbed Catt the wrong way and she declined to honor the boycott. Beto's second email was much shorter: *This puts us in an unfortunate position but we have to remain true to our ideals.*

Hosted by the Lost and Found Poetics Initiative at CUNY, the symposium on Kathy Acker's achievement felt like the high point of the book tour for Catt. A poetics grad student would

THE FOUR SPENT THE DAY TOGETHER

moderate; Catt would read from the book, and two prominent younger poets would talk about Acker's work and her influence. The first poet was actually a friend.

Brilliant and moody, she'd reached out to Catt a decade before while she was still one of Mikal's PhD students. Since then, they'd shared dinners and long emails and slept in each other's homes. Catt had never met the second poet but she was widely admired for her graceful and passionate prose and her principled stand against capitalism. Catt and Poet 2 chatted uneasily until Poet 1 arrived late, and then the event started.

Everything went according to plan until the moderator opened the floor up for questions and a young couple unfurled a white banner with the words *I Love Dicks-Ploitation* painted in red. Friends of Beto's and East Coast affiliates of the Boyle Heights Guardians, they'd come down from Yale to protest Catt's refusal to cancel the 282 Boyd book event. For a moment she was confused. *I Love Dick* was the TV show . . . hadn't she come here to talk about Kathy Acker? Still holding her half of the banner, the young woman accepted the mike from the moderator.

Hi, Catt. This question is for you. You're having a show at 282 Boyd where basically that place is displacing people. And there's a boycott by activist groups in Boyle Heights. I just wanna know if you're gonna pull out of that.

Catt could not hear the question and she asked Poet 2 to rephrase it for her. *It's a question about the Boyle Heights boycott and whether you're gonna relocate your event so you don't cross the picket line.* Catt said no, they were maintaining it. *What compels you to think it's okay,* the young woman continued, *to displace people, to be part of this organization that is displacing a neighborhood?* Poet 2 paraphrased, *She wants to know why you won't do it. And particularly about the displacement that the art gallery is part of.* Catt fundamentally disagreed with the question but saw no point making that point at the moment. Instead, she tried getting the Q & A back on the rails. *You know,* she began, *why don't we have this debate some other time? The two poets have joined me to talk about Kathy Acker and I don't want to hijack that conversation.*

Catt expected support from the poets but to her surprise, they chose to jump ship and stand with the protestors. *I think we're living in a time where the envelope of reality is shifting,* Poet 1 said, *and people are trying to respond to it in a new way. Gentrification doesn't have to be this inexorable thing, Puerto Rico doesn't have to be underwater—*

I've been thinking about the relationship of the displacement boycott, and Acker, and politics, and all those little competing lies inside the big lie, about the respectability of politics around breast cancer, around women's death, all of it. And I support the boycott, Poet 2 said.

What I wish people would do when they write is ransack themselves a little harder. Because this whole holograph we're in is like, sketchy, Poet 1 added.

We can have places to talk about books, Poet 2 said. *We don't have to destroy neighborhoods to do it. We have to find ways of thinking outside this monstrous trap of capitalism.*

Do you think we can wrap this up? Catt asked the moderator. The two poets remained onstage after she'd left the roundtable. *Aren't you glad that you heard about this beforehand?* Poet 1 whispered to Poet 2.

THE FOUR SPENT THE DAY TOGETHER

I knew— Poet 2 said.
Before you came here? Poet 1 asked.
I know, I know, right? Poet 2 replied. *Like twenty-seven minutes before, on my phone.*

The next morning video of the event was posted on YouTube and the Boyle Heights Guardians issued a new communiqué across all social media platforms:

THE 282 HYPER BEASTS ARE TRYING TO THROW A BIG CATT GREENE ART PARTY IN OUR HOOD IN BOYLE HEIGHTS. CATT GREENE REPRESENTS THE LA ARTIST/REAL ESTATE FLIPPER PERSONA. SHE'S PART OF THE ORIGIN MYTH BEHIND NIHILIST WHITE APOLITICAL EDGELORD MANDARINS THAT SNEAK INTO LA VIA MFA ART PROGRAMS AND INFEST THE CITY WITH THEIR TONE DEAF AND BRAIN DEAD TRUST FUNDED ENTERPRISES. FLIPPING HOUSES IN HIGHLAND PARK IN THE 90S WHILE FETISHIZING BROWN BODIES IS HER REAL LIFE AND IT IS THE META-TEXT OF ALL HER SELF-SERVING SO-CALLED CONFESSIONAL WRITING.

When she saw this on Facebook, Catt was beside herself. She'd never flipped a house in her life. "Trust funded enterprises"? As far as she knew, none of the former MFA students behind BHG had actual jobs. Her dream of rehabbing the buildings in Albuquerque began not just as a means of supporting herself but as a small social project. Unlike stock market investors, sole-proprietor landlords knew where their money came from and how it was spent. They could decide to sometimes put people before profit, waiving late fees, forgiving back rent, and leasing to people with less-than-great credit or felony backgrounds. And "fetishizing brown bodies"? Did they mean Paul?

These people are pit bulls, he emailed from Balsam. *It seems like they're really responding to Trump . . . they can attack you and get away with it, as opposed to having to sit by and watch their families being taken away by ICE. If the current political climate didn't exist this wouldn't be happening. Just move the event and do not respond.* She saw Paul was right and she did that.

Back in LA Catt collapsed with a 103 fever during a string of hundred-degree October days. *I feel mostly ashamed*, she wrote in her notebook. *Also: dirty, exhausted.* She did a few West Coast events in a fugue state, avoided seeing her friends, and then fled to Balsam. *The Fake News is going all out in order to demean and denigrate! Such hatred!* Trump tweeted. The stock market soared. In New York Galen Stein, the copublisher of *Artissues* magazine, resigned in the wake of a sexual harassment lawsuit. The magazine issued a statement: *Regretfully this behavior undermines the feminist ideals we have long strived to stand for. In response, we are creating a special task force of women.* An open meeting of the larger *Artissues* community debated how to divest him of shares in the company. An elfin man in his sixties, he wore bright orange suits and engaged in sexual banter that in some ways brought a much-needed levity to the magazine. Before assuming his role in high art, he'd founded and sold a successful sock brand.

THE FOUR SPENT THE DAY TOGETHER

Competition was fierce for poorly paid entry-level editorial jobs at *Artissues*. The successful candidates were often conscientious, expensively educated, and anxious young women. Galen paid keen attention to them, breaking the ice by unexpectedly sexualizing the most mundane conversations. He saw himself as their champion, and they saw him as a joke, rolling their eyes at his oafish behavior while at the same time enjoying his unfiltered advice and professional favors. Clearly, Galen's gonzo behavior needed to stop; it had no place in the workplace or anywhere else. Still, Catt was amazed by the global extent of his exile. Women who'd once joked about him were now recovering memories on social media, their annoyance reborn as trauma.

Galen had helped and supported many artists over the years. Catt wondered why no one argued for moderation or clemency. But then again once the trolling began, every stance instantly froze into affect. What you said didn't matter, the meaning was elsewhere.

In Balsam, it snowed. *Finally here, and finally happy!*, Catt wrote in her notebook when she arrived in mid-October. On the first morning, she and Paul went for a run while the stars were still out and then she went back to sleep after Paul left for work. She dreamed she was driving around near MacArthur Park with a single green fish in a bowl. She knew the fish needed food and clean water but she couldn't get to the store, there were too many people around it, lined up at food carts and tents.

Paul came home from work early and they drove to a feed store in Harding to buy grain for the deer. Since he'd be there all winter, he'd decided to feed them. And then they carved a fat pumpkin, played cards, and roasted a chicken.

He stayed sober until Catt left with Blaze in early November. Without them, it was so cold and lonely. When Paul left the house at eight it was dark and it was dark by the time he drove home at four thirty. The people who worked at the treatment facility were just normal North Country people—some of them nice, others less nice, but they all had their lives and their families.

The Lake Resort patients came from all over Minnesota, from small towns and cities with names like Red Wing and Thief River Falls, places he'd never heard of. Most of them came because of court mandates, meaning a judge let them choose between staying in jail and going to treatment. Hardly anyone sent by the judge ever made it. They'd be going to group and working the steps until they eventually figured out how to buy drugs—always meth— in the parking lot during the weekly van trip to the Walmart in Harding. Walmart was where everything happened. If they didn't run off that night with a friend waiting for them in the parking lot, they'd come back to get high and fail their drug test the next day or maybe get narc'd by a roommate. Sometimes they fled through the woods late at night, which was completely insane. They were never prepared—they always got turned around, none of them ever made it. And then in the morning Paul or somebody else would call for the sheriff. You had to wonder why they'd choose jail over treatment, especially since Lake Resort was so nice . . . a comfortable bed looking out at the lake, fresh organic meals, free Wi-Fi, and ice fishing. Or then again, not. In any case, it affirmed something Paul had always known: that treatment was pointless.

On weekends he drove to Greatwoods or Harding to pick up some groceries. *Why don't you join the Greatwoods Y*, Catt nagged from LA, *or go to yoga?* But as one cold gray day followed another, he couldn't be bothered. Except for shopping and the Wednesday night meeting, he stayed in Balsam. Each weeknight he'd come home, feed the band of eight deer that arrived every night, microwave himself a burrito, and watch *Fear the Walking Dead* or *The Office*.

As the snow froze into mountains of ice he began hearing noises.

He was upstairs in bed when he heard a loud stomping sound from the deck . . . was it the deer, coming all the way up to the house? The stomps came in patterns of three, repeated over and over. He got up to check but there were no footprints. When he went back to bed the howling began . . . he couldn't tell if it was an animal's call or a yell mixed with crying. It was the crying that got to him. He remembered the neighbor's story about the drowned boy in the lake. But then the sounds stopped and he forgot about it.

A month later he was upstairs in bed when the knocking began. Knock knock knock—again, patterns of three—coming from inside the closet. He forced himself to get up and look but when he opened the door nothing was there and the sound stopped until he got back in bed again. That night he slept with the lights on because he was scared. And then for a week or two, nothing—and then it happened again. He could never completely relax because he never knew when it would start again. And then the knocking moved into the walls—as if there was something, a mouse or a rat, trapped inside there.

He never drank Wednesday nights because that was his night for AA. Sometimes he'd hold out a week without drinking. But eventually the thought would arrive, like the knocks in the wall—*I'll just pick up a six-pack.* And then there was no getting rid of it. Inside the store he realized he might as well save a trip and buy twelve, or a case and maybe a fifth of tequila to enjoy over the weekend. His rule was to drink only beer on the weeknights, but sometimes after the ninth or tenth beer he'd take a shot to slow himself down, and then another. The next thing he knew it was too late to sleep and he had to call in to work sick or else go in smelling like alcohol. The days he went in he was on edge for eight hours hoping no one would notice . . . and they did not. Or maybe they did? The center was so far out in the sticks the owners were constantly struggling to keep licensed clinicians.

Sometimes he wondered if Catt had installed a camera somewhere to check up on his drinking . . . because there were these little soft beeps coming from inside the kitchen cabinets, but when he got closer the beeping would stop. The house was making him crazy. He considered smashing the cabinets.

THE FOUR SPENT THE DAY TOGETHER

The house torture stopped in December when Catt and their dog, Blaze, arrived for the holidays. For a while, Paul stopped drinking. He was finally happy. Catt wrote her art catalog essays while he was at work. On weekends they went cross-country skiing and made spaghetti and meatballs. He longed to be free of his job at the treatment center. Why did he have to work? Catt came and went as she pleased. He dreamed about becoming a miner or truck driver or boat captain.

The day after Christmas they drove up to Winnipeg for a few days. Catt booked a room in a great old hotel with a restaurant and bar. Paul saw this as his chance and he took it. He begged off the first dinner with her Winnipeg friends and went to the bar to get wasted. The bar was the first place she looked when she came back to their room. Seeing him at the bar was like being hit by a truck, but on the drive home he repented. Being around addicts all day had destroyed his recovery—he just had to get out of the treatment center. When they got back to Balsam, she helped him revise his CV. By the time Catt left to teach in LA, he had a new job in Greatwoods.

Paul loved his new job with North Country Kids Care. For the rest of the winter, he visited schools all over the county to do therapy sessions with young children. For the first time in a long time, he felt somewhat hopeful . . . but by March, everything changed again. North Country Kids Care had a contract with the juvenile detention center. Given his race, gender, and background, they thought his credentials could be better used at the River Road Center for Teens. Housed in a former jail, the center held the most troubled kids who'd been sentenced to juvie.

Paul moved from the main center downtown into a former jail cell that had been turned into a windowless office. Most of his job entailed doing intake interviews with the young inmates to assign diagnostic codes the agency needed for billing. Most of the time he had to make the codes up because none of the kids wanted to talk to him. Silence was their only weapon. Their mottoes were, "Don't Snitch," "Don't Talk," and "Don't Tell." Day after day he sat in his cell with clients who hated him. *Why don't you get to know some of your colleagues?* Catt brightly suggested. And he tried, but they all had their families and lives. When he invited a female clinician for lunch, she acted as if he was hitting on her.

Catt and Blaze came back to Balsam in May and Paul forced himself to stay sober. He knew if he drank she would leave, and Catt and the dog were his only real family. Eight hours a day, he worked in his River Road cell while Catt stayed at home writing an art monograph. He went to AA twice a week, and she went to Al-Anon meetings. On weekends they barbecued, kayaked, and drove up to Canada to go canoe camping.

In August 2018 *The New York Times* published a long story about former NYU grad student Nimrod Reitman's Title IX complaint against the philosopher Avital Ronell: "What Happens to #MeToo When a Feminist Is Accused?" Two years before that, she'd been his dissertation advisor. The piece had been arranged by Reitman's personal publicists and it quoted freely from his legal complaint: the emails she'd sent, the camp terms of endearment. The *Times* portrait of thirty-four-year-old Reitman showed him aggrieved but sharp, trim and fit, while their unflattering image of sixty-six-year-old Ronnell at a conference was grabbed from the internet. Her black beady eyes flamed behind a big pair of black plastic glasses.

A gay man abused by a queer woman? This was an exciting, salacious new spin on #MeToo. Reitman, who seemed to come from, or enjoy, access to great wealth, was also filing a civil suit seeking unspecified financial damages for the mental anguish he'd allegedly suffered. The London *Sunday Times* picked up the story: "Groping professor Avital Ronell and her 'cuddly' Nimrod Reitman see kisses go toxic." The same week the FBI agent who'd led an investigation into 2016 electoral interference was fired and Trump revoked the security clearances of several intelligence agents for prying into activities of his administration.

Catt didn't know Avital, but they'd met years before in Saas-Fee and she seemed like a nimble and generous spirit, a philosopher-pixie. However flawed and confused her behavior with Reitman had been, he was a consenting adult in this midthirties. She was his thesis advisor, but no one had forced him to stay at her Paris apartment. Surely she didn't deserve to be pilloried like this. Why did the *Times* accept Reitman's account as the baseline reality? Many of Catt's younger friends had studied with Avital and adored her. She wondered who would step up to defend her but except for a letter signed by a group of distinguished professors—and later, partly recanted—nobody did.

When an ex–Saas-Fee student asked her to post on a blog he'd set up in Avital's defense, Catt didn't think twice about doing it. *No one*, Catt posted, *stopped him from changing advisors . . . he is an empowered and privileged actor. His feigned helplessness after the fact is transparent to anyone who cares to consider the situation.*

Within hours, Twitter rose to attack her. *Pathetic . . . Double Pathetic . . . So underhand sly and misleading. Oh god oh wow . . . Catt Greene just showed her whole ass . . . Why is this not surprising?*

All this might have died down in a week were it not for a second incident. In New York, a new clique of hip, smart, youngish book critics had started meeting for drinks every week. With Yale PhDs and legions of Twitter followers, they brought an exciting new edge to the doomed art of reviewing. The critics courted the favor of the most wrongly ignored, brilliant, and mordant American writers, with whom they identified. Among these writers was Catt's friend G., a self-declared recluse in his late sixties who did not use social media. They invited G. to their table for drinks, and when Catt's name came up G. drunkenly quipped, *Oh, Catt Greene? She's a landlord, not a writer.*

The next morning, one of the critics tweeted G.'s drunken remark to her twenty-thousand-plus followers: *The funniest thing G. ever said to me was, Catt Greene is a landlord, not a writer*, deftly asserting her proximity to G. and her contempt for an older white feminist. *She's not a landlord, she's a slumlord*, a friend of the critic's who was also a critic for various high-profile media outlets added a few minutes later. *No*, a Princeton classics scholar amended, *Catt Greene is a POS slumlord.*

Twitter found this hilarious. The critics, who published in outlets like *The New York Times*, *The New York Review of Books*, and *The New Yorker*, soon deleted their tweets, but not before they were liked, loved, and shared by their thousands of followers. These followers—graduate students, writers for less A-list outlets—asserted themselves and their names by hate-reading Catt's writings and interviews. To people who'd come of age during the 2008 crash, Catt's novel *Summer of Hate*, about meeting Paul and renovating the Albuquerque apartments, seemed totally damning. Accompanied by various interviews where she'd talked freely about how she made a living—a political act, she believed, given that all but the most commercially successful artists enjoyed invisible means of support—the novel became Exhibit A in their case. Observations she'd made concerning money and class, culture and race, were ridiculed. She struggled to understand where her critics were coming from. Were they opposed to all rental housing? Should it be run by the state? Did they believe that the buildings maintained themselves? Sometimes the tweets had a point, but most had no point at all beyond mindless hatred. *Catt Greene put the first stone in Virginia Woolf's coat*, an ex-student tweeted. *& turned on Sylvia's oven*, Poet 2 from the CUNY event added.

I'm tired of radical white feminism that mostly ignores questions of race, wrote a PhD student from Berkeley.

She's a shittier person than I ever thought.

Tuesday. Catt clicks onto the landlord forum, someone has replied to her post asking how to make her tenant pay for new lightbulbs in the walkup.

It's fun knowing Catt Greene and Donald Trump could trade pointers about property management.

Catt Greene, people said, had been canceled. Someone went into her Wikipedia page and changed her occupation from writer to landlord.

On the Tuesday after Labor Day weekend, Paul dropped Catt at the Thunder Bay airport in Canada. They'd just had a beautiful week of canoe camping. She was going to Toronto and then back to LA. Until the end of November, he'd be alone again. The idea of drinking called out to him like a beautiful siren. Tomorrow, he'd be back in his cell at the River Road Center for Teens. In a month there'd be snow and another North Country winter.

After crossing the border he bought a twelve-pack of Molson and a fifth of Canadian Club in homage to their holiday. He drank half the bottle and chased it down with a couple of beers before leaving the parking lot. *Now we're talking.* His body was flooded with warmth: the onset of lovely oblivion.

He drove all the way home to Balsam in perfect control without any incident. But as he approached the Four Corners Store in their pickup loaded with kayaks, a big semitruck came out of nowhere and hit him. His pickup collapsed. No one was hurt, but the police and an ambulance came within minutes.

THE FOUR SPENT THE DAY TOGETHER

Just before going onstage to read in Toronto Catt got a text from Paul's sister: *Hi, I just wanted to let you know that Paul is in jail. He was in an accident and he was drinking.*

They paid bail, they paid a good lawyer, and Paul got off fairly easily. He did not lose his job. North Country Kids Care was desperately short of clinicians. Since this was his first DUI in more than ten years, the judge gave him home monitoring in lieu of thirty days' jail time and three years' probation. He'd have to install a breath-test device in his car and check in every day for random drug and alcohol testing for the next year. This left him no choice but to stop drinking.

Catt stayed with Paul from the Thanksgiving break until after New Year's. Drinking was no longer an option for him and their time in the gray house was peaceful. They cut their own Christmas tree, roasted a turkey, and went cross-country skiing.

Catt Greene's name continued to pop up each day on Twitter. The Avital case had long since been forgotten, but as the lack of affordable housing grew more intense, artists, musicians, and writers who'd dabbled in real estate became targets. Housing was a human right, and the very notion of owning and renting a house or apartment—and clearly, for profit—was now considered immoral, depraved, because landlords evicted those who defaulted on payment and eviction meant homelessness. Every day, someone retweeted *Catt Greene is a landlord.* A recent Sarah Lawrence grad sold anti–Catt Greene stickers on Etsy.

CHRIS KRAUS

In the dark every morning, Paul went out to the shed, loaded pails up with pellets they bought at the feed store, and spread the grain out on the hill for his small herd. Catt watched the deer feed as the sun rose and she sat in the kitchen drinking her coffee. Home alone until Paul got back from work at five thirty, she wrote a text for the artist Kate Newby. They subscribed to the *Harding Tribune* and the *Duluth Daily News* and every day around noon she walked a few hundred yards out to the mailbox to pick up the papers.

On Tuesday, January 8, 2019—a few days before she flew back to LA—the front page of both papers announced a spectacular murder.

COUPLE CHARGED IN NAGAMO TRAIL MURDER

A 33-year-old Iron Range man was blindfolded, marched into the woods, and shot twice in the face on Sunday morning for allegedly pursuing another man's 17-year-old girlfriend.

Micah Waldon, 18, Evan Stanton, 20, and Brittney Linn Moran, 17, all from Harding, have been charged with second-degree murder, kidnapping, and robbery of the victim, Brandon Halbach, of North Star. Halbach's ordeal began with a visit to Moran at Stanton's apartment on Saturday morning.

According to the accomplice Evan Stanton, the four spent the day together and Waldon, who carried a gun, talked of a plan to kill Halbach in retaliation for unwanted sexual advances and inappropriate touching of Moran, who was his girlfriend.

Halbach's body was discovered on the Nagamo Trail on Sunday by a snowmobiler with two gunshot wounds to his face, according

THE FOUR SPENT THE DAY TOGETHER

to court documents. The suspects remain jailed in lieu of $1,000,000 bail ahead of their January 19 court date.

The Nagamo Trail death was the second homicide reported in the Harding area in less than two weeks. On December 25, Jesiah Augustus Benedict, 34, of Harding, was shot and killed outside a residence. Marsell Darik Atkins, 29, has been charged with second-degree murder and second-degree assault in that case.

The case caught Catt's interest. Who were these people? The assassination-style shooting occurred on the same eighty-mile trail where she and Paul rode their bikes through the woods every summer, looking for foxes and eagles. Balsam was cabins, woods, and small farms—a whole other world, just twenty-two miles away, from the shooting in Harding. Micah and Brittney, the two kids in the case, could have been clients of Paul's at the River Road Center for Teens. They must have been high—on what drugs?—and what did they do with the victim for almost a day between the time he arrived at their place and the time that they shot him? The newspaper article said, *The four spent the day together.* Were they friends? What did they talk about? She longed to investigate.

Catt's novels had always evolved from her life, but now her life seemed redundant to the grotesque image of her as a landlord. Since Trump's election and the Twitterization of everything, she'd started to wonder if there was even a point to writing books anymore. And who for? The directionless cruelty of the Trump era tore the veil off social behavior and destroyed the illusion that any one human life mattered. *All we ever really wanted to do,* she wrote in her notebook, *was watch* Survivor *and* The Apprentice.

Catt remembered some lines from a book by her friend, the late Erje Ayden, published in the mid-1960s.

Each time a bus stopped at a Howard Johnson's of a new town, I was more convinced that there was an America I never saw before. It was not only the different appearances and faces of the people but the mysterious coldness and anger. This America with no artists and no Italian restaurants was a little scary. But I suspected that I had to learn about this America immediately if I was to succeed in my future projects.

Of course—the cruelty had always been there. She tried imagining America through Erje's eyes, arriving in New York from Istanbul in 1957—the tight pinched faces of upstanding citizens, the casual sadism of the high school party crowd. She thought about the distances between LA and the gray house in Balsam and the lives of these four young people on the Iron Range and decided she would try to bridge them.

PART 3

HARDING

"The Four Spent the Day Together"

1

... Brittney's family moved into the mustard-beige house in East Harding when she was seven. It was one of about three hundred houses in an old mining location built by the mines to house immigrant workers in the 1920s, a short walk to downtown. With a few variations, the old mining houses were similar: deep cellars, wood siding, set close to the street with an extra half story for kids' rooms squeezed out of the attic. Brittney, the youngest, had to wait till her two older sisters moved out to have her own room. The houses all had tiny front yards and short cement walkways up to the front doors or porches. The backyards—backing onto a series of alleys that divided the streets—were ample. Over the years people had added garages, workshops, and swing sets. By the time Brittney's family moved into the house it had been foreclosed on. The mines were long out of business and the financial crash gave her parents the chance to buy their own home. Neither of their families went way back on the Range—they'd moved up when Brittney's mom, Erin Page, and her father, Jeff Moran, were still kids.

CHRIS KRAUS

The Moran house was a five-minute walk from Harding's two main downtown streets, First Avenue and Howard Street. Although "downtown" hadn't been much for as long as Brittney remembered. There was Nick's Bar, for the old-man day drinkers; a veterans' thrift store; a Goodwill; and a Salvation Army. The Mexican restaurant, the chiropractor's office, the shoe store, and the hair salon were all closed. But there was a China Buffet and two pizza places as well as Andy's tattoo parlor, two liquor stores, a bike store, a pawnshop. Everything else—the places where everyone went, the Walmart, the Lowe's, the hospital and municipal center, the Chevrolet dealership—had moved out to the two highways that circled the town. At the beginning of 2019, when Brittney and her boyfriend Micah and their friend Evan kidnapped Brandon Halbach and shot him in the head at close range, no one had thought of turning East Harding and the old brick buildings downtown into a historical district. Harding's professional class—the doctors and lawyers, the judges and district attorneys consigned to pursuing careers in a spent mining town four hours north of the Cities, more like six in the winter—kept themselves hidden in big homes on the most popular lakes. There were no private schools for their children, no front doors painted Christmas red or canary, no planter boxes, no rainbow-heart yard signs proclaiming, *Everyone Welcome*. The only yard signs were the Trump/Pence signs left over from 2016 and the signs handed out by the multinational mining company who were seeking exemptions from a state fracking ban—*We Support Mining / Mining Supports Us*, which was no longer true, not even remotely. Fifty percent of the town's jobs were in health care and the rest were in retail or service. But mining remained Harding's origin myth, the myth that Trump spoke to: a time when a churchgoing working-class one-paycheck family needed only one car, because Mom could walk down to the Red Hen IGA for groceries while dad was at work and the kids were at school. Evenings and weekends, they all went to hockey games, and Knights of Columbus and church functions.

On the Friday late afternoon before Brittney met Brandon Halbach and everything happened, she and her friend Misty were home alone in Brittney's small attic room working their phones. Her parents were both still at work and the dull granite sky outside the house had nearly faded to black.

Hey, Tyler from Moose Lake messaged Misty. They'd met on LiveMe just an hour before that. This was Misty's first time on LiveMe. She'd never do it at home because she lived with Evan, her new boyfriend. They'd been living together less than three weeks and it was too risky, him seeing it.

Heyyy, she messaged him back. LiveMe was a site where guys PayPal'd girls money for doing stuff. If Brittney hadn't helped her sign up she would never have dared, never thought about doing it.

Gonna bend over for me is the question?
Maybe. Depends.
So you're a bratty lil girl huh
Oh yeah
I won't have any problems making u submit

Misty wasn't sure how this should go or what happened next. The space heater purred, turning the small room into a sauna. Brittney was on her twin bed, already changed into a tank top and busy with someone. Misty sat on the floor, her back leaning into a pouf, sweating hard in her fleece leggings.

Pinning you down

Kissing your neck

She instinctively held the phone back at arm's length and slipped out of her sweater. Did this make her a whore? Brittney had helped her set up a secret PayPal.Me for the money.

I'll pull your hair

Misty was a plump strawberry blonde.

Mmmm, she said, shaking it.

Are you gonna send me those pics here? And also a list of your kinks?

LiveMe wasn't actually live because just doing stuff on-cam wasn't enough to make any real money. As Brittney explained, you had to send pictures. Brittney was fearless. Her friends all thought she had a body count over one hundred and that wasn't even including online. And it wasn't as if Misty was actually doing anything with this guy, it was invisible.

You have to pay first. Misty copied and sent him her PayPal.Me link. As soon as *You've Got Money* popped up on her phone, she began taking photos and sending.

Want me to slide my head back and forth over your pussy until you're dripping then slide in really fast causing you to gasp—Tyler messaged, but she'd already X'd out to message Micah on Facebook.

Hey, I'll have that $60 tonight.

THE FOUR SPENT THE DAY TOGETHER

Misty's real thing was babysitting and selling weed since being laid off after Christmas from Walmart. Brittney's new boyfriend Micah was her supplier. Really the weed came from his parents—his mom, Crystal, and Quinton, her boyfriend. Supplying Micah with weed was one of the many ways Crystal cared for her son. He'd been bullied so much as a child and a teenager. He was already eighteen and she wanted him to feel independent but stay living at home long enough to get his diploma.

To Misty it felt strange, but in a good way, being here in this room with Brittney and having adventures as if they were little kids again.

If you asked Misty, she'd tell you that Brittney was her best friend forever. They'd been in diapers together! They'd climbed trees in Grandma Ann's yard, made weird things to eat in the kitchen, told secrets, chased chickens. Brittney was the friend Misty remembered the most from her childhood—a childhood that was cut short when she was eleven and came home from school to find her mom on the kitchen floor, dead of an overdose. After that, she'd bounced around group homes and foster care within north-central Minnesota—never in juvie—before moving to Harding last August with her then-boyfriend Fernando, just in time for her eighteenth birthday.

When Misty moved back to Harding, Brittney was still in the Duluth Juvenile Detention Center. She'd been sentenced to treatment but she'd waited five months until early September, when a bed opened up at the Prairie River Youth Center down in the Cities. Brittney hated the rich girls in treatment on their parents' insurance, but during her ninety-day stay she finally quit meth. Before she came home, just in time for Thanksgiving, her parents painted her room a beautiful pale shade of blue to surprise her. And except for some weed, she'd managed to stay totally clean since returning. Brittney was a year younger than Misty but way more adult in just about every way. She kept her little blue bedroom cozy and minimal: her old desk and bed, a few anime posters, a sheer orange scarf hung over a lamp. Brittney was skinny and short, a fast skater but never a jock. In treatment she'd toned down her skater-punk/biker style but she still razor-cut her own hair and wore a black leather jacket. Misty shopped at the Walmart. She liked T-shirts and fleece but beyond that, she had no special style.

Brittney's take on her friendship with Misty was noncommittal. To her, Misty was just someone she knew from around. So much had happened since she was ten. Misty hadn't been part of her old high school friend group and the fact that Misty had her own apartment was the only reason Brittney decided they should hang out. Micah—whom she'd been seeing for less than a week, maybe two, no one could really remember—was an old friend of Evan's, so of course the four of them kicked back together. Brittney had a key to Misty's apartment and used it to take care of business and also get away from her parents. Her dad had a temper and her mom just got so sad whenever she got into trouble. When she was fifteen they'd ruined her life by taking an order of protection out against Dylan, her much older boyfriend, the love of her life.

Misty couldn't really understand what Brittney saw in Micah. She'd never known Brittney to date someone so close to her age—all of her boyfriends were older. Micah was pale and intense, with raven-black hair like Edward Scissorhands. He wore an old man's wool overcoat. Some of the people in town were afraid of him, but really he was quiet and loyal and nice. She and Micah had actually hooked up a couple of times before she met Evan and before Brittney moved back. She'd never told Brittney or Evan this and neither had Micah . . . because really there was nothing to talk about.

Misty's phone buzzed. It was her girlfriend Rosetta wanting twenty dollars of weed. Two days ago, Rosetta sold Misty a half gram of crack that she'd shared with Evan. Rosetta wanted to stop by Brittney's and give Misty the money, but Misty didn't think that would work, because she'd never told Brittney she was selling weed for Micah. Would she even care about that? She wasn't sure, Brittney could be hard to read. Just to be safe, she asked Rosetta to come by her and Evan's apartment.

Misty got up and put on her powder-blue parka and gestured to Brittney that she'd be back, but Brittney didn't look up from her phone.

Do u cheat, Justin Cole messaged Brittney—her name on LiveMe was Cherry—from his mom's basement in Biwabik.

No but I work

Wat u mean work wat kinda work.

Duh, what kind of work do you think we're talking about, Brittney thinks, but instead she texts back—*I blow glass* (which she actually does, she has a friend with a bench and a blowtorch)—*I'm a Personal Care Attendant* (a thing she'd set up with her grandmother Dee, $140 a week from the state, which of course they would split)—*and I also sleep with people for shit.*

Ok if we were together would u ever do that knowing ur wit me? Justin Cole wants to know. Clearly he doesn't mean personal care. What is his point? Does he think they're dating?

I would let you know but cash is cash to me, she texted back, and then shut down the app. This guy seemed even more stupid than most.

Misty was gone and she was alone, restless and anxious. She tried calling Micah's phone but it went straight to voicemail. She wondered where he was now and what he was doing. *What you doin,* she messaged. Maybe he was at home, in the basement of Crystal and Quinton's new house two blocks away, where he'd set up his room, the Wi-Fi there wasn't great.

A half hour later Micah messaged her back, *Everything good sorry phone died.*

I figured

The 20 Brant gave me fell out my pocket and now I can't reup until tomorrow. He *was* messaging her from his room: a twin bed and blankets pushed up against the cold cellar wall to turn it into a sofa. He had his mom's gun that she kept in a brown paper bag on the fridge and his own black nylon holster. *I'm having the worst day.*

I'm sorry love

I just really wanna shoot someone

It's a figure of speech—it doesn't alarm her. Micah is a wannabe thug. Part of him truly believes he's on the verge of being invited to join the Minneapolis branch of the Gangster Disciples,

THE FOUR SPENT THE DAY TOGETHER

but he also calls himself Pineapple Man from the dumb stoner movie he watched with his biological dad when he was eight.

That cant be your go-to every time you're upset

Micah, Brittney knows, is an innocent soul. He'd do anything in the world to protect his siblings and mom.

But it helps the anger go away

Yeah so does sex

Tru but your grounded

Upstairs, Crystal and Quinton were watching TV with Micah's younger siblings Paisley and Zeke and his baby half sister Cheyenne. Micah's family had split, almost in half, when his mom and ex-stepdad Pete King divorced a year ago. Pete had moved back to the Cities with his new fiancée—Crystal's former best friend—and the two other kids he and Crystal had had. Micah couldn't be bothered going upstairs so he messaged Crystal—*I'm having Brittney come over everyone can criticize but I love her*

Nothing came back.

And she makes me happy

He waited a moment, then typed: *And I need happy right now I'm getting really depressed*

It's ok if she makes you happy, Crystal replied.

You got 2 g's? Micah asked his mother.

Ya

Can I sell it

Pause.

Give you the money

Ya I guess

Later that night when her parents were in their converted garage drinking with some of her dad's friends, Brittney slipped out and walked to Micah's house. They hung out and smoked weed with his mom and Quinton and his sister Paisley. When Brittney left to walk home at one everyone at Micah's was still up except for the baby, Cheyenne.

Nine hours later, Brandon Halbach left a note and a handful of Marlboro Reds on the kitchen table of his apartment in Beulah. *Borrowing the car to go get laid FR be back in a couple of hours.*

Ten o'clock Saturday morning, the first weekend in January, he was the only one up. His roommate Pixi was sleeping and her boyfriend Mikey, the Harding Deputy Chief told Catt later, was in jail for the weekend, knocking another three days off his sixty-day sentence of intermittent confinement for DUI 2 on a suspended. The car, an '02 Chevy Malibu, was actually Mikey's, not Pixi's. It was on its last legs but Mikey had always been generous about loaning it.

Brandon was thirty-three, turning thirty-four on Monday, and it was embarrassing not having a car, but since he'd gone back to school he couldn't even start saving up for one. Back in July he'd been arrested for failure to pay child support. Since he was still on probation (he'd caught a second-degree burglary charge for driving the car when his friend took a flat-screen TV from someone who owed him $140) the judge gave him a choice: a month at a work farm downstate or another four years on probation. Brandon chose the farm. Everyone knew

THE FOUR SPENT THE DAY TOGETHER

probation was quicksand and by then he felt ready to get off the Range and get clean. At the work farm he made pizzas for everyone, passed the test for his GED, and walked through the meadows looking for four-leaf clovers. After everything happened no one who knew him could believe that Brandon had come anywhere close to raping Brittney. He was chronically shy; he'd been a virgin until he was nineteen.

After the work farm he moved back to Beulah and enrolled at community college for heating and cooling. When he passed the exam in six months and got his license things would be different. Until then he'd have to get by on food stamps, a few loans from his dad, and selling small bags of meth for old friends who wanted to help him.

The Malibu started up right away. It wasn't that cold yet for January. He drove the twenty-five miles over to Harding nice and slow, taking it easy, but even so, the check engine light started flashing in Colberg and the engine was squealing. Brandon had no clue, cars weren't his thing. He was relieved the Malibu made it to the address this girl Cherry—probably not her real name—gave him and around 11 a.m. he parked out in front of Misty and Evan's duplex apartment.

On a warm late July evening in 2004 in Gilbert, Minnesota, a small town of about two thousand people on the northeastern edge of the Range, Frank Miller, Jesse Ridlon, and Jason Anderson jumped twenty-five-year-old Travis Holappa outside the Gladiator Bar on North Broadway and forced him into the trunk of Frank Miller's car. The only strip club within a two-hundred-mile radius and fully licensed, the Gladiator was a popular place. On this midsummer Saturday night there were plenty of people out on the sidewalk, smoking and milling around. It wasn't pitch-dark. Burnished gold light hovered low in the sky, bathing the beat-up main street in a liminal glow. No one outside the bar tried to stop them; no one called the police.

The car, a dark blue late-model Cadillac, sped off into the twilight and drove seventeen miles southeast to Jesse Ridlon's in Makinen. When they arrived, the three men moved Travis Holappa out of the trunk into Ridlon's garage. After binding his ankles and wrists tight with duct tape, they passed a meth pipe around and took turns beating him with their fists, an old fan belt, and the butt of Frank's .44. As Holappa began to lose consciousness, they doused him with battery acid and locked him back up in the trunk of the car. Then they went into the house to get high. As the sun rose on Sunday morning, they realized they might have a problem. Frank Miller went outside to solve it, popping open the trunk and shooting the still-living Holappa ten times in the head. "I wasn't gonna have anyone else do my dirt," Miller bragged later on to his brother. "I filled his head with the clip. Just kidding. I sent him to Colorado."

Six weeks later, four days into bear-hunting season, Holappa's remains were discovered, unburied, next to a reservoir a few miles away.

According to people whose families went way back on the Range, 2004—when Brittney and Misty were toddlers—was when everything changed. Holappa's gruesome death occurred just thirteen months after the disappearance of five-year-old Susanna Martin in Colberg, where she was abducted in broad daylight while walking home from a friend's house. Search parties, bloodhounds, and helicopters went out to find her but her body was never recovered. It wasn't exactly the drugs that freaked people out, people like Brandon Halbach's two aunts in North Star insisted. Everyone knew there were drugs, the drugs had always been there. But this time in Gilbert in 2004 was different. The absolute horror of Travis Holappa's kidnapping and murder, the idea that someone could be grabbed off the main street in full public view and then tortured and killed for a drug debt, meant that no one was safe. Young people like Brandon Halbach's two older sisters picked up the message and fled: the era of the small-town, free-range childhood was over. Both girls had grown up with their mom and as soon as they finished high school they moved far away from the Range. Brandon stayed with his dad. He loved the outdoors, collecting feathers and rocks, camping and fishing. He imagined becoming a wilderness guide in the Pacific Northwest but he had no idea how to realize this dream. How could he save up enough to move somewhere where he knew no one so far away? Besides, his dad's health was bad and he needed his help, so he stayed.

On January 11, 2019, the day that Brittney, Micah, and Evan were arraigned, Paul drove Catt to the Cities to catch the plane back to LA. As they were approaching the terminal he saw the flashing red and blue lights of the airport police. His plates had been flagged and the officer wanted to see if Paul had installed a breath-check device as the judge in his DUI case had ordered. The breath-check device would have cost two hundred dollars a month for monitoring, not to mention embarrassing huffing and puffing into the thing outside of work in full view of his colleagues. He'd worn the electronic ankle monitor that chafed his leg and blipped all the time for a month—surely that was enough? When the officer saw that he hadn't installed the device she suspended his license. But instead of impounding the car she let Catt drive it away. As soon as they were out of the airport she gave Paul back his keys and caught a Lyft back to the terminal.

With his license suspended Paul couldn't legally ever leave Balsam for groceries, let alone get to work. *Just try and keep your head down*, his attorney advised. For the next thirty days he drove with no license until he installed the device and the judge gave him permission to drive.

By the third week of January the temperature dropped to minus 32 degrees Fahrenheit. The radio called it a polar vortex. Snow piled up six feet high, blocking the windows, frozen too solid to move. Every day, Paul gamely posted a picture of his car's thermometer on Facebook—minus 27, minus 38, minus 32—but he felt abandoned and sad. Every two weeks for the foreseeable future, he had to leave work to check in with probation. The office felt sickly familiar: the same dirty floors, folding chairs, and tan paint, the same metal stall where he had to pee into a jar with somebody watching, that he remembered from being on parole and probation in Albuquerque. In the waiting room, he sometimes sat next to his former clients from Lake Resort. Paul was fifty-two years old, soon to turn fifty-three, and he wondered if all of his life would consist of these repetitions. *I don't know, Catt,* he emailed one Saturday morning, *I guess I'm getting a little depressed. I just fed the deer and did my routines but I feel a little like Jack in* The Shining. *It's day after day of gray, freezing, snowy cold and dangerous driving. I keep hearing these weird banging sounds in the house after I go to bed. It stopped for a couple of nights and then last night it started again. Am I going nuts? It's actually pretty scary and I wish you were here as a witness* ☺

Catt felt terribly sad and sorry for Paul. She wondered if he was drinking again. The same week, on January 17, Micah Waldon and Evan Stanton had their first hearings in court. Several new facts emerged. Brittney, who was being held at the Juvenile Detention Center in Duluth while the prosecutor made up her mind whether or not to charge her as an adult, told the police that the three of them kidnapped Brandon Halbach and drove him to the Nagamo Trail. Evan stayed in the car while she and Micah took Brandon into the woods. They walked uphill for a while and then stopped near the dim flashing light of an electrical substation. The light cast a diffused but triangular beam onto the trail almost like a theatrical spotlight and it was there at the edge of this light that Micah shot him. Two bullets discharged at close range entered Brandon's head, one in the forehead, one in the left temple. Thirty-six hours after the crime, the police found Micah's mom's gun underneath Brittney's bed. Evan, the first of the three to be arrested, told the police that "Halbach had attempted unwanted sexual contact with Brittney." He gave the police Brandon's maxed-out EBT card, which the three of them used once he was dead.

Catt had two teaching jobs that semester: her usual art college job and a prestigious visiting chair at a liberal arts college that paid very well. She decided to use the funds to build a small house at a campo in Baja five hours south of LA. She'd need someplace to go if Paul started drinking again once he moved back to LA. To her, both of those possible futures seemed inevitable. She'd tried and failed so many times to leave that living alongside Paul's drinking seemed like a fait accompli. Each time things got really bad she waited for someone, anyone, in her life to say plainly, *You need to leave*. But nobody did and she stayed.

After the hearings, everyone had something to say about Brittney on Facebook:

Murderer . . .

Just disgusting

I've known her for yrs, she's always been trouble, dating guys causing them jail time lying about her age . . .

apparently she's had a problem with drugs for quite some time

She's real nasty

Shes never seem to be to be right in the head either

She sleeps with older men! She does it all the time!!

Poor Brandon just made the mistake of getting involved with the wrong skank—

The look in her eyes says it all.

Evil

Underneath these remarks Brittney's mom posted a photo of Brittney taken when she was five: asleep underneath a white quilted blanket, her sweet peaceful face burrowed into a soft white duvet.

Paul went several times to the courthouse in Harding to request transcripts of the Nagamo Trail hearings. After the murder, Catt had begun reading everything that she could find about the case and the people, and Paul was excited that she might actually write a real true-crime story. But teaching three classes a week and driving to meet the builder in Baja whenever she could, for the next several months she lost track of it.

Less than two weeks before the Nagamo Trail murder, two doors away from Misty and Evan's East Harding duplex, Marsell Atkins shot and killed Jesiah Benedict on the sidewalk. It was Christmas Day 2018. Marsell Atkins got out of his SUV and walked up to Benedict, who was talking with neighbors. *What up now?* Atkins asked Benedict before firing shots that killed him and injured two others. The autopsy showed a mixture of methamphetamine, weed, and amphetamines in Benedict's body. Friends told police the two men had a long-standing beef, presumably over a drug debt.

A year before that, Bobby Horvat killed his former landlady Jessica Lenske, seventy-one, in her home in Clifton, an old mining location adjacent to Harding. Believing she kept "buckets of cash" in her house, Horvat bound, gagged, and strangled the woman and then left her for dead with her savings of three thousand dollars. He was arrested three and a half years after that when police picked him up on separate charges of methamphetamine distribution.

The same year, on July 8, 2017, Jay Simic was found stabbed to death in his apartment behind his small liquor store in East Harding. On January 17, 2017, Everett Sundquist stabbed fifty-four-year-old newspaper deliveryman Lou Grainger to death fifteen times in the back and the chest in his room, number 12, at the old Sky Motel in Harding. High for five days and suffering from methamphetamine psychosis, Sundquist told the police that *everything came to twelve* and that Jesus told him to do it.

About eighteen months before that, on June 24, 2016, Charles Gunnarsen, thirty-six, and his girlfriend, Joleene Muller, twenty-two, kidnapped and killed twenty-year-old Bryce Hartman of Harding, decapitating him in the woods outside of Greatwoods with a machete. Hartman was the younger brother of Tiffany Hartman, one of Charles's former girlfriends, and he'd had a crush on Joleene. The three bought and smoked meth together a few times and one of those times Joleene had sex with Charles and Bryce together under Charles's direction.

Leading Joleene through her plea hearing the following year, Greatwoods public defender Todd Sterling—who was also Paul Garcia's attorney—asked if she could recall when she moved in with Charles Gunnarsen but Joleene couldn't remember the month or the day. She said, *Snow was melting.*

Do you remember Mr. Hartman coming to your home?
Yes.
Do you remember what time of day it was?
No.

THE FOUR SPENT THE DAY TOGETHER

Do you know if it was dark or light out?
I don't remember.

After smoking meth together in Joleene and Charles's apartment, the two bound, gagged, and punched Bryce Hartman and then carried him out to the car. They drove over to Blue Lake and untied their victim when they arrived at the home of a friend, where they all, including Bryce, smoked more meth together. As the day drew to a close, they went to another friend's trailer nearby and did several more lines of meth. Then Charles and Joleene borrowed the friend's four-wheeler. During their ride, Charles Gunnarsen told Joleene that they were going to kill Bryce Hartman together. He didn't say why. Later on, when the three of them left in Charles Gunnarsen's car, Charles said to Bryce, *We could have avoided all this if only you'd told me Tiffany was messing around while we were dating*, which made no sense because when that happened, the two of them still hadn't met. Smoke poured out of the hood when they went through some mud and Charles told Bryce Hartman to get out and check the oil. Charles hit Bryce over the head with a baseball bat while he was looking around under the hood. Bloodied and stunned, Bryce looked up from the ground and called Joleene's name, and then she stabbed him.

What did you use to cut his head off?
A machete.
Where did the machete come from?
I don't remember. It was just in my hand.

After that, Charles used a filleting knife to remove Bryce's head. Once it was fully severed Charles put it into a bag and threw it out in the woods.

Awaiting her plea hearing in the Greatwoods jail, Joleene turned her life over to Jesus.

A month before that in Harding, Dustin Christensen, nineteen, stabbed and then clubbed his twenty-year-old roommate Jacob Fenn in the downtown apartment they shared with some friends in a dispute over an iPad. Two other roommates, including a sixteen-year-old girl, were arrested and later released. The girl, whose name was Mariah, told the police how she'd come home and stumbled onto the murder-in-progress before fleeing. When she arrived Dustin had already beaten Jacob beyond recognition and was strangling him with an electrical cord on a La-Z-Boy recliner. He had *a methamphetamine-induced crazy look*, she reported. Dustin then drove Jacob's corpse to the Mount mine pit in Oreville, doused it with gas, and then set it on fire. A dog walker found Jacob's remains the next day.

Meth leads to a possession by evil, one of the prosecutors would tell Catt a year later when she finally got around to researching the Nagamo Trail murder. *Up here, it's the drug of choice, $100 a gram. It leaves people very aggressive and angry. Meth captures the evil spirit hovering and activates it, catalyzes it.*

When she interviewed Harding homicide detective Matt Rogers, he said that he couldn't recall any cases during his eighteen-year-long career that didn't involve methamphetamine.

Two grand juries convened on February 26, 2019, to review the state's cases against Micah and Brittney, and the charges against them were upgraded to first-degree murder. The new first-degree charge meant that seventeen-year-old Brittney would automatically be tried as an adult. Perhaps poorly advised by her public defender, she *shuffled into the courtroom wearing blue jeans and a black T-shirt displaying a gray skull*, the Harding paper reported. After the hearing she was transferred from juvie to the county jail in Duluth, where she mystified everyone.

According to a friend who'd been in jail with her, Brittney bragged that she'd slept with more than two hundred people and got locked down immediately for sexual behavior, rubbing girls' backs and trying to kiss them. And then she did it again as soon as she moved back to general. Her grandmother Jean put $300 a week on her books that she used to buy drugs and friendship.

Brittney couldn't handle her drugs. She stayed up all night making noise and fake-laughing so hard she peed herself. She blabbed every day about Brandon's murder, as if it was one more boring day with a little more blood in it. Her cellmates all warned her not to ruin her case, there were microphones everywhere, but she did not seem to care.

On the other hand she was easy to talk to. Brittney knew right away when someone was down and stepped up to comfort them. If someone liked playing cards she'd play cards with them.

It never crossed Brittney's mind that she'd ruined her life. Or maybe she did know. She told people she'd get a slap on the wrist, maybe five years, and the boys would be sentenced forever to prison.

She did not understand, in the most basic way, what was going to happen.

The day after the two grand juries upgraded the charges against Micah and Brittney, their friend and accomplice Evan Stanton accepted a plea in exchange for his cooperation.

Evan was the first of the three to be arrested, leaving Brittney's house on Monday night at six thirty in the '02 Chevy Malibu. By then Brandon had been dead for about thirty hours. Late on Sunday afternoon, a Harding couple discovered Brandon's body out on the Nagamo Trail while they were snowmobiling. Blood clots around his head weren't yet completely frozen and the coroner placed his time of death between two and three on Sunday morning.

Since Brandon had prior arrests, the Harding Police and the Minnesota Bureau of Criminal Apprehension identified him through his fingerprints on Monday morning. By noon the murder was announced on Harding Crime Alert on Facebook and investigators were interviewing local Harding businesses where Brandon Halbach's EBT card had been used since the time of his abduction. On Saturday at 3 p.m., Brandon, Brittney, and Evan went to the East Harding Short Stop to buy snacks and vape cartridges. After shooting Brandon, at 4:08 on Sunday morning Evan, Brittney, and Micah stopped at a Holiday gas station and used his EBT card to purchase chips and Monster energy drinks. And then again that night around eleven, Evan and Misty went to Walmart, where they maxed out the

THE FOUR SPENT THE DAY TOGETHER

card with a case of ramen noodles and some sodas. Meanwhile, Brandon's roommates reported Mickey's Chevrolet Malibu missing . . . but the police already had the plate because the car appeared on all three stores' parking lot surveillance videos.

By time Evan left Brittney's house that Monday evening, police all over the county were looking for the '02 Chevy Malibu. The Harding police officers who stopped him asked if he'd mind coming down to the station. He didn't know what to think. He'd been high and awake several days and complied and went willingly. There, homicide detectives from the BCA and Harding police interviewed him for several hours. They ordered food from Taco John's and Evan soon told them everything. Putting bad things into words was a way to stop the chaos inside his head and leave it behind him. Besides, they hadn't arrested him yet. Evan truly believed that as soon as he finished his story they'd drive him home and he could finally crash and the whole thing would be over. He'd been in Harding less than a month and didn't know much about the people and places, but he struggled hard to remember everything. *I don't know* or *I can't remember* was his reply to most of their questions.

Eventually the prosecution would use Evan's statement as the master narrative in all three of their cases. As soon as he finished, the police read him his rights and placed him in handcuffs.

As the long winter of 2019 dragged on Paul went to work every day at the River Road Center for Teens. Except for the pay that arrived every two weeks he had no idea why he was there or what he was doing. North Country Kids Care was a liberal, progressive employer. The owner, Eddie Whitsen, was a local philanthropist. They sent him on trainings to Duluth and the Cities where everyone talked about positive outcomes and treatment modalities, but there was no treatment to speak of. The anger management workbook they gave him to read aloud to the kids said, *Successful people have a plan to be successful. Now it's time for you to develop a plan in order to be successful in managing your anger. Identify your anger triggers, keep a list of positive thoughts to produce positive outcomes, and create a positive message . . .*

Paul just couldn't do it. All of his juvenile clients had shuttled between foster care and group homes after being abandoned or sexually abused by their fucked-up parents, who were either dead or in jail or in rehab. The only treatment modality that achieved a positive outcome for him was taking the kids to the gym and shooting baskets. Sometimes in between shots they'd actually say something. But even then nothing changed. As soon as a few kids were out-placed a new group came in. From his windowless cell at the River Road Center for Teens he observed a perpetual stream of dysfunction and misery.

In late April, Micah's Rule 20 Evaluation came back to the court. The county psychologist deemed him mentally fit to stand trial. Micah had been diagnosed with paranoid schizophrenia in Lincoln, Nebraska, when he was four after threatening to stab both his parents with scissors while they were sleeping. A year later, clinicians in Minneapolis amended his diagnosis to what was then called Asperger's syndrome, which they said, at least in his case, was untreatable. With his murder trial looming, his mother, Crystal, convinced an attorney

THE FOUR SPENT THE DAY TOGETHER

from the Autism Advocacy and Law Center, Justin Wiedel, to represent him. On June 13 Micah pled not guilty against his attorney's advice and filed a demand for a speedy trial, but within two weeks he withdrew it.

Paul was still sober when Catt arrived for the summer. Between probation and randomized testing and blowing into the breath-test device whenever he started his car, there were no drinking opportunities. He still went to AA twice a week but he and his sponsor agreed it would be foolish to share about his desire to drink or his relapses. *Loose lips sink ships.* The Iron Range was one big small town. Why risk losing his job and shooting himself in the foot even further?

While Paul was at North Country Kids Care, Catt flailed around, wondering what she should work on. All of her summer assignments were finished and she was tired of writing catalog essays that would only ever just be PR for the artist. She considered writing something about the Nagamo Trail murder and made a few calls to the police and public defenders but the kids' cases were pending and until they concluded no one could talk to her. For the time being, she dropped it. Well-meaning friends suggested she try writing short stories but she could not grasp the form or the point. She'd never studied creative writing, joined a group, or even taken a workshop. To her, writing was research. She had no writing practice. The only way she could do it was by default—the times when she was possessed by an idea too large and upsetting to formulate.

For years, she'd thought about writing something about her family's flight from Milford, Connecticut, and their first year in New Zealand. But the starts that she made while Paul was at work sounded quaint and contrived, they didn't go anywhere. Catt's only agenda in writing was truth; her sad family life had been structured around an ethos of unspoken secrets and pretense. Deep down she knew that so long as her dad was alive it was impossible. *Your sister is perfectly normal*, he sneered whenever she brought up support groups and treatment for autism.

The summer settled into the kind of placid routine Catt had longed for. Paul came home from work every day at four thirty or five. They had dinner and then watched TV until nine thirty. On weekends they kayaked and some evenings they drove up the highway to get ice cream at the Antler Lake store. It was as if Catt's dream of a pleasant domestic life and Paul's alcoholism had reached a détente. But at the same time a dullness settled like dust over everything. After spending two winters in Balsam, the long summer evenings had lost their magic for Paul. They were a countdown to darkness and suffering. Old men at the Balsam Four Corners café talked about selling up and leaving for Arizona. Thickets of MAGA signs still lined the roads, as if the election had never happened. The loud shrieks of laughter that rose from the Lapke float on the lake struck them as simulated. Catt still went to Greatwoods for yoga and the vegetarian café and took bike rides, but she was aware of the gap between the world of her summer vacation and the one that Paul worked in.

THE FOUR SPENT THE DAY TOGETHER

In August their torpor was shattered by a letter Paul got from the Minnesota behavioral health state licensing board. After receiving complaints from a Greatwoods physician, they were placing his license under review. This particular doctor had refused to approve his credentials to treat low-income subsidized patients because of his DUI history. Since most of their clients were low-income, North Country Kids Care chose to ignore this, assuming approval was pending. But now the physician accused him of practicing under the influence—a career-ending allegation that came out of nowhere. There'd been no complaints and he'd been sober the whole time that he'd worked for the agency.

Paul spoke no Spanish and had never considered himself especially Mexican but would this have happened in the 96 percent white town of Greatwoods if he weren't brown, if his name weren't Garcia? His bosses at North Country Kids Care said not to worry. Paul was still paying his bill to Attorney Todd Sterling for his DUI back in September and now he had to hire another attorney, a licensing specialist in Minneapolis, to help him defend his license.

By the time Catt left in September they'd agreed that he had to get out of this hillbilly elegy and back to LA, where things were more normal.

On September 25 Micah accepted a plea bargain. The state dropped the grand jury's charge of first-degree murder committed during a kidnapping in exchange for his guilty plea of first-degree murder committed during a robbery. The logic of this was, instead of serving a mandatory life sentence for murder and kidnapping, the robbery charge would let him petition the court for early release after three decades in prison. Life without parole was the state's harshest available penalty. Convictions receiving a mandatory life sentence were often appealed. Given Micah's young age and mental health background, the prosecution probably thought that convicting him of the downgraded charge could pre-empt his chance for a later, successful appeal.

Was Micah aware of these implications? Maybe he was. The prosecutor had to approach him from multiple angles before he confessed to a theft of five dollars.

Did you take any items that belonged to Mr. Halbach?
I did not.
Did anybody that you were with take from him some personal property?
I can't answer that question.
At any point did you come to be in possession of his personal property?
No.
You were never in possession of any cash that belonged to him?
Yeah. I was in possession of five dollars cash.
Can you describe for this Court how he was threatened into giving his cash to you?
I don't know how to answer that question.
Did you show any force upon Mr. Halbach?
I was an intimidation factor.
You were an intimidation factor?
Yes, ma'am.

In what way?
I'm just a big guy, I guess. I mean all I did was sit there.
Were you in possession of a firearm at this time?
Yes, ma'am. It was concealed, though.
How were others threatening or intimidating Mr. Halbach?
I really can't answer that question. It's all kind of faded.
Was he prohibited from leaving?
No. He was free to leave.
What were the others saying to Mr. Halbach when they took money from him?
I really wasn't paying attention.
After this money was taken did you cause the death of Mr. Halbach?
Yes, ma'am.
How did you cause Mr. Halbach's death?
I shot him twice in the head.

"Shooter Pleads Guilty," the front page of the *Duluth News Tribune* announced the next morning.

Brittney and Evan's public defenders sat through the hearing and were less than impressed by Attorney Wiedel's performance. *He didn't talk to anyone here during any of these proceedings,* one of them said. *He was just up and down from the Cities, in and out of the courtroom. Some of us wondered if he was autistic.* Micah begged to be sentenced to prison immediately. That, the judge said, was impossible. Brandon's friends and relations needed time to prepare their victim impact statements so the sentencing date was set for a month later.

Brandon's big sister read their father's statement out to the court at the sentencing hearing. *I can't say what I wanted to say* but . . . this has impacted me really bad. *I sit on the corner here in North Star for hours and hours. When people ask why I say I'm bored and I don't have a TV. But the real reason is I'm meditating, trying to keep the demon in check. They killed my son. They killed a part of me and I will never forgive them.*

Before being sentenced Micah stood up and said, *There's a lot in the paper and the investigation—the police did not investigate on this case. There's a lot that was not said. I was manipulated into doing this. I—I mean—I don't really know what to say other than I'm a man that was raised on my principles and morals. And what I did was bad but at the time what I thought I was doing was right. I apologize to the family.*

Before reading the sentence the judge told a story about an uncle who suddenly died in the prime of his life from an aneurysm. *There is no good explanation for this*, the judge said, *and no reason why this happened other than senseless reasons.*

Catt was in Balsam with Paul for Thanksgiving break when Evan Stanton was sentenced. An early Arctic blast kept them indoors. Temperatures dipped to minus 18 degrees Fahrenheit, breaking all records, the *Duluth News Tribune* reported. Paul kept the wood furnace stoked and they sat near the vent playing checkers and talking. There were no deer to watch in the yard. Paul had decided not to start feeding them because he knew he'd be leaving and he didn't want them to starve. He'd already handed in his notice to North Country Kids Care and planned on moving back to LA before Christmas.

THE FOUR SPENT THE DAY TOGETHER

That month, a young New York–based Russian cultural writer that Catt admired brought her name back into circulation by tweeting *Catt Greene is a landlord* and a new generation took up the banner. She wondered if it was the proximity to poverty she allowed herself that enraged them.

We NEED to talk about Catt Greene & her odd landlord politics . . .

Catt Greene being a landlord in LA is just one of a few things I don't like about Catt Greene

Catt Greene is a LANDLORD???? In MEXICO???? WHAT???? SCREAMING!!!

Probably the worst kind of people on earth: artists who become landlords to sustain their creative work

If you read any of her books, you'll know Catt Greene is a landlord!! She writes about it all the time!!

Imagining a biography of Catt Greene but only the part where she is a landlord

The foremost landlord of American letters

Catt Greene defending her slumlord activities by saying she's better than the average slumlord so her slumlording is a net positive

I also happen to think her work sucks because it's historically batshit and DIRECTLY racist & homophobic

Catt Greene being terrible comes as no surprise but MY GOD recommending becoming a landlord "as a way of engaging with a population completely outside the culture industry"!!!!!

I mean I was literally reading Sebald's Natural History of Destruction until seconds ago and this is a far more damning indictment of all humanity, well done CG!

CHRIS KRAUS

Saw her defend this in person and it was as grim as anything

lmao Catt Greene literally makes her money as a landlord for low-income tenants but, sure, a TV show based on her monument to mediocre heterosexual schtupping is a feminist issue

I have to say it was really me who disliked her first

The day after Evan's sentencing hearing, the *Harding Tribune* ran a several-page story summarizing all three of the cases. New details emerged that hadn't appeared in previous coverage. The four of them spent the day together, the newspaper reprised, until 2 a.m., when they drove to the old Kerr mine location outside of Harding. They parked on a dead-end road off the highway alongside the trail and Brittney used her bandana to blindfold Brandon. Brandon did not seem to mind this, which was maybe not so surprising given that Evan recalled *he was mostly out in space, just not paying attention, I knew he'd smoked meth or something like that*. But also, before that, before leaving Misty and Evan's upstairs apartment in the Chevy Malibu, in order to coax Brandon to walk down the stairs, they'd told him they were taking him out to the woods to sell weed to the Mexican cartel to get money for gas so he could drive home to Beulah. So—perhaps for that reason Brandon didn't resist when Brittney tied the bandana and scrunched up his hood, because they'd already said the cartel did not want to see him, that *nobody could see his face*. The other reason could be he was scared shitless. In any event, Evan recalled that *he was quiet the whole time, he did not question it.*

Micah was already out of the car when Brittney asked Evan if they could switch shoes because there was snow on the ground. *I put her high heels on and she took my shoes*, Evan remembered. And then Brittney and Micah helped Brandon out of the car and walked him into the woods. Evan didn't remember how long he waited but some time later he heard two distant shots. And then Micah and Brittney came back to the car and they stopped off at a Holiday gas station to buy snacks and some energy drinks.

Catt was intrigued and confused by this story. She was even more struck by the statement Evan's public defender Chad Thayer read to the court.

"Addiction is a terrible thing, Judge. It puts you in places you would not otherwise be. Mr. Stanton's addiction put him in the wrong place at the wrong time, with the wrong people. Beyond that, Mr. Stanton's life has been one of victimization that resulted in his removal at age six from his parents' home and into the foster care system. As a result of being perpetrated upon, he's had to deal with mental health issues. I look at Mr. Stanton as being vulnerable because of his addiction, because of his victimization, because he wanted to belong. He's wanted to be loved and supported by somebody and that vulnerability put him with people and places that were no good for him.

"We have to ask ourselves how this could happen. We should all weep, we're all involved here."

Family and friends of Halbach gasped and whispered expletives as the defense attorney continued, the newspaper reported.

"Evan weeps for Mr. Halbach. He weeps for the entire family. We also know that fewer people will weep for Mr. Stanton but, Your Honor, I do. I weep for Mr. Stanton. Mr. Stanton stands ready today to accept his consequences. But, Your Honor, we should weep for Mr. Halbach. We should weep for the families. We should weep for these kids, these three kids, and we should weep for society."

Who was Attorney Chad Thayer? Roughly Catt's age, he'd finished law school in Minneapolis in the early nineties. Had he protested apartheid, demonstrated against the CIA's covert operations? He was an old-fashioned humanist, and his heartfelt speech conjured the world of her parents, which was anomalous anywhere but especially here on the Range.

Catt had just finished *Hinterland*, a book by the geographer Phil A. Neel, who'd grown up in a trailer in eastern Oregon. Neel defined "hinterlands" as the regions remote from the cores of the global post-industrial economy—rural regions abandoned as wastelands—the sites of "tweaker demographics," white meth addicts whose forebears had once used speed to get through long mining and logging shifts. *I am convinced*, Phil A. Neel wrote, *that the eyes of tweakers see something that other eyes do not . . . as if the eyes are sunk straight back into the brain . . . the iris black like a single, dilated pupil open to the world's many wounds and thus capable of seeing that world as it is: a congress of explosions tearing bodies apart all at different speeds and in different directions.*

Throughout the Thanksgiving break Catt continued thinking about the Nagamo Trail cases. It was clearly a book that had to be written and if she didn't write it, who would? Researching

THE FOUR SPENT THE DAY TOGETHER

the lives of these kids was a way to crack open the flat frozen landscape and understand what went on inside the trailers, the abandoned community centers, the old wood-frame mine houses. Paul would be moving back to LA, he'd get another job and they'd most likely sell the gray house and leave Balsam. It occurred to her that before leaving the region forever she might be able to learn something about an America that her Twitter detractors would not understand, would not even see.

One week before Christmas Paul closed up and drained the house, loaded up the car with all his personal belongings, and drove back to Los Angeles. In January he'd be starting a new job as the clinical director for a psychiatric felony-diversion program in South Central. By the time that he arrived Catt was totally immersed in the Nagamo Trail cases. She'd found Brittney, Micah, Evan, and Brandon's now-dormant Facebook pages and followed the links to the social media of all their friends and families. She found their playlists and their favorite shows and movies; she took screenshots of their cover photos of Confederate flags, gangster rap stars, and cats surrounded by massive displays of automatic weapons stretched out on comforters.

January 6, 2020—the first anniversary of the crime—was fast approaching. She considered flying out to Harding, smoking meth, and visiting the crime scene at two thirty in the morning. Paul talked her out of that. Still, she craved a ritual—anything to rouse her from the somnambulant state she'd lately fallen into and bring her closer to the kids, because her distance from them seemed unbridgeable. And then the spring semester would start and she wouldn't be able to do anything.

Finally, she booked a plane ticket to Harding for January 8, a rental car, and a motel room. Then she emailed the reporter on the *Harding Tribune* who'd been covering the cases.

Changing planes at MSP, Catt felt an abrupt shift when she walked over to the regional wing from the main section of the airport. The seamless string of high-end boutiques, bookstores, and organic restaurants gave way to something that felt more subconsciously familiar, sullen, and shabby. A long flight of descending steps dead-ended in an amphitheater with a sports bar. Beyond it, a fluorescent-lit corridor led to a long row of gates where lonely, overweight men in work boots and parkas sat slumped in plastic chairs awaiting flights to places like Bismarck, Thief River Falls, and Bemidji.

It was the second Wednesday of the year, one year and three days since the day the four had spent together. Catt had a copy of *Hinterland* in her backpack and a lunch date with the *Harding Tribune* reporter. Beyond that she guessed she'd see. She knew the address of the duplex apartment Evan had shared with Misty and the addresses of the East Harding houses where Micah, Brittney, Evan, and Misty lived within two blocks of each other. She'd even found the old address of the single-wide trailer in North Star where Brandon lived with his dad before they were evicted in the wake of Brandon's arrest in 2017 for methamphetamine possession.

In Harding she picked up her Nissan Sentra and drove over to the Rodeway Inn. Even though the Rodeway was Harding's last functioning motel, it was three-quarters empty. She woke up at eight and looked out the window. The sky was grayer than a pigeon's breast and tinged with pink at the horizon. A strip mall sat on one side of the junction of two rural highways. Across the street there was a car wash and a body shop and beyond that, only desolate snow-covered prairie. A slow stream of cars on their way to work clipped through the fog.

Harding's a cemetery, the *Tribune* reporter would eventually tell her. He'd moved up to the Range after some family troubles forced him to leave his former home in Boulder, Colorado. He'd grown up in Livermore, California, and gotten his BA from Berkeley. He'd won awards, published important stories about the gas and oil industries for major publications but the associate editorship of the *Tribune* was the only full-time journalism job that he could find. *The whole court*, he'd continue, *was flummoxed when Justin Weidel introduced autism in Micah's defense. You've got to understand—up here it's like 1980. They don't know what autism is, or that there's any difference between it and mental illness.*

Catt's first stop was the Harding Historical Museum, a tribute to the town's mining history, open three days a week for three hours. She bought a collection of notecards by local artist Ron Durham. Durham painted his scenes of 1930s small-town Americana in the mid-1980s. His work was a product of Reagan-era nostalgia. Because by that time, the magnificent old Palace Hotel had already been turned into low-income apartments and the mines that hadn't already shut down were being automated, as the museum booklet explained, to *face global challenges*. Given the extremely short generational span on the Range, the mid-1980s had been the era of Micah and Brittney's grandparents.

A swathe of pale orange light glowed beneath gray-purple masses of cloud when dusk fell at four thirty. Walking the alleys in between Evan and Misty's apartment, Micah's house, and Brittney's, Catt felt a gravitational pull back to her childhood in Milford. There were the same metal clotheslines in scabby backyards, the same electrical power lines drooping between old wooden poles, the same bare skinny bushes and glassed-in porches. She remembered the mud-smell of spring and the kickball games that went on until dark in the Tiermans' side yard. She remembered how everyone knew it was the Shaminskis who'd spray-painted the N-word on the garage of the neighborhood's only Black family and how no one said anything.

Standing in line at the Caribou Coffee in the strip mall near the motel the next morning, Catt watched three high school juniors or seniors getting out of a late-model Toyota RAV4 to pick up their coffee drinks. Two boys and a girl, all wearing navy blue varsity jackets with the name of the school's ice hockey team, the Harding Blue Jackets. Tall, blond, and lean, they looked just like the 7-A kids at Kay Avenue School except for their teeth, which were whiter and straighter.

Watching the three of them, Catt felt a slow wave of shame. She thought she understood then what Brittney had been up against.

In early March, just before the COVID shutdowns, Paul flew to Minneapolis to defend his state license at a board hearing. The board members were four white men, a middle-aged white woman, and a lone Latino man. Paul wore a jacket and a tie, sat beside his lawyer, and answered questions about his background dating back to 1985, when he'd been less-than-honorably discharged from the navy. Yes, he'd had a drinking problem. Yes, he'd gotten five DUIs in New Mexico. Yes, he'd driven on a suspended license and gone to prison fifteen years ago for using his employer's credit card during a relapse. Paul had gone to graduate school hoping to redeem his past by helping people, but every step forward he took in the profession involved a new scrutiny of his background. After he received his PsyD the California Board of Psychology refused to license him because of his felony conviction. He'd had to settle for the MA-level license in marriage and family therapy that the California Board of Behavioral Sciences had finally granted when he appealed their first rejection. Paul had turned his life over to God, he'd paid all the fines and fees and restitutions, and yes, he'd relapsed, drinking was the thing he feared the most, it was also what he most regretted, but he'd never practiced under the influence, there was no evidence of that. It would be so wrong! It was something he could not imagine. The board discussed his case for fifteen minutes. When he came back into the room they said that he'd receive a formal reprimand and pay a fine of one thousand dollars. His lawyer hugged him, shook his hand, and drove him to the airport. To her, this was a happy outcome.

Paul hit the airport bar as soon as he got through security and drank four Bloody Marys. He got so drunk they wouldn't let him onto his flight. Determined to get home without missing more work, he took the shuttle to Hertz and rented a Ford Taurus. Leaving the parking lot, he banged into a fence and the police came immediately. That night Catt received *a call from an inmate at a Minnesota correctional facility* and paid the bail, twelve thousand dollars.

2

Misty moved into the big upstairs apartment at 2659 East Fifth Street on September 1, four months before the murder. She was about to turn eighteen and she'd just eloped from her last and worst group home with Fernando, her boyfriend at the time, and his brother Diego.

They'd moved to Harding from Thief River Falls, a small town of eight thousand people two hundred miles away, landlocked on all sides by frigid prairie. She'd failed her sophomore year at Thief River Falls High School and was working at Dairy Queen. The group home kept half her wages.

Fernando was twenty-three and he'd grown up in TRF. Except for a couple of trips to concerts in the Cities he'd never left, but he knew he had to disappear when a probation violation triggered a warrant for his arrest. The cops in TRF were assholes but the original charge, buying alcohol for minors, was so petty no one would bother traveling the state to look for him.

Micah and his siblings and his mom, Crystal, and her boyfriend, Quinton, were all living in the apartment downstairs when the three of them moved in. Fernando's occupation, to the extent he'd had one, was selling weed to kids in TRF and they all became good friends and started hanging out immediately.

Things went south between them two and a half months later. Fernando liked to drink and when he drank his affable demeanor turned murderous and stupid. The Sunday night before Thanksgiving, Micah was hanging out with them upstairs. The four of them were bored, just kicking back— some weed, some lean, some vodka—when Fernando cracked a dumb joke about New Genesis, Crystal's part-time massage business.

Hey, homie, good thing your mom keeps the lights out when she's giving those massages cuz nobody would get off if they saw her ugly face, haha.

You better take that back—
And I should know, yo!
Fuck you beaner!
You know it's true.

Fernando grinned and sank back on the couch, waving his beer like he'd just won a medal, and Micah did not think twice about knocking the bottle out of that fat fucker's hand. A pool of foam and glass formed on the floor and Fernando got up and grabbed Micah's throat, pulling him up off the armchair—

You better check yourself, retard.

Misty begged them to both stop but Fernando was no fool, he knew there was a backstory and the backstory was that Misty had hooked up with this freak at least once, maybe twice.

THE FOUR SPENT THE DAY TOGETHER

The image of this was so distasteful he couldn't bear to look at her face so he threw her down to the floor where the spilled beer was. The broken glass gashed Misty's leg, and now there was blood. Misty whimpered. Being a man of honor and principle, Micah head-butted Fernando, but then Diego got up and pinned Micah down to the couch, slamming his fists into his shit-ugly face over and over.

When Crystal heard Micah's screams an electrical charge shot through her body. She ran upstairs, pounded the door, and finally kicked it open.

You asshole! You pussy! You're beating up a kid!

Crystal screamed when she saw Micah's bloodied face and tried to separate them with her body.

Misty was down on the floor, crying. Diego pulled Crystal off Fernando and threw her against the wall, pounding her head into the plaster. Crystal's screams reminded Fernando that Misty was just a cheap whore, he had to do something to hurt her—so he reached for the tank with her pet gecko and smashed it onto the floor. Misty, now sobbing, cradled her lizard but Fernando kept hitting her. When he thought she'd had enough he was still all wired up so he punched out some windows.

The neighbors heard this and police were called.

POLICE REPORT—11/19/2018—2659 E 5TH STREET HARDING

As I exited my squad car I heard a bunch of people yelling. One male, identified as Fernando Jesus Cortez, was yelling loudly and stumbling around. When Sergeant Amherst told Fernando we were going to place him in handcuffs Fernando began yelling loudly and then punching Sergeant Amherst. At this point I observed Officer Hermann deploy his Taser to Fernando's stomach. I placed rubber gloves on and picked up Fernando with Officer Benjamin. Fernando was yelling racial slurs calling me "a fucking white person who must hate Natives and Mexicans." He also stated he was "going to fucking kill" me and then he spit in my face. My glasses were covered in Fernando's spit which I believed entered my mouth and eyes . . .

The police questioned Misty but she refused to snitch. Still, the spit and racial slurs and death threat, plus the outstanding warrant, put Fernando in jail for the foreseeable future. The next day Diego moved back to TRF, leaving Misty on her own to pay the rent, which was eight hundred dollars.

At that time, Evan Stanton hadn't met Misty yet. He lived three hours south in Isanti County but the very same night she was being beaten up by Fernando, he'd posted:

Feeling it it hurts I'm scared on Facebook. He'd just had another awful fight with Kristen, his girlfriend. *Every time my life gets better and I'm happy it gets shot right out of my life I just don't know what to do*

For the last few weeks they'd been staying in a camper van with friends and smoking meth. Before that, he'd been sober and working full-time for a moving company in Fargo, North Dakota, with Kristen and their baby daughter, but everything had gone to shit when they moved back to Minnesota.

THE FOUR SPENT THE DAY TOGETHER

Evan and Kristen had been together ten months and they'd already been through so much together. She was pregnant and living in a homeless shelter when they'd first met. Kristen's case manager advised her to give up the baby, and she was ready to do that. But to Evan, meeting someone like Kristen, who was pregnant and even worse off than him, felt like destiny. He'd just turned twenty and all his life since being placed in foster care, he'd dreamed of having his own family. We can do this, Evan told her, and in the beginning they had. They moved in with Kristen's mother in Fargo, worked and stayed sober and got into taking care of the baby . . . But then the parents of their child's bio-dad lured them back to Isanti, promising Evan a well-paid construction job. When they arrived there was no job. They had nowhere to stay and they were running out of money, couch-surfing among friends. The grandparents called CPS and were given immediate custody.

Everything fell apart after that. The car they'd bought in North Dakota got impounded since they hadn't been able to afford reregistering it in Minnesota. There was no way of getting to work. Eventually they moved into the camper with some friends of friends and went back to smoking meth.

The night of the big fight Kristen got too drunk and started screaming at Evan that he'd been cheating on her again. It was too much. He wanted to hit her but instead he ran out to the pole barn and banged his head against the wall. He couldn't stop, over and over. It hurt so much he started weeping and when Kristen saw him she was so terrified she called 911 for help.

Evan was calmer by the time the cops arrived but they said they couldn't leave the scene of a domestic without making an arrest. Protecting Kristen, he stepped up and went.

Five days later the prosecutor dropped the charges. Evan was released but he had nowhere to go and for a few nights he slept in a shed. Eventually he called Josh, one of his ex–foster brothers. Josh let him crash for several days but when his roommates started talking about kicking them both out, he put a status update on his Facebook page—*Hey can anybody help my brother Evan out? He needs a place to stay*—and Crystal saw it. She and Josh were old friends—they'd gone to the same church when she and her first husband, Ray, lived down in Pine County. Evan, when she knew Josh, was still just a kid—two years older than Micah—but he'd seemed nice, quiet, and polite. He'd even been protective of Micah, kind of a big-brother figure, because Micah was always being bullied.

Crystal liked to think of herself as a kind of universal mother, a MILF, of course. She was thirty-eight and she'd given birth eight times. She'd taken beautiful care of her son Callan from the time he was born with severe cerebral palsy and epilepsy until he died before turning ten. Crystal considered her friend Josh's post. Misty upstairs seemed like a nice girl, she knew that Evan was nice, and they were almost the same age. Misty needed a roommate, Evan needed someplace to live. Plus, Evan was cute and Misty deserved someone nice after that monster Fernando so she messaged them both:

Hey, I think you guys should meet

THE FOUR SPENT THE DAY TOGETHER

They swapped DMs for a while and then they talked on the phone. Within a day they switched to FaceTime and decided they should live together.

On December 20, 2018—one day before the winter solstice and sixteen days before the crime—Crystal, Quinton, and Misty drove down from Harding to pick Evan up in Isanti. It was already late when they arrived. Evan gathered up his stuff and for the next three hours he and Misty sat in the backseat of Crystal's old Expedition holding hands. They drove about two hours north. When they got off the interstate at Moose Lake there were no other cars for the next sixty miles. Driving further into the darkness alongside Misty, Evan felt happy and peaceful. He'd never been to Harding, didn't know much about the Range. But he'd been clean since staying at Josh's place. In Harding, he thought, he could make a fresh start, begin his life all over again.

Crystal and her second ex-husband, Pete King, moved up to the Range in 2015 to make another fresh start. In their eight years together they'd been through a lot. Still caring for Callen and her two other kids when her first husband left, she'd been forced to put Micah into a Catholic orphanage, the last orphanage in the state. Giving up on her son broke Crystal's heart but his rages were out of control. When Micah pushed her down a long flight of stairs, something snapped: she had to be there for her other three kids and with Micah, she just couldn't cope. And then Pete King stepped up to help. They took Micah home and within two years they had another son of their own. After Callen died their daughter Onyx was born and they moved to North Carolina so that Pete could study to be a mechanic at the NASCAR Technical Institute.

But when Crystal found out Pete was cheating on her she went back to Minneapolis with the kids. Pete followed her there and they got back together. Then they broke up again.

Pete started therapy in 2013 and they decided to make a fresh start. For a year things were good but then Crystal saw some red flags and she made him move out.

A few months later she realized that she'd made a mistake. She begged Pete to come back and they reconciled in 2015. This time they'd get out of the Cities, forget the past and make a truly fresh start. They wanted a home of their own and things were cheaper up north. They kept driving north until they found a rent-to-own house in Colberg, a few miles from Harding, and it was there that their daughter Cheyenne was born.

Micah had his first encounter with the Colberg police when he was fourteen. Crystal called 911 because she was scared: Pete was at work and Micah was threatening to jump out the upstairs window he'd just smashed out with a chair. He was refusing to take his new medication because it muddied his brain and made him so fat he'd begun to grow tits.

Throughout the course of his childhood, Micah was hospitalized twenty-three times—sometimes to prevent him from hurting other people and sometimes to prevent him from hurting himself.

THE FOUR SPENT THE DAY TOGETHER

After Christmas in 2017 Crystal and Pete finally divorced. He moved back to the Cities with two of their kids and she lost the house. She and Micah and his three other siblings and her new boyfriend Quinton moved across town into the Sunny Slope projects, a festering tract of city-owned town homes, some boarded up and some burned. Five miles northeast of Harding, Colberg was one of the worst towns on the Range and the Sunny Slope projects were the slum of its slums, with plenty of drugs, kids running around, and fights breaking out everywhere. Crystal didn't feel safe so she bought the .22 Ruger that Micah would eventually use to shoot Brandon Halbach twice in the head.

At first, Micah rebelled against living with Quinton. His stepdad Pete could be tough but Micah knew that he cared and wanted the best. The night Pete King left, Micah tore up the house when he walked in and saw Quinton having sex with his mom. Quinton was just twenty years old; Micah was then seventeen. Until that point, Quinton had been one of his closest friends. Still, Micah soon accepted Quinton as his new stepdad. He reasoned it out. Because wasn't it better for Crystal to be with someone he liked than with some asshat he didn't know?

By the time they moved into the projects Micah had stopped going to school but he was busy all day, seeing his two closest friends, selling weed, and helping Crystal take care of the kids. Like his dead brother, Callen, his little sister Cheyenne had special needs. His mom had always stood by him and family was everything to him.

Some of their Sunny Slope neighbors were gangsters. But Micah, who'd been bullied all of his life, wasn't afraid. He was attracted to them. These people had honor, they took care of their own. To these men in their thirties who'd moved up to the Range to get by and sell drugs, Micah was a mascot, a freak. He was—as per reports filed by the Colberg police when they picked him up drunk—*a tall youth with a shuffling gait*. Micah was volatile, pale, with wild raven-black hair, and his neighbors liked fucking with him. Jamal from upstairs let him in on a secret: in his youth he'd belonged to the Gangster Disciples, the notorious gang from Chicago. Jamal showed him his GD tattoo, the star with six points, and explained how, if Micah ever got into GD, they'd take care of his family for life. It wouldn't be easy. Micah could get past being white, it wasn't an issue, but to get into the gang he'd have to kill someone first. Of course there'd have to be proof, Jamal said, so he'd better remember to video it on his phone.

Crystal was desperate to get her kids out of the projects. In August she met Landlord Mark . . . a nice guy who lived up to his name. Having grown up poor outside of Harding with a father who drank, he believed in free enterprise and giving people a chance. Mark managed or owned about a third of the East Harding houses—places that no one would touch.

When Mark Tomek met Crystal King, he knew right away she was having hard luck. She was wearing a wig so he assumed she had cancer—and then, she had all of those kids.

Mark assumed she was on disability, which he knew was enough to cover the rent. Crystal did collect disability payments, but this was only part of the way she supported herself and the kids. There was also the weed and PCA—a government scheme that paid $15 an hour for the personal care of someone with special needs. All you needed to do was go online, fill out a form, and pass a short test. Micah served as the PCA for Cheyenne and Crystal, and Crystal was the PCA for Micah, which brought in another couple thousand a month. Crystal was also a licensed masseuse but the money for that wasn't great without happy endings, which she mostly preferred not to do, so she also sold Mary Kay to her friends. Despite all of this, she and Quinton drove rusty old cars and were forever broke.

Crystal told Mark that no one in Harding would rent to her so he decided he would. On September 1 he moved them into the downstairs apartment on 2659 East Fifth Street.

Crystal *was* wearing a wig when she met Mark but it wasn't because she'd had chemo. The wig (a blond shag) belonged to Penelope, one of her multiples. Over the years, Crystal had been host to fifteen personalities but by 2018 she'd killed most of them off and was down to just four. Crystal's multiples were both a blessing and curse. They'd been with her since she was five and they helped her to manage the trauma she faced every day of her life.

Penelope was the little blond flirt. Jazmin, the sharp-tongued Black party girl, had bright purple dreads. Marcella, with long Gypsy curls, was moody and passionate, prone to falling in love, but Veronica, who wore a black pageboy bob, was the one who could get the job done. She was the ultimate manager, the one Crystal relied on when things spun out of control. Unlike

Crystal, a natural empath, Veronica was completely detached. It was Veronica who leapt forth to advise Crystal after Micah killed Brandon and the whole family began receiving death threats from all over the Range. Because Veronica was able to keep things at arm's length and assess likely outcomes after weighing the facts.

Paul missed two days of work due to being arrested in Minneapolis but the clients and bosses at his job in South Central liked him so much he didn't get fired. He went back to AA and found a new sponsor. The first COVID lockdown began in mid-March but it didn't affect him that much. As an essential healthcare provider he went to work every day and he Zoomed into AA meetings all over the world every night. Because of COVID, his new DUI case in Minneapolis was postponed for nobody knew how long.

Catt taught on Zoom and took long walks every day. She drove past the growing homeless encampments on Alvarado Street and Glendale Boulevard on her way to the iconic stair walks in the Echo Park and Silver Lake hills. She copied the words of a child's handwritten sign taped to the fence of a beautiful two-story Tudor into the spiral notebook she carried—

Dear Amazing Delivery Person!

   Thank you for taking time out of your day and risking getting COVID to help people! I think that is super helpful and nice! Thank you for putting yourself out there! ♥

THE FOUR SPENT THE DAY TOGETHER

The sign struck her as an insult not just to the Amazon guy but to anyone who'd ever worked for a living. These people were tone-deaf.

Catt didn't know what to do about Paul's chronic drinking so she didn't do anything. Since her short trip to Harding she couldn't stop thinking about the Nagamo Trail kids and the cases. She read Stephen Montemayor's investigative series about the methamphetamine pipeline from Juárez to the Cities in the Minneapolis *StarTribune*. Located in between high-demand areas like Fargo, North Dakota, and Milwaukee, Wisconsin, Minneapolis served as a trans-shipment point for the Sinaloa cartel. The drive from the Juárez / El Paso border was a pretty straight shot, from I-25 to I-40 to I-35 North. Sometimes drugs moved up to the Range from Duluth, other times local suppliers drove down to Minneapolis stash houses. Still, the Harding police couldn't recall arresting any local suppliers who were not also addicts. Catt listened to Misty Starr's Facebook playlist (PJ Harvey and Marilyn Manson). She found Brittney's ex-boyfriend Dylan's Facebook page and watched his videos.

Since she was teaching on Zoom Catt could have left LA for Balsam anytime but the house was closed for the winter, the water shut off. Besides, juggling the world of the Iron Range kids with the world of her MFA students just felt too weird. She decided to wait until the semester finished.

Meanwhile, she emailed a Balsam neighbor who taught at the Harding community college and asked if he could recommend a part-time research assistant. He asked his best ex-student, Cameron Lusk, if she'd like to do it and she agreed.

Cameron would be home all summer waiting to leave for Madison to start college in the fall. She planned to be a lawyer. She was eighteen and she'd just graduated from Harding High School. A middle child in a big Colberg family of nine, Cameron knew everyone.

When Catt arrived in Balsam in mid-May, the Minnesota lockdown order had been extended twice. When it expired again on May 18 it was renamed Stay Safe Minnesota. The order didn't seem to matter much on the Range. Some people, including Cameron and Catt, wore masks and others did not. The region was already isolated. Except for Grace Church, the county fair, and the rodeo, there were never large crowds. All of the stores put down plastic marks six feet apart near the checkouts but besides that, nothing much changed.

The first thing Catt did was rent a small basement office on Harding's main street. When she mentioned she was researching the Nagamo Trail cases, the skinny, chain-talking part-time manager told her right away that the snowmobiler who'd discovered Brandon's body was her cousin, which seemed encouraging. Catt's plan was to interview as many local kids about Micah and Brittney as she could find. Cameron talked everyone she knew into coming into the office and Catt paid them each twenty-five bucks. People in town trusted Cameron even though she'd been on the academic track at Harding High. Cameron's dad worked for the mines and she had many friends, including people who'd been on the edges of the meth crowd.

A slow and steady stream of kids passed through the office. Some were attending community college. Others worked part-time at Walmart, Holiday, and Short Stop. All of them knew who Micah and Brittney were but nobody really knew them, it seemed. Micah was remembered as being "quiet," "bullied," "nice," and Brittney was remembered alternately as "a freak," "a pathological liar," and "a troubled little one." Catt hoped to talk with Misty Starr but she'd left town. After Evan's arrest Fernando had gotten out of jail and moved back in with Misty. She'd gotten pregnant and had their kid. When he hit her again and threatened to take the baby back to TRF to his mom, Misty fled and no one knew where she was. Brittney was in Duluth County Jail awaiting trial and Micah and Evan were serving time in separate prisons.

Catt put up flyers in the Harding Laundromat and Walmart—

METH USERS AND FORMER METH USERS WANTED
Writer-researcher working on book about the
Iron Range wants to hear about your experiences.
$50 for 30 minutes of your time
Anonymous and respectful

—but no one replied.

Meth is, sort of, niche? Cameron diplomatically explained to Catt. *You don't really just mention it—like, yo, anyone know a good place for meth?*

Catt called and emailed the detectives and police but since Brittney had so far refused to take a plea bargain and her case was pending, no one could talk to her. Instead, she spent hours pulling records at the courthouse until one afternoon the masked guard passed her a note:

We need to talk about your business here at the courthouse. The courthouse is currently closed due to the pandemic. This computer is not for research. If you need court records you may contact the administration but you may not continue to spend the time you are spending at this computer doing research.

Instead, she moved over to the Municipal Records Center to look at grant deeds, bankruptcies, and divorces. Catt could not believe her good luck when she found Mark Tomek's name on the deed for Misty and Evan's East Fifth Street duplex. She knew Mark Tomek—he'd helped Paul install a shower at their Balsam cabin.

Mark was happy to help Catt with her research. He and his son were hard at work repairing their old family house on East Second Street, which Crystal and her family had trashed. After Fernando's big blowout that November night, Crystal and Quinton begged Mark to move them to a safer place. Since Mark and his wife no longer lived in the house, he'd agreed to rent it to them. They'd moved in on December 1, a month before the murder, and left him with a $2,036 heat bill that May when they fled the Range. There'd been death threats, she said. Mark's friend Chad Thayer—Evan's former public defender—was helping him challenge the bill. After Brandon's killing Mark decided to get out of property management and took a job at Lowe's. Now he was trying to fix up his old house to sell. He was sixty-two, still working for the foreseeable future, and he wished he had funds to hire a crew and fix the house right. As it was, he and his son were just chipping away at the mess.

THE FOUR SPENT THE DAY TOGETHER

In the six months they'd lived there, Crystal's family had done a decade's worth of damage to the old house. The maple floor was stripped with ammonia, the glass-fronted built-in cupboards were smashed. When Crystal's German shepherd had eight puppies, she'd transformed the old dining room into the Dog Room. They'd left missing doors and broken windows throughout the house.

Catt wondered why Mark hadn't just thrown Misty out after the big November fight when all the front windows were smashed. *My heart sank when I saw it*, he told Catt. But then again, he'd felt bad for Misty. *I didn't even recognize her, that first time when she came to rent from me in August. It had been several years since I'd seen her. What I remember of Misty was—a little kid running around the yard. And then her mother died, and she got put in foster care after all that trouble with her grandma Ann, who had the same drug problem as her mother. I figured, Fernando and Diego had already left. She was a good girl and I didn't want to see her hurt.* Besides, he didn't want his investor-partner to hear about what had happened, at least not yet. His partner was an independent TV producer in Los Angeles who'd believed the old East Harding houses had potential. Someday, they'd told each other, Harding—the childhood home of a great musician—might become a haven for creative people from all over the world. That dream died when Micah was arrested and they saw the photo the police retrieved from Evan's phone of Brandon Halbach bound with duct tape and gagged in the East Fifth Street upstairs living room.

Catt asked Mark what he thought about the Nagamo Trail cases.

My opinion, he replied, *is something's gone wrong with the way we're educating our local kids. I hear such strange stories as I deal with people in our rental properties. People do such strange things—there's a new norm out there, a norm you and I wouldn't recognize. Their thinking ability, how they perceive life—it's kind of depraved. And I'm not just talking about moral thinking, what's important to them. One of our tenants did not know how to mop a floor. We had to teach someone else how to mow their front yard, she did not understand what a lawn mower was. It's a complete lack of common sense.*

But that isn't fatal. There's something else lacking now that leads to situations like this. And that part, whatever it is, that part is fatal.

Cameron and her brother Tim took Catt on a walk to a pit lake where kids liked to hang out in the summer: a vast hole in the earth formed when a pit has been thoroughly mined and the company stops pumping out groundwater. Kids jumped fifty feet from the rocks into the deep ice-blue lake. At night, they hauled kegs to the woods, smoked weed, and built bonfires. The pit wasn't far from the spot where Dustin Christensen had dragged and burned Jacob Fenn's body four years earlier. No one their age had forgotten it because everyone knew them or knew the apartment on the main street above Blue Moon Appliances where it had happened.

Cameron had been friends with Mariah, the sixteen-year-old girl who walked in on the murder-in-progress. After Mariah told the police everything, she'd been arrested and placed on probation. They released her in January and she immediately fled, drifting around the US with a guy in a camper. Cameron took out her phone and showed Catt some of Mariah's Instagram stories . . . photos of her and her boyfriend camped out in a desert near Tucson, in a fishing boat somewhere in Louisiana. She'd gotten clean and looked happy.

Tim was still haunted by the Greatwoods murder of Bryce Hartman in June 2016. He'd been in middle school and Bryce's younger sister had been his first girlfriend.

Walking around the pit lake, Cameron and Tim tried to explain the setup for kids on the Range as they understood it. Kids could choose to attend any school in the district. No one who hoped to do well went to Colberg—the school was known for its drugs and the kids there were notorious for being involved in not-so-great things: of course weed, but also pills, meth, and crack. Cameron and Tim lived on the "good" side of Colberg but when they chose to attend Harding High the kids there called them "hood rats" and "Colberg trash" at first. This was completely unjust—they had a good home life, plus they were still friends with the neighborhood kids who didn't bus over to Harding.

Harding High School had all the Advanced Placement classes. Cameron had earned her associate's degree while she was there through a program called PSEO, where faculty from the community college came to the school to teach college classes. If Harding High was the best school, then IRTT (Iron Range Tech & Trades) was hands-down the worst. Located in Beulah, it was designed as an Alternative Learning Center, or "Asshole's Last Chance," as the Harding High teachers liked to say. IRTT was for people who couldn't cope elsewhere. The kids there could smoke and they made their own schedules.

Tim had two Colberg friends who'd been abandoned in their midteens by single parents but escaped CPS when other kids and their families looked after them. His friend Barrett had recently passed from an overdose. *The Colberg kids stick together,* he said, *but in Harding, there are the preppies, the jocks, and the druggy art-emo kids.*

Caribou Coffee is where the preppies hang out, Cameron continued. *It's very stereotypical. You see the economic gaps among kids, how much their parents make, by who they hang out with. All the lower-income kids band together. The upper-income kids have lots of different groups, but the lower-income kids just have one group. It all seems to be part of the same thing. If you're lower income then you're part of this group. Anyone from a middle- or upper-class family goes to Harding. They're not gonna send their kids to Colberg or IRTT. There are kids who struggle to get good grades and go to college but if you're lower income you're just automatically exiled.*

Church, they agreed, was the only place these divisions evaporated—it was the only uniter.

The next day Cameron got a text from an old classmate—

> Hey Cam we had Sloan L. come over to the apartment to get his stuff and we were all just making small talk and he brought up the writer. He said people have told him that she's a fed and that he knew you were involved. He was acting a little like he was on something and I know he has more than a couple of friends in the meth community.

THE FOUR SPENT THE DAY TOGETHER

> Will doing this potentially bring up other cases like the decapitation? I'm just afraid working with this author could be potentially dangerous for you or me. People already know you're working with her. I don't mean to say this to scare you, I just wanted you to know . . .

Thinking it best to back off from the kids for a while, Catt met with Ellen Broyard, a senior teacher at Harding, and Avery Corradi, the director of IRTT.

The school year was over but Ellen Broyard was still working. The school had just changed direction, she said. The new Harding principal took a closer look at the Range and saw that 40 percent of the parents were working part-time, if at all, for minimum wage. Within that demographic, many had drug and alcohol issues that affected their kids, parents and teens getting high together. Instead of "Let's punish," her new policy was "How can we help?" In addition to AP and community college, Harding High School offered targeted learning for special needs students and an Academy for the Trades, where kids could get licensed in welding, electric, and plumbing before graduating. They partnered with Range Mental Health to set up a clinic on-site where kids could get help with their problems.

Avery Corradi grew up in the Colberg projects, had her son when she was seventeen, got her master's degree, and became the director of IRTT. She knew exactly what she was dealing with—20 percent of her students were already parents; 10–15 percent had been in foster care or juvenile detention.

You want to help a kid academically, she told Catt, *but you also want to help them have a plan after school. A lot of the kids have no form of ID, and so we work—it sounds crazy, but one of our goals for twelfth grade is for everyone to have ID. Because you can't get a job without your Social Security card, and to get it, you need your birth certificate. Kids really struggle with that. They struggle with things some people take for granted—driver's education, getting a license.*

We have a lot of kids that'll be bouncing around, sleeping place to place, and we try and connect them with housing. Instead of just giving them a phone number, we bring them to Housing and help them fill out the forms. All those little things—without them, you can't take the next step.

We have kids who are sixteen, seventeen years old and their parents will leave for thirty or sixty days to go into treatment. We try to make sure they have food, keep the heat on in the house, because very few kids of that age want to go into foster care.

Brittney Moran attended IRTT for a few weeks in between juvie and treatment and being arrested on January 7 for Brandon's murder. Avery remembered her well. Brittney was very adult—*She dressed like a thirty-, maybe forty-year-old woman, with her black leather Harley jacket, razor cut, leather pants. I had no issues with her. I helped her with math. She was a really nice kid, sweet to the teachers, and she seemed like she wanted to do well.*

By the end of the summer IRTT itself was threatened with homelessness: the Beulah school board wanted to reclaim the campus to build a new school for the district. Corradi fought and the lease was extended one year. She is no longer working at IRTT.

3

When she was little Brittney was the girl no one sat next to on the bus. She carried strange things in her backpack—open cans of things like SpaghettiOs and tuna. For the whole ninety-minute bus ride across the five miles from Harding to Colberg School she kept her nose in a book. The fishy smell in her bag stank up the bus and when she talked, which wasn't that much, it was always about things like spirits and ghosts. She said crazy things like *The dead live amongst us*, and said she talked all the time with the ghosts in her grandmother's house. Also, she lied. She told people she was really eleven when she was eight because she'd been in a car wreck that left her in a coma, which was where she met the ghosts. Sometimes when people called her a freak she just stared at her book but other times she got really mad, as if she were possessed, and threatened to beat people up. The kids on the bus told her she stank so she stopped taking showers. If they were going to call her a monster, she'd show them what monsters were like.

In seventh grade Brittney got into anime and cosplay. She wore a Little Red Riding Hood costume, paired with her mom's stripper boots with high platform heels, laced up to her thighs. When that costume wore out she switched to Little Bo Peep. She was creative and kind. She picked up on her dad's favorite bands—Five Finger Death Punch, Black Veil Brides, and Disturbed.

Like everyone else, Brittney followed the story of the two Wisconsin girls who lured their friend Payton into the woods and stabbed her nineteen times to appease their leader and friend, the internet character Slender Man. *Slender Man is my boyfriend*, Brittney told her teachers to see what they'd do. But no one was scared. They just laughed or they sighed.

In eighth grade, Brittney challenged Sophie, the biggest girl-bully at school, to a fight. Everyone gathered at lunch and Sophie punched Brittney out within seconds. When the cops came Sophie had already run and Brittney was given a warning. And then she did it again. Brittney put the word out she'd be fighting Tanisha, a basketball star known for picking on weak younger kids. No one at school thought Brittney was brave for challenging the two meanest girls. They just thought she was weird. Tanisha trained every day and all Brittney knew how to do was pull hair. Still, everyone gathered to watch. Tanisha finished with Brittney in minutes and fled, leaving her too bloody and bruised to run away from the cops.

Suspended for a week, Brittney decided to switch over to Harding High School and it was there that she found her real friends. In Harding she fell in with an artistic clique of working-class kids who liked to build things, draw their own comics, and dress up for photo shoots. They loved Drama Club,

THE FOUR SPENT THE DAY TOGETHER

cosplay, manga, and anime, invented their own Homestuck avatars, and played games with Magic cards. The group spent so much time at the vintage clothing store on Harding's main street that the owner gave them a key. The best thing to do on Saturday night was hang out at the store playing video games and ordering pizzas. (Later, even though the charges were dropped, the store owner would abandon his business and leave Harding forever after one of the kids accused him of sexual harassment and attempted rape.) Brittney dreamed then of studying art in Japan or Korea. And then she'd come home and open her own tattoo shop with her friend Ruby. The two girls spent hours in each other's rooms drawing up plans.

The only thing that set Brittney apart from this new group of friends was her side gig in prostitution. When she was thirteen, an old man in East Harding who had a thing for young girls offered her money to visit with him. The old man was slow and confused and Brittney had a big heart. She longed to swoop in and rescue any living thing that seemed frail. When he offered a bonus to show him her tits it didn't seem like a big deal—hadn't Janet Jackson done the same thing in front of millions of viewers with her wardrobe malfunction at the Super Bowl? And then there were others . . . It didn't take much to zone out and let these guys touch her and take out their dicks. Like her friends, she smoked lots of weed and she found that things could just blur together when she hit the right spot. And then she had plenty of money to buy what she liked and share with her friends.

Without really trying, Brittney was gaining a reputation for being reckless and wild. *Brittney just seemed to stir up the pot and do whatever she liked . . . She was an outcast . . . She just didn't care.*

There was something perverse and oppressive about the value everyone placed on the idea of the innocent young girl. Speaking out against this was something only a preppie would do—it was much smarter to use it. After a few old-man encounters Brittney set up new social accounts under fake names like Jailbait, Cherry, and Cupcake. *We are talking*, Crystal's friend Peyton told Catt on the phone, *about someone who's known that the fastest way out of trouble is to cry rape since she was twelve.*

Others saw Brittney's behavior as a plea for attention. She'd been shunned for being ugly and weird for so long, she was just seeking some kind of validation from these older guys. Had she been abused? Anonymous posters on the Minnesota News and Gossip Facebook page liked to think so—but others who'd known the family for years saw her dad as a regular guy, committed to raising his family. Unlike Micah and Brandon, Evan and Misty, Brittney's parents were married, with stable jobs and a home. They could be strict but they wanted the best for their daughters.

When she was thirteen, Brittney began going out with nineteen-year-old Damien. Damien wasn't a client—he was a friend of her friends who worked at the Salvation Army thrift store where they bought vintage clothes. Damien liked all the things that they liked—anime, cosplay and Magic Cards. Soon, they were in love and Brittney carved the date that they'd met into her thigh. More than anyone else, Damien saw Brittney as someone at risk and kept her from getting in with a much heavier crowd. Brittney told anyone who would listen they'd had a baby together . . . which became too much for him, especially when he came out and began to transition. Already on T, he told Brittney *they had to break up because he was gay.*

Brittney's first thought was, maybe she could transition as well? If she was a boy he could love her the same as before. She changed her name to Cole and got rid of the Little Bo Peep dress. *Respect My Pronouns, he/him*, she wrote on her new Facebook page. They went back and forth for a while but soon it was over for good.

After their final breakup Brittney sought a reprieve from the pressures of Harding. In ninth grade she transferred to Lisbon-Tioga, a much smaller school several miles west of Harding. The school had only two cliques—preppies and bad kids. Brittney wasn't a preppie. She bought a longboard and changed her look to something more goth, wearing high-collared black dresses and Converse to ride around town on her board. On a bleak winter day she found a broken-winged pigeon outside in the snow, smuggled it into her locker, and built a nest for it.

The summer when she was fourteen, Brittney met Dylan Modich in the park with some friends and they fell in love right away. Dylan was twenty-two and he'd just arrived on the Range. He was living with friends in one of the big apartments above Blue Moon Appliances on Harding's main street.

Nobody knew exactly where Dylan was from. He was a drifter. He'd moved to the Cities to be with a woman he'd met online and they'd had a baby together. He started getting in trouble when their child died . . . no one knew of what causes, but he was arrested for passing bad checks and possession of methamphetamine. Friends of Crystal's friend Peyton suggested he move up to the Range to make a fresh start and avoid the warrants. Dylan could be kind of slow and depressed but Brittney's friends liked him at first. He seemed like a good person: moral, correct.

The day Brittney met Dylan they talked nonstop for four hours. Dylan was *exactly* her type: a stoner-skateboarder-gamer with long thick dark hair, piercings, and a little beard. Until this time, weed was the only drug Brittney had ever tried. They hadn't been dating for long when he asked if she wanted to smoke meth with him. Meth and heroin were the two drugs Brittney swore she'd avoid but she thought it over and decided to do it with him.

After that she stopped coming home for days at a time. She'd get grounded and then do it again. *It was hard to tell Brittney anything*, Brittney's mom, Erin, told Catt. *She was a stubborn, hard-hearted girl and if she wanted to do something, she did.*

At first, Brittney's dad added, *she was kind of helping him out. Because he was slow. Dylan would freak out and she was the only one who could calm him down.*

Brittney loves you deep down in your soul, her mom said. *She doesn't care what you look like or what's going on—she cares about what's in your heart. So Dylan must have had something good in his heart. He had a lot of problems—mental health, other things. And he played off that.*

She had no problem disclosing her meth use to her old friends. *I want you to know it's okay*, she would say. *I can do stuff without anyone knowing. I'm very high-functioning.*

THE FOUR SPENT THE DAY TOGETHER

The summer and fall of 2016 were the honeymoon of Dylan and Brittney's new love, and her meth habit. In her heart they were married and she set up a new Facebook page as their album, using her new married name, Modich.

Labor Day weekend—they're in her grandmother's van, their wrists handcuffed together and their fingers entwined.

Mid-October, four days before she turns fifteen—they're holding each other close in a kitchen. He's love-dazed and grinning, wearing a black porkpie hat, black shirt, and super-low-riding black jeans. Brittney's eyes are alight. She's smiling demurely and wearing a floor-length black dress.

A month later they're together again, eyes swollen and heavy with cavernous rings. He holds her tight to his chest, exhaling vape smoke. They were inseparable. Brittney's parents gave up *because the more you try and push them away, the worse the kids get.* They brought Dylan with them on a family trip to Duluth and in Brittney's album they're standing together at the winter Tour of Lights, sharing a kiss. Later that night, Dylan wrote, *My real queen bitch of this universe.*

Three weeks later, when the police pulled him over for running a red light at 1:30 a.m., his old warrants came up. Because of the old pending charges he was arrested, held without bail, and remanded back to the Cities. When Brittney watched Dylan climbing into the van in handcuffs and shackles, she was destroyed. She assumed, because of the warrants, he'd be in jail for a very long time, maybe sentenced to prison.

Since meeting Dylan Brittney had stopped doing sex things for money. And once he was gone she stopped using meth altogether. But one day at her weed dealer's house, Blinky, a much older guy who was part of the meth crowd, stopped by to sell some WIC vouchers. She followed him out to the street and asked if he'd get her high. *So he got me high*, she told Catt on a phone call from prison, *and I started talking to him*. After Brittney was sentenced to prison Catt wrote her a letter and they began corresponding and talking.

Straight off Blinky tried to get her into a threesome with him and his overweight girlfriend, which she declined, but he had a more interesting side. Blinky knew how to tattoo, and he had a glassblowing kit at his place to make pipes and other drug paraphernalia. He gave Brittney her first tattoo—a wolf, her totem animal—and let her blow glass at his place whenever she wanted. She began making fantastic creatures, like Mexican alebrijes, two or three different animals melded into one. Until then she'd only smoked meth but Blinky taught her how to shoot up.

There's a north side of Harding, and a meth side of Harding, Brittney's friend Ruby said. *Brittney started out as a casual user but then she got much more into it, hanging out with that crowd.*

The meth community is very tight, very scary up here, Cameron's friend Bethany told Catt. *The people are dangerous, it's very heavy up here. Things get weirdly violent. It's easy to get involved with them if you're the odd one out, but it's hard to get out. If you're already an outcast, it's your community now.*

I was so upset about Dylan getting arrested, Brittney recalled, *I got my ass tattooed and started shooting up! People were saying Dylan was going to be in prison for years. But I was young, not even sixteen—I*

THE FOUR SPENT THE DAY TOGETHER

wasn't going to wait for him. So I started prostituting again, she told Catt during one of their phone calls.

But then three months later, Dylan got out of jail and returned to Harding. They decided to get high one more time before starting their new sober lives.

After that, Brittney started getting in trouble all the time with meth, Brittney's mom remembered. *Getting caught with it, brought home with it, stuff like that. She started doing short stints at juvie when she wasn't running away. She was always running away. After her first arrest, we put a restraining order out on Dylan. There are no dates I can give you. It went on for a long time, here and there. She wouldn't come home, ran for three days. It wasn't even running away from home by then—she would just not come home. Then she'd come home and we'd ground her. As soon as we let her out, she'd be going back out with him again.*

In December 2017 the two were picked up in a parked car at a trailer park outside of Harding. *I observed*, the police report read, *that the sixteen-year-old girl appeared to be tweaking. She had meth marks all over her skin. I retrieved her belongings: a coat, two blankets, and a brown wolf backpack* . . . Dylan was booked into Harding Jail again for possession and violating a restraining order. The police took her home and she posted on Facebook:

> Dylan's in jail again for basically nothing . . . They never asked me about the restraining order and if they don't remove it I will sue them. Nobody understands how good our relationship is, how happy and strong we are together. I will do anything for Dylan. This is the fifth Christmas

where I've hated everything, my household and the world, the whole set-up. I will not give up on him!

Dylan got out of jail two days later. But the next time they were arrested, he was held until trial and Brittney was sent back to juvie, where she remained until going to treatment down in the Cities. Thanksgiving arrived and she came home sober and clean to her freshly painted blue room. And then sometime between Thanksgiving and New Year's she met Micah.

It wasn't as if Micah got Brittney back into meth, and in fact it was the reverse. Micah was all about being a stoner—*he hated the meth crowd, called them tweakers and crackheads and pieces of shit*, his friends told Catt.

Brittney was supposed to be sober at that time. She promised him that and I think she actually was, Micah's best friend Amanda, who'd since become a drug and alcohol counselor, told Catt. *He was a caring person—he connected strongly with people who were trying to overcome bad pasts. She was someone to hang out with who'd been through it, who'd dealt with mental health issues and bullying, who understood.*

On Sunday, most likely after Brandon Halbach was shot, Brittney changed her cover photo on Facebook to an image of her and Micah. The photo must have been taken before the shooting, because Brittney's still wearing the bandana she used in the woods to blindfold Brandon. Micah's hood is pulled up and their faces are pressed close together, their mouths are relaxed, beautiful, and soft. In the GIF underneath it, two hearts are pierced by the words *my baby*. They share a great love, their destinies joined.

4

On August 13, 2020, Brittney pled guilty to aiding a second-degree murder and kidnapping. She was sentenced to prison with an expected release date in 2044.

The four spent the day together on January 6, 2019, but during those sixteen hours, what did they do? Now that the three cases were closed Catt was allowed to speak with detectives and view the reports.

She tried constructing a timeline but it was hard. The job of the police was gathering facts that could lead to convictions. Beyond that, they didn't care what the kids were doing that day. She reached out to Evan, who'd already begun serving seventeen years at the MCF Stillwater prison, and they met several times but by then he'd blocked most of it out.

He remembered how he'd been sober and clean for five days after arriving in Harding, until a party at Micah and Crystal's the day after Christmas where he got drunk and high. He remembered believing at first that Brittney was Misty's real sister, and then he remembered how strange it all seemed arriving up north where everyone called each other sister and brother, uncle and aunt, as if they were related when they were not. So when Brittney came out of the spare bedroom where she'd been *taking care of some business* with Brandon and said that he'd tried to molest her, his first thought was, *This asshole is trying to rape my sister-in-law.*

Of course he'd assumed that their business was drugs. Before that, he'd just been hanging out on the living room couch being productive, playing games on his phone and messaging Misty, who was over in Colberg. They kept a candy dish on the table alongside the couch where everyone pooled their gabbies and K and ADHD meds and he was already wired from sampling them. Evan didn't hear any noise from the room because he'd had his buds in playing some Skrillex songs on his phone. He was being polite, respecting their privacy.

Although, actually, thinking back—the time of the rape wasn't the first time Brittney came out of the room. She'd come out before that after an hour or two and said she was hungry so they all walked down to the store. She wasn't mad then. Brandon had arrived at eleven or so, so he guessed it must have been around noon, one o'clock when they went to the store? (Surveillance tape reviewed by the police showed Brandon, Brittney, and Evan entering Short Stop gas at 3:06 and charging $44 of items on Brandon's EBT.) And then they all walked back to the house. Brittney and Brandon went back in the room and then Evan guessed he went back to the headphones and couch but he didn't remember.

The reason they walked instead of driving Brandon's car to the store was because the Malibu was having some problems.

THE FOUR SPENT THE DAY TOGETHER

Evan knew a lot about cars. He remembered talking to Brandon, helping him diagnose it. The sound that he'd heard—was it a squealing or was it a squeak? Because a squeal probably meant the alignment was bad but Evan guessed it was the serpentine belt when Brandon said it sounded more like a squeak.

Anywayyy after getting back to the house Brittney and Brandon went back in her room. When she came out again it was like night and day, her mood had done a 180. She was really upset and kept calling and texting Micah, saying he had to come over right now because *that creep just pinned me down, he had his hands all over me.* Facebook accounts reviewed by the police recorded a DM exchange at 4:15 p.m. between Micah and Brittney. Beneath a photo she'd taken of Brandon, Brittney messaged:

That's him.

He has a very punchable face

I need to talk to you in person asap please I'm freaking out

What's wrong

I want it to be in person

Right—come to the house

I'm too upset to leave

Wya

Misty and Evan's

OK

i'm sorry i'm being needy and annoying but i'm really upset and about to explode

I'm omw

Ok [pause] . . . Make sure you got your strap

But Micah didn't come right away and Brandon left the apartment. When Micah finally showed up, Evan heard him and Brittney talking about where to find Brandon. And then he remembered—Brandon had told him he was going to stop at O'Reilly's! He told Micah that and the three of them walked to the auto parts store.

They found Brandon fumbling around under the hood of the car, trying to install a new serpentine belt. Evan remembered being pleased that he'd been right, it *was* the serpentine belt. He even helped Brandon install it. Meanwhile Micah and Brittney were inside the car talking and texting until Micah got out and said, *There's been a change in the plans.* They were all going over to someone named Erik's, a guy Brittney said was her uncle. They didn't tell Brandon anything then except they were going to hang out and maybe get high.

But why, wondered Catt, *did Brandon agree to go with them when he could have just driven off?* Evan couldn't remember and the police never pressed anyone on that point, it was irrelevant.

Micah turned his music up loud while Evan drove. Brandon was in the passenger seat alongside Evan, and Brittney was in back with Micah, calling out the directions. Evan couldn't remember if it was dark out or light but when they got there, he parked and there was a small group of guys working on cars. So maybe still light? Brittney, Brandon, and Micah went inside Stan's house but he stayed out in the driveway thinking he'd watch, maybe help with the cars. Whatever Brittney and Micah had going on inside with Brandon didn't really concern him.

THE FOUR SPENT THE DAY TOGETHER

The house was on the outside of town, the last row of houses backing up to a pit. One of Erik's friends—a skinny young guy with white hair and deep eyes—had a pit bull named Butch. The friend showed him Butch's best trick. His girlfriend's mom taught the pit bull to bark out *I love you*—ruff-RUFF-ruff—whenever anyone held out their arms. And it was hilarious, the dog did it over and over again. And then Evan started to think about Misty.

There was one point—by then it must have been dark—when Evan actually left. He started driving around circling the streets. There was an old Quonset hut building, like from World War II, with a yellow light next to the door. And then he really didn't know where he was so he kept driving around until he got back to the house, which he would never have recognized except that Brittney was standing out in the driveway, waving him down.

Inside the house there were all kinds of people milling around, girls and their kids. Erik and some of his friends pushed Brandon around, took his wallet and phone and what remained of a small bag of meth, and told him to stand in the corner. And Brandon did it.

This gave Erik a better idea. He didn't really know Brandon but he knew his friend Harlan, so he used Brandon's phone to text Harlan:

Can you get me some drugs?

Erik knew Harlan sold meth in North Star and Beulah.

Where you at? Harlan texted back.

Yo, I'm in Harding.

Erik's "yo" was a fatal mistake. Harlan knew Brandon would never say "yo" and assumed someone had taken his phone. To his forever regret he thought he'd better stay out of whatever it was so he never texted Erik back.

Erik was pissed about that. He and Micah took Brandon down to the basement and locked the door from outside. Upstairs, one of the girls at Erik's party overheard Micah and Brittney talking about killing Brandon. And she'd seen Micah's gun. When no one was looking she snuck downstairs, unlocked the door, and told Brandon, *You have to leave now. They're going to kill you.*

Brandon just could not believe it. He didn't really know Erik but they were around the same age and he knew who he was. Why would Erik do this? He'd never tried to rape Brittney— she'd invited him over for sex and he'd just gotten her high, just like they'd talked about. If he'd known she had a boyfriend he never would've stepped into this mess. His best guess was, they were trying to scare him. It was cold and he couldn't just leave without Mikey's car so he decided to stay where he was.

Brandon was still in the basement when Evan came back into the room. There were security cameras all over the place. Erik rolled a joint with some weed and the dregs of Brandon's meth and everyone kicked back for a while and felt good. And then Erik told them all to get out and take Brandon with them. They'd already taught him a lesson. If they wanted to really drive home the point, they could drop Brandon off somewhere outside of town and then ditch the car in another place. So they all left together but Micah did not want to do that.

He told Evan to drive them back to the duplex. When they arrived Misty still wasn't there and again, just like at O'Reilly's,

THE FOUR SPENT THE DAY TOGETHER

Evan felt the temperature shifting. Micah took out his gun and told Brandon, *You're not gonna live one more day.* Later on, Evan realized that he could have called 911 and gotten out of it, but they were in his apartment, nothing made sense and he had nowhere to go, so he put on his earbuds.

After that, they all tied Brandon up to a chair with duct tape and rope. Evan took a photo and put it on Snap: *He tried to touch Brittney*

Misty was overnight babysitting for some neighbors a few streets away. *Who the fuck is that?* she messaged him back. And then Brittney got hold of the phone and told Misty they were going to take care of some business.

It was late and things soon got even stranger. Micah and Brittney were sitting there on the couch just texting each other, not talking out loud.

> I need to take a video of me shooting him to send to my crew—they're killers they love this shit

> No

> It's a respect thing—

(And wasn't that what Jamal said about getting into GD? Catt thought when she read this.)

> —I can do it on Snap it won't be tracked

> No

CHRIS KRAUS

I'm shooting him anyway your not gonna tell me I'm not
You tell me no I'll shoot him right here

Brandon was pretty sketched out and Evan asked if they could just let him go but Micah and Brittney said it was too late for that. Brittney said they should take him out to the woods but to do that they'd have to get him out of the house.

And then Micah came up with a plan. They could tell Brandon they were taking him out to the woods to meet up with the Mexican cartel so Micah could sell them a half ounce of weed to get Brandon some gas money. Brandon seemed okay with that.

Waiting out in the car by the trail Evan turned off the engine to save gas. He saw an electrical beacon flashing far away in the trees, making him even more scared. After a very long time he heard a couple of pops from out in the woods and after that Brittney called to say they were done. The whole tiny village of Kiernan, where they'd entered the trail, was still fast asleep when they left—nobody heard.

After that, they stopped off at Holiday to buy energy drinks and then they went home again.

The Harding Police and the BCA picked Evan up in the car Monday night and brought him down to the station. For the next several hours they drove him around to the various scenes of the crime, asking him questions, recording it all.

Catt was certain the answers to all of her questions must be on that tape. She emailed and phoned the entire chain of command but no one answered.

5

The Minneapolis prosecutor was insisting on thirty days' jail time for Paul's DUI 2 at the airport. COVID restrictions had put his case on hold for a year but by the spring of 2021 they were pressing his lawyer to give them a date. Paul was in total despair. He'd tried setting up a $100-per-night weekend stay at the Harbor Point Jail in Newport Beach but they had a long wait list, it was harder to get into than Yale. The thought of being locked up for a month horrified him—it was a giant step back. Plus, he'd lose his job if he left for a month, and where would he be after that? Given these facts, there was no reason not to start drinking again, so he did.

Catt's plan for the summer was to fly back and forth between LA and Harding to finish researching the case and start writing the book. The gray house in Balsam had been sold early that year so she rented an East Harding bachelor apartment from Landlord Mark.

She arrived at the beginning of May. After a few trips to Walmart to set the place up she became stuck in an uneasy feeling about Paul. When she'd left things had seemed off. He sent the same short cheerful emails and texts but she knew something was wrong. The thought that Paul was probably drinking again bothered her so much she couldn't start working.

This time, she needed the truth and the truth couldn't wait. After so many years of Paul's drinking she was embarrassed to ask one of her friends to check things out. She found a PI online who agreed to examine the trash bins that would be set in front of the house that Tuesday night.

At ten o'clock Tuesday night a series of photos popped up on her phone. The blue recycling bin was full of empties of Paul's favorite drinks—vodka, Jack Daniel's, Bud Light. As smooth and numb as an assassin, Catt threw some clothes in a bag and drove down to MSP to catch the 6 a.m. flight to LA.

Why, kitten duck, what a surprise, Paul slurred when she walked through the door. The house was a mess. As soon as she'd left he'd been free to start smoking meth and crack. She told Paul to get out and that they were getting divorced. This time she called a real divorce lawyer and filed immediately.

The lawyer advised her to stay away from the house. The best outcome, she said, would be to leave Paul alone and hope that he'd sign an uncontested divorce.

Catt made the best settlement offer she could afford and went back to East Harding to pick up her research. Cameron was no longer there but she interviewed Brandon's father and sisters and cousins and all the detectives involved in the case. Mark Tomek put her in touch with Brittney's parents, and she drove down to the Cities to meet Crystal three times. She bought an adult coloring book from the store at Scenic State Park and a deluxe box of crayons at Walmart. Most evenings, she sat in the tiny apartment coloring pictures of birds.

The three of them did this for their own amusement, one of the former public defenders told her when she cornered him outside a courtroom. *They did it because they wanted to. They wanted to do something sinister, something bad.*

In August, a year after Brittney's sentencing hearing and just before Paul signed the divorce papers, the deputy district attorney called Catt and said he had something for her. She met him at the Municipal Center and he handed over a fat file of text messages exchanged several days before, during, and after the crime, from Misty and Brittney and Micah and Evan's phones. The texts—bought from T-Mobile, Catt imagined, at considerable taxpayer expense—contained everything the DA's office needed to get their convictions, and more.

The "more" was what Catt wanted and so the folder of texts was a real treasure trove. What were Brittney and Misty, Micah, Brandon, and Evan really like? What were their jokes, who were their other friends? Whom did they envy, what were their dreams? She wondered where Brandon and Brittney had met. Was it on Tinder, LiveMe, or Facebook? What did they buy when they went to the store? At what point did everything change from a crazy idea to an accomplished fact?

Catt went home and read the eighty single-spaced pages right away and then she read them again but she could find no answers there.

Appendix

Friday, January 4, 2019
2:45 p.m.
Brittney Moran's "Cherry" Facebook Messenger account

JC: (Greatwoods, MN) Do u cheat
BM: No but I work
JC: Wat u mean wat kinda work
BM: I blow glass I also sleep with people for shit
JC: Ok if we were together would u ever do that knowing ur wit me
BM: I would let you know but cash is cash to me

Friday, January 4, 2019
4:10 p.m.
Brittney Moran and Micah Waldon — Facebook Messenger

BM: What you doin
MW: Everything good sorry phone died

BM: I figured

MW: The 20 Brant gave me fell out my pocket and I can't reup until tomorrow

I'm having the worst day

BM: I'm sorry love

MW: I just really wanna shoot someone

BM: That cant be your go to every time you're upset

MW: But it helps the anger go away

BM: Yeah so does sex

MW: Tru but your grounded

Friday, January 4, 2019
7:23 p.m.
Micah Waldon and Crystal King—Facebook Messenger

MW: I'm having Brittney come over everyone can criticize but I love her

And she makes me happy

And I need happy right now I'm getting really depressed

CK: It's ok if she makes you happy

MW: You got 2 gs?

CK: Ya

MW: Can I sell it

Give you the money

THE FOUR SPENT THE DAY TOGETHER

Friday, January 4, 2019

9:42 p.m.

Brittney Moran's "Cherry " Facebook Messenger account

  JD: (Ely, MN) Do I pay for pics
  BM: Yeah $5-$20 depends on the request
  JD: Just pussy
  BM: Oh ok
      Yup

Saturday, January 5, 2019

9:33 a.m.

Brittney Moran's "Cherry" Facebook Messenger account

  JH: (International Falls, MN) Hey
  BM: Hey
      What kind of video you looking for
  JH: Strip and pussy play
  BM: Ok
  JH: How much? Are you going to do it now?
  BM: (link) www.paypal.me.Moran360 and type in the amount.
      Since it's PayPal it's easy and secure
      How long of a video?
  JH: Probably enough to make yourself cum
  BM: Ok
  JH: Are you doing it?
  BM: Getting ready to

JH: How much

BM: I'm gonna make the video and after I look at it and make sure everything is good I'll give you a price and once PayPal gets it I'll send it to you

JH: Hot

(12 minutes later)

BM: Ok I'm thinking 60 for the video along with 5 pictures of your choice so long as it's not my face

I'm willing to bargain a bit

JH: Can you do $40

BM: Yeah but only 2 pictures of your choice

JH: Ok

BM: Let me know when you send it

JH: It's gonna say Tracey Blandin

BH: Ok

JH: That's my ex

Saturday, January 5, 2019
10:19 a.m.
Brittney Moran and Misty Starr — Facebook Messenger

BM: I got $40 on my PayPal I just gotta go to Walmart and cash it out

MS: How you get 40?

BM: What can I say except I know how to make shit happen

MS: True

THE FOUR SPENT THE DAY TOGETHER

Saturday, January 5, 2019
10–11:00 a.m.
Pixi Ryan (Brandon Halbach's roommate) Facebook page, posted January 8, 2019

BB left me a note SATURDAY MORNING stating he was going to be using my car to "go get laid. FR. See you in a few hours."

The 3 of them weren't "hanging out" . . . he went to meet her with the intentions of hooking up, and she was portraying herself as an older "legal" adult.

So . . . she either lured him in WITH THE INITIAL INTENTION of ROBBING AND KILLING HIM, or, she was caught being a little HO ASS SLUT by her "boyfriend" panicked and screamed rape.

Brandon wouldn't have knowingly made a sexual advance toward a 17 year old and he wouldnt have been so goddamn stupid as to do it with 2 other dudes around.

BB aka Brandon left our home with the intentions of meeting to engage in VERY CONSENTUAL SEX with a woman believed to be of legal age on Saturday morning!

Saturday, January 5, 2019
11 a.m.–12:30 p.m.
Evan Stanton, prison visit with Catt Greene, October 28, 2020

Brittney came over to my house, and then Brandon showed up about a half an hour later. They went into the spare bedroom to "take care of business," Brittney said, which was something to do with drugs, I guess, although I didn't think about it then because since relapsing at Micah and Crystal's party I'd been drinking and getting high every day.

After a while Brandon came out and asked me if I wanted to walk down to the store, he was not from Harding and he didn't know where one was. So the three of us walked down to the gas station on First Avenue to buy some chips and drinks.

Saturday, January 5, 2019
Harding Police Department Narrative Report filed by Inspector Bruce Kovacek, January 7, 2019:

Through the course of our investigation it was determined that Halbach's financial card was being used at the Short Stop gas station located at 2202 1st Ave E in Harding.

Surveillance video from the Short Stop showed Halbach, Stanton, and Moran purchasing chips and energy drinks at 12:46 p.m.

Inspector Salerno collected a DVD of this surveillance video. This DVD is logged in evidence as Item #9.

THE FOUR SPENT THE DAY TOGETHER

Saturday, January 5, 2019
1:06 p.m.
Micah Waldon and Crystal King—Facebook Messenger

MW: Can you get me two things of the cough syrup adult robitussin

I'll pay you back

CK: Ya I gotta go back already in checkout I forgot

I grabbed one

MW: Damn

CK: I'll go back later

MW: Thanks mom

I gotta leave at 3

Saturday, January 5, 2019
1:00–2:45 p.m.
Evan Stanton, prison visit with Catt Greene, October 28, 2020

So we get back and Brittney and Brandon went back into the bedroom.

After about ten minutes or so, Brittney comes out alone and says, You've got to help me get rid of this guy. She told me he'd been groping her, molesting her, and that made me really mad.

I wasn't really sure exactly what was happening but she was upset so I told Brandon that he had to leave because we were expecting a family member to come by. Except he didn't leave. He just went back into the spare room and Brittney started texting to Micah.

Saturday, January 5, 2019
3:00 p.m.
Brittney Moran and Micah Waldon — Facebook Messenger

BM: I have someone your gonna wanna take care of
MW: Who
BM: Brandon something, goes by the name of BB
MW: Don't know him.

Saturday, January 5
3:11 p.m.
Brittney Moran's "Cherry" Facebook Messenger account

JD: hi sexy
BM: sup
JD: wyd
BM: chilling
JD: fun

THE FOUR SPENT THE DAY TOGETHER

Saturday, January 5, 2019
4:15 p.m.
Brittney Moran and Micah Waldon — Facebook Messenger

BM: (texts a photo of Brandon Halbach on the couch)
   That's him
MW: He has a very punchable face
BM: I need to talk to you in person asap please I'm freaking out
MW: What's wrong
BM: I want it to be in person
MW: Right — come to the house
BM: I'm too upset to leave
MW: Wya
BM: Misty and Evan's
MW: omw
BM: . . .
MW: 20 minutes
BM: Ok
   I gotta go home and check in at 5
MW: Hang on
BM: Ok . . . i'm sorry i'm being needy and annoying but i'm really upset and about to explode
MW: I'm omw
BM: Ok
   Make sure you got your strap

———————

CHRIS KRAUS

January 5, 2019
4:21 p.m.
Brittney Moran and Erik Dorland—text messages

ED: Sup
BM: Not shit . . . What about you cat in hat?
If you're still on good terms with me I'd like your help with some plans
ED: Of course
What you got in mind?
BM: Can you call or possibly meet up?
[Phone call, duration of 2 minutes, unrecorded]
BM: Call me back in a minute
ED: I am pooping in a minute
BM: Lol ok I have updates for you
ED: Ok text me at this other number—218-421-5559
[ten minutes later]
BM: On our way

Saturday, January 5, 2019
4:39 p.m.
Brittney Moran and Misty Starr—text messages

MS: I'm stuck here in Colberg lol . . . Might just stay at a friend's
BM: Ok do that cause we got work shit going on
MS: Huh?
BM: I'll tell you later ok love

THE FOUR SPENT THE DAY TOGETHER

MS: Good? Or bad shit?
BM: Both

Saturday, January 5, 2019
4:30–5:30 p.m.
Evan Stanton, prison visit with Catt Greene, October 28, 2020

So then there was the whole thing with O'Reilly's and the car. When it was finished Brittney and Micah told me there'd been a change of plans and we were going over to Erik Dorland's house—they didn't tell me anything except that we were going to hang and maybe get high.

We're driving over to Clifton and Micah has his music on. I parked and the three of them went inside and then there was the whole thing in the yard with all those other guys fixing cars.

At one point I actually left and started circling the streets and then I wanted to go back but I couldn't find Stan's house until I saw Brittney in the driveway waving me down . . .

Saturday, January 5, 2019
5:45 p.m.
Micah Waldon and Brittney Moran—Facebook Messenger

MW: Say when
BM: 👍

[Micah calls Brittney but no one answers]

BM: Trust me ok my plans have never gone wrong the only times they have is when people went against what I said and made impulsive decisions

MW: I better not get caught

BM: Wym

MW: Nothing just tell me when

[Eight minutes later, Brittney gives her phone to Erik to text Micah]

ED: We're gonna bring her home and you and him come back here and we can put him on the block without kids or girls around n take his shit n send him out without a beating or with one depending on how he reacts and what he says

BM: My brother Erik typed that

MW: All right I'm down I still wanna pop him

BM: We'll talk about that while y'all drive me home

MW: And am I working with your brother

BM: Yeah

MW: So we taking him out

BM: Not yet tonight we scare him our next move is annihilation we gotta plan that out

MW: Why not take him out now I can do it it's not hard

BM: Trust me

THE FOUR SPENT THE DAY TOGETHER

Saturday, January 5, 2019
8:13 p.m.
Misty Starr and Evan Stanton—text messages

MS: Where the fuck you at
ES: At Brittney's friends

Saturday, January 5, 2019
9:27 p.m.
Misty Starr and Brittney Moran—text messages

MS: Brittney your mom is wondering where your at
She was just asking if I was with you and I guess you said you were on your way home from Clifton around 8:30
She said you need to get home
BM: I'm gonna in a bit
MS: Okay lol be prepared to be grounded or something again

Saturday, January 5, 2019
9:52 p.m.
Evan Stanton and Misty Starr—text messages

ES: Love you
MS: I love you too baby
Hey the people I gotta babysit for tomorrow picked me up I'm staying there tonight cause they leave around 6 a.m.

CHRIS KRAUS

ES: Ok

I'm fucking pissed rn but not at you

MS: Why you pissed

Saturday, January 5, 2019

10:58 p.m.

Micah Waldon and Brittney Moran—Facebook Messenger

MW: He knows to much I gotta take him out
BM: We were gonna lol
MW: I need to take a video of me shooting him to send to my crew
They're killers they love this shit
BM: No
MW: It's a respect thing I can do it on Snap
It won't be tracked
BM: No
MW: I'm shooting him anyway your not gonna tell me I'm not
You tell me no I'll shoot him right here
BM: It's not a good time yet besides I have a plan that will make him wish you did shoot him
MW: No I'm shooting someone tonight he knows too much
BM: If you wanna do it so bad you take care of it
MW: I need you to find a spot we can go to dump
BM: I have multiple spots in mind but we'd have to bring him in the woods . . . all my places are cliffs and pits
MW: All right let's do that

THE FOUR SPENT THE DAY TOGETHER

    Which one woods or cliffs
    I've got a spot let's go
    At 2
BM: You have to go through the woods to get to a cliff
    We need rocks and garbage bags
    Or ropes and bricks
MW: I know a spot
BM: Where
MW: By Lucky 7 — the giant mountain a ways up
BM: Nope that's an apartment building and after that we got some bears, coyotes, and cougars
MW: The side of the mountain with the pond and baseball field
    The bears and shit would eat his remains
BM: In Colberg?
MW: No Harding it's right by Lucky 7 I hiked trust me it's a perfect spot
BM: Dude I grew up on these trails that's called Boy Scout Hill its one of the snowmobiler routes
MW: Damn right well I'm capping him tonight
    You know anywhere?
BM: Go to Snap
[Snapchat, unrecovered]

Sunday, January 6, 2019
1:33 a.m.
Micah Waldon and Brittney Moran—Facebook Messenger

MW: If I go up alone he'll suspect something
BM: He's already sketched out
  We gotta walk pretty far cause of the sound

Sunday, January 6, 2019
2:29 a.m.
Evan Stanton and Micah Waldon—cell phone

Evan calls Micah [unrecorded]
  They talk for 45 seconds
  Evan calls Micah three minutes later [unrecorded]
  They talk for 91 seconds

Sunday, January 6, 2019
3:18 a.m.
Micah Waldon and Crystal King—cell phones and text messages

Micah calls Crystal but it goes to voicemail so he texts—
MW: I wouldn't call if it wasn't important can we talk
[three minutes later]
MW: Nvm

THE FOUR SPENT THE DAY TOGETHER

Sunday, January 6, 2019
4:03 a.m.
Police transcript of Holiday gas station surveillance cameras

On January 6, 2019, at 4:03 a.m. the maroon Chevy Malibu was seen entering the north entrance of the Holiday gas station on 13th Avenue E. opposite the police department. Arrested Party Stanton exits the vehicle and wipes off the headlights and then proceeds to park in front of the store.

Stanton then enters the store and removes a Gatorade, a Monster Zero, two Monster Hydros, and two Monster Import drinks and proceeds to pay for these drinks with victim's EBT card.

Stanton leaves the store at 4:08 a.m.

Sunday, January 6, 2019
4:18 a.m.
Evan Stanton and Misty Starr—cell phones and text messages

Evan calls Misty's phone but it goes to voicemail so he texts—
   ES: Hey babe

Sunday, January 6, 2019
5:25 a.m.
Micah Waldon and Crystal King—cell phones and text messages

Micah calls Crystal's phone, it goes to voicemail, then she texts—
  CK: I was asleep I'm so sorry

Sunday, January 6, 2019
6:41 a.m.
Brittney Moran and Evan Stanton—text messages

BM: Hey
    Why haven't you slept yet
  ES: Cuz I'm wide awake
BM: Me too tho
  ES: Come out in the living room if you want
BM: I'm trying not to wake Micah
    Any idea on a cigarette?
  ES: I'm still trying to figure that out
BM: Damn
    Is that you making noise?
  ES: Idk
BM: Weird
  ES: Right
    Come here
BM: Kk

THE FOUR SPENT THE DAY TOGETHER

Sunday, January 6, 2019
9:49 a.m.
Evan Stanton and Misty Starr — Facebook Messenger

MS: Are you coming over?
ES: Ok I'll be over soon
MS: When you coming
ES: I'm working on a car right now but I'll let you know when I'm there
MS: Why
ES: Cuz
  I'll tell you when I'm there
  I love you
MS: Uggghhhh
ES: What
MS: Idk

Sunday, January 6, 2019
12:15 p.m.
Micah Waldon and Brittney Moran — Facebook Messenger

MW: You told Raven.
BM: Well you see here we were talking and it sorta slipped out, yesterday's events
MW: Now I gotta deal with him

BM: I'm sorry he's my best friend
MW: Omg I cant deal with this

Sunday, January 6, 2019
12:36 p.m.
Brittney Moran and Erik Dorland — text messages

BM: Hey Evan wondering if he can swing by for his jacket
ED: Yes of course Ill stuff it in the mailbox tell him we can kick it later
or whatever im in bed

Sunday January 6, 2019
1:01 p.m.
Micah Waldon and Brittney Moran — Facebook Messenger

MW: Evan went looking for his coat fuck he took off I'll try and find him
He wanted to drive the car I said I don't really wanna ride in it
BM: Damn

THE FOUR SPENT THE DAY TOGETHER

Sunday, January 6, 2019
3:05 p.m.
Micah Waldon and Evan Stanton—Facebook Messenger

MW: Hey get a hold of Brittney
 ES: Y
MW: Coat
 ES: Ok

———————

Sunday, January 6, 2019
3:15 p.m.
Evan Stanton and Misty Starr—Facebook Messenger

 ES: I'm going to get my coat from Brittney's brother Erik's house be right back
MS: Ok

———————

Sunday, January 6, 2019
4:37 p.m.
Evan Stanton and Brittney Moran—text messages

 ES: It wasn't there

Sunday, January 6, 2019
5:19 p.m.
Micah Waldon and Crystal King—Facebook Messenger

MW: I might have to dip
CK: Y what's up?
　　What's wrong

Sunday, January 6, 2019
5:25 p.m.
Micah Waldon and Brittney Moran—Facebook Messenger

MW: I love you but I can't risk him snitchin
BM: Ok
MW: Are you ok
　　I need to see you
BM: I'll be ok I just woke up
　　You'd have to come see me
MW: Ya will they let me in the house
BM: I was gonna say bring the car
MW: Evan has keys
BM: I want you to have them
MW: I didn't do it for payment I did it cause I love you
BM: I only want the car being driven for important shit
　　It's a waste of gas and we don't know how long that car will last

---

THE FOUR SPENT THE DAY TOGETHER

Sunday, January 6, 2019

5:45 p.m.

Brittney Moran and Evan Stanton — text messages

BM: Hey

   Dude

ES: Hey

BM: Give Micah the keys and could you give him like 2 smokes hes gonna come see me

ES: Yeah well he's not getting the keys no one is

   I'll bring him there

BM: Wya

ES: Still at the house

BM: Uuuugggghhhh

   Could you grab the crushed up gabby off the coffee table at your house please and thank you

---

Sunday, January 6, 2019

7:36 p.m.

Evan Stanton and Crystal King — Facebook Messenger

ES: Hey

   Can I use your number so the junkyard can call me and give details tomorrow

   Since I don't have phone service

CK: Yeah

Sunday, January 6, 2019
9:25 p.m.
Evan Stanton and Misty Starr—Facebook Messenger

MS: They ain't back yet
 I'll walk over to Crystals it's not that bad out
ES: It's fuckin' cold out no
MS: OH MY GOD
ES: Babe no
MS: UGGGGGGHH
ES: I love you
MS: I love you too
 Where you at

[Evan sends her a location pin. Then he calls but she doesn't answer]

ES: Wtf
 And we have to go to Walmart when I pick you up
MS: Why???
ES: Cuz food
MS: Why not get it tomorrow?
ES: Please please baby tonight I want real food
MS: Ok

THE FOUR SPENT THE DAY TOGETHER

Sunday, January 6, 2019
Harding Police Department Narrative Report filed by Detective Chief Kenneth Fawkes subsequent to interview with Involved Party Misty Jane Starr on January 9, 2019:

. . . Starr stated she remembers Stanton talking to her saying "they" were going to kill somebody. Starr stated Stanton told her "they took care of business and the person won't be coming back." Starr said this was an in-person conversation she had with Stanton on Sunday night when they were on the way to Walmart.

Sunday, January 6, 2019
Evan Stanton, letter to Catt Greene dated September 27, 2020:

I think I brought her up to speed while we were on our way to Walmart. Misty wasn't trying to distance herself—it just happened that way cuz she was babysitting and she wasn't in the loop.

And then I think we drifted around the Walmart for about an hour playing hide-and-seek.

CHRIS KRAUS

Sunday, January 6, 2019
Harding Police Department Narrative Report filed by
Inspector Bruce Kovacek, January 7, 2019

Through the course of our investigation it was determined that Halbach's financial cards were being used at Walmart on 1/6/19. Investigator Horvat and I responded to Walmart and spoke with Loss Prevention Specialist Nathaniel Conner.

Conner was able to collect video of a male and female using Halbach's financial cards. These parties were later identified as Evan Stanton and Misty Starr. Using the surveillance system Conner followed the parties entering the store at 10:07 p.m. At 11 p.m. the two involved parties approached the register and attempted to purchase two cases of Mountain Dew and some boxes of Yakisoba ramen noodles for a total of $63.52.

At 11:07 p.m. they exited the store and entered a vehicle that appeared to be the maroon Chevrolet Malibu. They then drove off through the Murphy Gas side of the parking lot. Screenshots of the vehicle and the parties were taken and distributed to assist in identifying them . . .

Monday, January 7, 2019
9:52 a.m.
Brittney Moran and Evan Stanton—Facebook Messenger

ES: Hey
BM: What's up

THE FOUR SPENT THE DAY TOGETHER

ES: Nm

BM: How much gas we got?

ES: Why

BM: Cause I need to leave school asap I'm blacking in and out haven't eaten or slept in 2 days and I can barely walk without falling over
I'm trying to make this happen at exactly lunch cause that's when I go to treatment in another building and my school will think I'm there

---

Monday, January 7, 2019
Evan Stanton, letter to Catt Greene dated November 7, 2020

So yes "Evan" was going to bring the car to Brainerd but at the time "Evan" had no cash and nobody to follow him and everything that was happening was just going fast.

I think he was looking toward the future, not thinking in the moment, so he wasn't in the right mindset. "Evan" wanted to bring the car to Brainerd but his mind was scared and horrified cuz he didn't really know what was going on. He's never been in this situation before—and "Evan" is obsessed with any kind of vehicle with wheels so in the moment it was just about the car . . .

CHRIS KRAUS

Monday, January 7, 2019
Harding Police Department Narrative Report filed by Inspector Bruce Kovacek, January 7, 2019:

. . . Through the course of our investigation, it was determined that Halbach's financial card had been used again at Walmart at 12:28 p.m. today, 1/7/19 . . . Stanton entered the store at 12:29:33. As he left the store, he was again using the maroon vehicle (Evidence Item #10).

Loss Prevention Specialist Nathaniel Conner noted that two items that were attempted to be purchased had been voided off of the receipt. This included Monster Energy Drink and cheese sticks. It is believed that the financial card was now out of funds so these items could not be purchased. Total value of this purchase was $44.65 . . .

Monday, January 7, 2019
12:38 p.m.
Brittney Moran and Evan Stanton—Facebook Messenger

BM: Where is my car
ES: Wdym
[One hour later]
BM: You got my car right
ES: Yeah
BM: Are you gonna go get your coat today
ES: Yeah
BM: Ok let me know when so I can let my brother know

THE FOUR SPENT THE DAY TOGETHER

[One hour later]
ES: Where you at
BM: Why
ES: Hang out
BM: Still at school my mom wants me at home so you guys are gonna have to come to my house after school
ES: I'm going to go get my coat
BM: No wait for a response from him

Monday, January 7, 2019
3:04 p.m.
Misty Starr and Evan Stanton — text messages

MS: You gonna go get your coat?
ES: I can't till Brittney says I can
MS: She told me to pester you to get it
ES: Ok
MS: Idk lol

Monday, January 7, 2019
4:33 p.m.
Crystal King and Quinton Breyer — text messages

QB: Evan is heading out to Brainerd
CK: I know
QB: Ok

CHRIS KRAUS

Monday, January 7, 2019
4:50 p.m.
Evan Stanton and Misty Starr—Facebook Messenger

MS: Baby how long you gonna be at Brittneys
ES: Idk
MS: Well leave the door unlocked
ES: Ok I will go over there
MS: Wait what you mean? Are you at Crystals?
ES: I am at Crystal now but I'm going to Brittneys see you soon
MS: I love you baby
ES: I love you too baby can we hang out tonight
MS: When I get home yea

Monday, January 7, 2019
4:57 p.m.
Brittney Moran and Evan Stanton—Facebook Messenger

BM: Ok yall should actually park in the parking lot behind the flower shop across my house
ES: Ok
BM: Make sure you do that cause my dad might need the yard

THE FOUR SPENT THE DAY TOGETHER

January 7, 2019
Harding Police Department Narrative Report filed by Officer Ted Bracken subsequent to Evan Stanton apprehension

At 6:31 p.m. Officer Adler spots the Chevy Malibu parked on E. 29th Street. He parked a ways away from the car on W. 29th where he could keep it in sight without being seen. After reporting the sighting, backup was sent.

About a half hour later, Adler saw Evan Stanton get into the car. Evan drove north onto E. 5th Avenue and parked outside the duplex at 2659½ 5th Avenue E., followed by the police. It was now 7:01 p.m. Just as he turned off the lights, the backup officers turned on their blinkers, blocked the street, and told Evan to get out of the car.

He agreed to go with the officers and be searched. They found Brandon Halbach's EBT card in his pocket. He was apprehended and the car was towed to the police impound yard at 7:10 p.m.

Monday, September 7, 2019
7:49 p.m.
Misty Starr and Evan Stanton—text messages

MS: Hey

Monday, January 7, 2019
9:52 p.m.
Micah Waldon and Evan Stanton — text messages

MW: Cops outside

July 20, 2021
Attorney Kamal Dewan (initial public defender for Micah Waldon), interview with Catt Greene in the hallway of the Harding courthouse

KD: The world of crime up here is very small. Most crimes up here are committed by a small group of people. I grew up on the Iron Range and it is not the cliché of a small, close-knit community.

Micah was manipulated. He was told Brittney was assaulted — although he could have made that up, because the text messages don't fit the story that he was manipulated.

Evan Stanton wanted to leave, but Micah said, "No, let's do this." There was a point at which it could have stopped, but it kept going.

The three of them did this for their own amusement, because they wanted to. They wanted to do something bad. They wanted to do something sinister.

The cell phones are in storage now.

Acknowledgments

Special thanks to Hedi El Kholti who saw the book before I did, as he has so many times, and to Estelle Hoy and Ria Julien for their helpful notes at difficult points. Thanks to Luis Bauz for our correspondence while I was writing it and for the use of his beautiful illustrations. Thanks also to my friends and first readers Jennifer Kabat, Kim Calder, Robert Dewhurst, Marwa Abdul-Rahman, Philip Valdez, Colm Tóibín, Veronica Gonzalez Peña, Kevin Vennemann, and Juliana Halpert. Thank you to Carlo Craig for transcription, and to Bruce Hainley, Jane McFadden, Lorne Buchman, and Karen Hofmann at ArtCenter. I'm grateful to agent Laurence Laluyaux for her ongoing, insightful support and to editor Sally Howe for her belief in the book and inspired suggestions. Finally, thanks to Vermont Deputy Defender General Anna Saxman for sharing some of her knowledge about the trifecta of criminal prosecution, poverty, and mental health, and to Mark Wehrenberg and the dozens of others on the Iron Range who talked so clearly and freely about their lives and situations.

ACKNOWLEDGMENTS

Grateful acknowledgment to the editors and publications where portions of this book first appeared: David Everitt Howe, Pioneer Works *Broadcast*; Meeka Walsh, *Border Crossings* magazine; and Patrick McGraw, *Heavy Traffic* magazine.

Research for this book was partly supported by an ArtCenter Faculty Enrichment Grant.